WHAT DARK PASSAGES

BRYAN CLEGG

ISBN: 978-0-9939701-0-8

ACKNOWLEDGMENTS

This book would not exist were it not for the efforts of various people. I want to thank my parents, brother, and friends for their support and encouragement. My editor, Linda Lee, for her great work making this book the best it can be. And my beta readers for helping me find the holes that needed to be filled in the first drafts.

Most of all, I want to thank my partner, Kathryn, who worked harder than anyone to make this book happen, and who came home from work every day to read and give feedback on whatever I was able to write that day. We tested each other's patience, and may not have always agreed, but we're still here, and now so is this. Are you ready for another?

PROLOGUE

HE DIDN'T REMEMBER falling. But here he lay, cold pavement on his back and an annoying ringing in his ears. Must have bumped his head when he fell. His ribs burned, the way it offset the cold was kind of soothing, except…

He covered the sore area with one hand and tried to sit up. Extraordinary pain blossomed in his chest, forcing him to lay back down with a strangled cry. He lifted his hand, the dim light emanating from the street lamps made it hard to see, but it was covered in a warm, sticky liquid that was definitely red.

He laboured to breathe. Tiny beads of sweat formed on his forehead. The sound of rapid footfalls echoed as shock and fear overtook him. He closed his eyes, tried to think. *What happened?*

He remembered now. A stranger. A knife.

Rolling to his side, he began coughing, each one a painful convulsion that felt like a powerful current of electricity running through his body. When the pain finally subsided, he noticed the pavement in front of him was covered in red flecks.

His head pounded. The lamp above him buzzed almost in rhythm with the thumping blood rushing through his body.

He looked at his blood-covered hand again.

This wasn't supposed to happen.

Then a shadow descended over him.

ONE

ALEX

ALEX SAT AND sipped his coffee, savouring the bitter taste. Through the window in front of him people streamed past the shop in an unabated flow like a rushing river, the sidewalk trying—and often failing—to guide them along to their destinations. Sometimes the river would burst its banks, spilling out into the road with the angry honking of car horns doing nothing to contain the rush.

We run around like we're so important, he thought. *We have things to do, and they need to be done NOW. Yet, does anything we do have any real meaning? Are we any different from tiny drops of water in a river?*

Checking the time, he sighed inwardly and finished his drink before wading into the surge coursing passed, sweeping him–filled with meaninglessness and despair – back to the call centre.

Finishing his drink, he threw the empty cup in the garbage and opened the door. He dove into the lunch-time mob and headed back to work. Pushed around by the powerful ebb and flow of the current, the direction he was aiming for seemed contrary to the communal will of the horde, and it took what he felt was an absurd degree of effort to make a simple course correction.

Ten minutes later, having somehow extricated himself from the torrent of humanity, he was stepping out of the elevator on the tenth floor and heading to his cubicle. After walking past a half dozen rows of chattering people, he made it to his desk and sat down.

"Hey, Alex. How was lunch?" His office neighbour Zane leaned back, sticking his head beyond the partition.

"Good. They had a new coffee," Alex replied.

"Oh yeah. What kind?"

"Slow roasted something, I think. I don't know, I think they're trying to be more like Starbucks. Draw in the hipsters."

"Great, another place ruined. Well I'm going for lunch now. Have fun. We're starting to get a flood of angry calls about the new returns policy." Zane got up and walked away.

Alex put on his headset and punched his login into the phone. "Great," he mumbled.

* * * * *

Alex spent the remainder of his day fielding calls from an endless line of irate customers. Not a lot different from any other day, he supposed, but these calls were even harder to deal with because it seemed as though everyone had been given special training on how to be a difficult customer.

"I'm sorry, sir, but your device isn't covered under our return policy. You'll have to contact the manufacturer."

"I told you: they said it's not covered and I should return it to where I bought it from. I can't believe you would do this right before Thanksgiving! What the hell is wrong with you people? Always passing the buck! Just a bunch of scammers looking out for yourselves, you don't give a shit about customers!"

"I'm sorry you feel that way, sir, but there's nothing I can do."

"Why can't you make an exception?"

"We have millions of customers; making an exception for one is unfair to everyone else. It's important to treat everyone equal. We—"

"God. You know what? Fuck this! I want to speak to a manager."

Alex rolled his eyes and barely suppressed a sigh. "I understand you're frustrated, but—"

"Transfer me to a manager—now. Obviously, you aren't going to help me."

"Sir, even if I transfer you to a manager, they will say the exact same thing. It's not in our policy. There's nothing that I, or anyone in this office, can do."

"Why is it so hard for you people to listen? I'm not talking to you anymore. Get me a goddamned manager."

"I'll see what I can do. Please hold." Alex pressed hold and dialled a quick code into the phone. A woman answered.

"Hi, Alex, what can I help you with?"

"Hi, Becky. I've got another out of policy return. The guy's demanding a manager."

"You told him there are no exceptions?"

"Yes."

"What's his name?"

"Manwin Richards."

"Okay, send him through."

"Thanks." He wrote a quick note on the customer account and linked it to Becky's profile. He took the caller off hold and hit conference. "Hello, sir, I have Becky on the line now and she will be assisting you further."

"Hello, Mr. Richards. My name is Becky. How can I help you?"

"Are you the manager?"

"Yes, I am."

"About time! Do you realize—"

Alex disconnected the line and took off his headset. Five minutes until his shift was over, but he just didn't have another call in him; so he switched his status to busy and pretended to work on an account. When the five minutes were up, he wrapped up his company-issued headset and shoved it in his backpack, then punched out and grabbed his jacket. Zane was still on a call, he was leaning back in his chair, playing with the cord of his headset and speaking in a soothing voice: "Mmhmm. Yes, absolutely. I understand your frustration."

"See you later, man," Alex said. Zane nodded and made a face.

Alex squished into the packed elevator where a group of girls were chatting excitedly about their plans for the weekend. Apparently some nightclub was doing girls' night, drinks half off, and they planned to take advantage of it. He wished he was the sort of person who went out and had fun like that, but he wasn't.

Leaving the office building, and the soon-to-be-drunk girls behind, Alex walked to his bus stop and waited for his ride home. At this time of day, the streets were as packed as they were at lunch, if not more. The forty-four arrived and a portion of the throng disappeared into it, followed by the thirty-two. When the twenty-two came, Alex shuffled onto it with the same six people as every other workday. Actually, only five today; Cliff was missing.

Cliff probably wasn't his actual name, of course, but it might be; Alex really had no idea. He didn't know who any of them were, but since he commuted with them on a daily basis he had named them: Cliff, the tall guy with the big nose and dark hair; Kate, the cutie with short, blonde hair Alex had always felt a sort of kinship to, like they were cut from the same cloth. She was quiet, with scared eyes that always looked away from everyone, and kept to herself; Bill and Will, two businessmen who always wore suits and carried briefcases. They exchanged greetings with each other but never anything more than small talk. As though each respected the projected station of the other, but had no intention of actually becoming friends; Jane, who always wore a long skirt and walked with an air of assured self-confidence that said "I have climbed the ladder, I have earned my place, and you *will* respect me"; and lastly, Mitch, who always wore a hat and sat staring at an e-reader. Alex couldn't remember the last time he didn't have it with him. He often wondered if Mitch ever missed his stop because he was too focused on reading.

There weren't many empty seats on the bus, so Alex ended up sitting beside Bill who, like everyone else who rode the twenty-two, paid no attention to him. The ride passed in blessed silence.

Soon he was home, cooking mac and cheese while a rerun of *Friends* played on the TV, the soulless laugh track buzzing in his ears like a swarm of bees. His supper was bland, as always. No one would ever mistake Alex for a cook by any definition because, if anyone could screw up a simple pasta with cheese, it would be him. Nevertheless, he soldiered on until his plate was empty. He was good at that. Besides, he hated throwing food out.

A few hours later, after a series of increasingly mind-numbing sitcoms, Alex peeled himself off the couch and sat down at his computer. He checked his e-mail: empty. Logged into Facebook: no new notifications, but his friends were busy, incessantly posting about their mundane lives as if any of it really mattered. Julia bought new shoes today. Her status had six Likes and twelve comments. Josh used a public washroom and farted so loudly someone else laughed at him. He had eight Likes, but only three comments. How sad. You'd think something like that would elicit more conversation.

He minimized the browser and stared at his desktop background for a minute, then moved his cursor over to the My Documents icon and double-clicked. He navigated a complicated series of randomly titled folders within folders until he found himself looking at a document titled "Note." He opened it and started reading.

To Aunt Nikki and Uncle Phil,

If you're reading this, then it means I've done it—I've killed myself and my torment is finally over. Maybe you're wondering why I did it. Maybe you think I'm a coward for killing myself; that I took the easy way out. Isn't that what cowards do? But if that's true, why has this been so hard? Why has it taken me this long? I've been thinking about this since I was a teenager. I started writing this note years ago. Does that sound easy? Because I can say from experience, it is not. Anyone who calls suicide the coward's route has never truly contemplated it. Maybe the only coward is the person who can't do either: the person who wants to neither live nor die, but can't commit to one or the other. For most of my life, that's been me. But I'm done living on the edge.

My parents died when I was eight, killed by a drunk driver. It was the worst day of my life. I remember being at home with my babysitter Chloe, when the police showed up at the front door to tell us my parents had been in an accident, and that they were dead. I cried, of course, and Chloe hugged me. I'll always remember that because she was crying too.

Then you two came along and picked me up, saving me from entering the foster system. I guess I should thank you for that, but sometimes I wonder if living with strangers could have been any worse.

I've always wanted to ask you this: Why did you do it? Why did you take me in? Was it some sort of guilt or obligation that you felt? I obviously wasn't welcome. I could feel it every time you looked at me, Aunt Nikki, as if you were staring at someone with a contagious disease. I cried myself to sleep every night because I couldn't understand why you hated me so much.

It must have made you so happy when I moved out. I was finally out of your hair, a problem you didn't have to deal with anymore. Finally, you were free of me.

And I wonder if it would please you to know how much I hated being on my own; that I hated it almost as much as I hated living with you. Night after night I sit in this apartment watching shows about companionship, sad reminders of just how alone I am and what I've been missing for so long. Fully aware of the fact that I haven't had a meaningful relationship with another human being since my parents died.

As much as I'd like a girlfriend, I'm twenty-six years old and I've never had one. Do you think I could ever find a woman to love me? I don't know how to approach, let alone talk to, girls. They won't even look at me. Am I really that hideous? Is there something wrong with me? I think the answer is yes. I have no friends, and I work in a fucking call centre where—every single day— someone tells me they hate me. It's like living with you, except those people are more honest about their feelings.

To Oliver, Lance, and Austin,

You three were, bar none, the shittiest brothers I could have asked for. At a time when I really needed a family, you went to great lengths to make sure I was always left out. I'll never understand why you worked so hard to make my life at home and school so terrible, but you did one hell of a job. Maybe now you've got what you always wanted.

To Emily,

You are the only person in this family who ever made me feel like a person, and not a waste of space, and I thank you for that. I only wish you could have played a bigger part in my life.

Mom and Dad,

Please forgive me. I know this isn't what you would have wanted for me and I'm so sorry. But if it's true that departed souls meet again, I will see you soon.

I've gotten really good at blending in, at convincing everyone I'm just a regular person. But I just can't do it anymore. My life is worthless, and I'm pretty sure my death won't matter much to anyone.

Goodbye.

Alex Phillips

When Alex finished reading, he sat for a while, lost in thought. After all this time, the letter was finished. He'd said what he needed to say, no more revisions: adding a bit here, taking out something there, fixing spelling errors. The only thing left was to decide how and when it should be done.

He shut his computer down, turned out the lights, and went to sleep.

TWO
MELISSA

THE BARTENDER FINISHED pouring six shots of tequila. Melissa grabbed one of the glasses and raised it in the air, her friends joined her with their own. "To Lindsay," she said, "Happy twenty-second birthday! We love you Lins!" The others cheered their agreement. Melissa clinked her glass with the rest, tequila splashing over her hand, then downed the shot. She quickly shoved the lemon slice in her mouth. Not exactly high quality tequila, but you can't expect much at a dance club.

"We forgot the salt," Becky said as she coughed.

"Who cares?" Lacey replied.

They had another round of shots. Lindsay, not known for her alcohol tolerance, already looked half gone. "Let's dance!" Amy shouted.

The six of them moved out to the dance floor and formed an inward-facing circle, the most effective means of keeping guys from jumping in. Though as the night wore on it became less and less of a deterrent to the increasingly drunk men in the club. Melissa was approached more than anyone else, and on more than one occasion needed help from the others to push off some guy who didn't get the message that she wasn't interested.

"Whoever said that blondes have more fun is full of shit," Lindsay pouted.

Melissa replied, "I don't think they can tell what colour our hair is in here."

"Yeah, right," Amy said, rolling her eyes. "Your hair sticks out like a sore thumb no matter where you are."

"Admit it: you dye it anyway. Your natural colour is totally brown. You love the attention," said Cece.

Laughing, Melissa shook her head. Despite her protests, her friends had all decided she must secretly be using hair dye, as no one could naturally have hair such an outlandishly bright shade of red.

Melissa couldn't deny that, even with the unwanted attention, there were obvious advantages to her unique look. For one thing, it saved her a lot of money when she went clubbing. Drunk men were almost always free with their money, likely in an attempt to project an image of wealth and power. They usually came across as desperate, but who was she to let a free drink go to waste?

But tonight was all about Lindsay, so Melissa was buying her own drinks and ignoring all prospective suitors. It was more expensive, but sometimes you have to take one for the team.

When the club closed they pushed their way through the crowd of people milling around the front entrance. Closing time was always the most dangerous, as the remaining single men and women pulled out all the stops to earn themselves a last minute hook-up. Lindsay, so drunk she could barely walk, was singled out as the most vulnerable. Lacey was hammered, as usual; but being more of a functional drunk, her tolerance was higher and she didn't appear to be as intoxicated as Lindsay. Melissa, Amy, Lacey, and Becky formed a protective cocoon around Lindsay while Cece led them through the mob. When they broke clear Cece located a van-cab and waved it down.

As they piled in the driver called back to them, "Only five of you can get in. Regulations."

Melissa shrugged, "That's fine, I'm not getting in."

"Why not? Of course you can get in."

The cab driver began to protest, "I'm sorry but it's the law—"

Becky cut him off: "And a healthy tip wouldn't change that, would it?"

The driver stopped and considered.

"It's okay. I only live two blocks from here. I'll be home and asleep long before you are."

Amy looked concerned: "Liss, it's late. I don't think you should walk home."

Melissa rolled her eyes. "Don't worry about me. I do it all the time. It's perfectly safe." Amy and Becky looked at each other then back to Melissa, seemingly ready to argue more, but Melissa didn't let them. "You better get going; Lindsay doesn't look good. You need to get her home."

The driver turned, "Hey, I don't want anyone making a mess back there."

"As long as you don't drive like an idiot, she'll be fine," Jess responded. He still appeared worried.

"Go!" Melissa urged. "Love you girls. See you tomorrow."

"Bye. Love you," came the chorus from inside the van. The door closed and they left. Melissa watched as the cab drove away, then began walking home.

It was a clear night, and the air was crisp and cool—a welcome change from the stuffiness inside the club. Refreshing walks like this were one of Melissa's favourite things. It didn't take long for the bar crowd to thin out, as most of the parking was in the other direction. Soon she was completely alone on the sidewalk, which she didn't mind. She enjoyed socializing, but she also enjoyed her solitude every now and again, looked at it as time to relax, think, and reflect on her day.

Now, thinking about the good time she'd had with her friends, she strolled along with a smile on her face. Before she knew what was happening, a man darted out from the alley and grabbed her by the hair, savagely yanking her head back. She screamed but his other hand covered her mouth so that only a muffled squeak escaped. The hand holding her hair had no sooner let go when it wrapped tightly around her midsection and dragged her backwards into the darkness of the alley. Handicapped, with her right arm being held fast against her side, she tried frantically to hit her attacker with her left arm, swinging it behind her. But the angle was all wrong, and she couldn't make contact. She tried grabbing the hand that covered her mouth, to pull it away so she could call for help. When that didn't work, she jerked her head back as hard as she could, and connected with his jaw. It hurt like hell, but his grip loosened slightly and she was able to pull his hand away long enough to scream. It was louder this time, but they were deep in the alley now and no one would hear.

He covered her mouth again but this time her mouth was open. She bit down as hard as she could. He grunted and yanked his hand out of her mouth, nearly taking her teeth with it, then he spun her around and backhanded her across the face, knocking her into a brick wall. She almost fell, but he grabbed her again and pulled her close. "Don't fight it. This doesn't have to hurt," he said softly into her ear.

Her face burned where he'd hit her and the taste of blood filled her mouth. But those terrifying words converted her fear into anger. She began to kick, swing, and twist in every way possible, trying to escape the vice-like grip he had on her arms. She stomped her high heel onto his foot and heard him cry out in pain; she scratched at any piece of exposed skin she could find, digging her recently manicured nails into him like a feral cat. When he pulled one arm back in pain, it gave her the freedom to shoot her elbow back, catching him in the ribs.

She managed to break free, but he blocked any escape, forcing her to back into a corner. He started to laugh. "You're a feisty bitch, aren't you?" he said.

His face, she thought wildly. *I need to see his face.* She tried to wipe the tears from her eyes but, between her blurred vision and the darkness, it was difficult to focus.

He came at her again. She swung at him, but he sidestepped and punched her in the gut, the impact stealing her breath away. She doubled over, struggling to breathe, then she realized she was in midair. He slammed her against the wall, her head cracking violently against the brick. She coughed and sucked in a few hoarse breaths. The world was spinning. Tears streamed down her face, mixing with the blood from her split lip. He punched her again in the gut and tossed her to the ground. She landed awkwardly, a stabbing pain lanced up through her arm. She took giant, wheezing breaths, but none of them seemed to enter her system. It felt like her lungs had collapsed. She tried to crawl away, but two hands grabbed her legs and dragged her to the corner. She was flipped onto her back and he was on top of her. Her arms lifted in a feeble defence, but were swatted away.

"Please." It was barely a whisper.

He leaned close. "What was that, missy?" His breath was hot on her face, it smelled like dirt and rotting onions.

"Please don't."

"I told you not to fight, didn't I? But you did anyway. You earned this. You deserve it!"

"No," she croaked, trying to push him away. But she was too weak, and had no strength left. His hand was around her throat, choking her. His other hand ripped open her shirt, and then it was down in her skirt.

"You deserve this." He said again. And then he bit her, hard.

* * * * *

She bolted upright, screaming. Blinking rapidly, her surroundings slowly came into focus. It was her bedroom. She was in bed, covers bunched up and tossed to the side. She was soaked in sweat, her heart racing and breathing heavily. She closed her eyes and tried to calm herself. *It was just a dream. It's not happening; it's not happening.*

She got up and walked to the kitchen to pour herself a glass of water. Her heart had yet to slow down, the force of its constant beating made her skin feel like it was jumping off her bones. The water was refreshing, but she had to put the glass down as she didn't trust her shaky hands to maintain a strong enough grip. She went to the bathroom and splashed cold water over her face. Her breathing had calmed now, and she watched her reflection in the mirror as water droplets fell into the sink.

She ran her hands through her hair, untangling the knots. Then she reached down, down to the top of her breast, her fingers passing over the red indents of two ragged, semi-circular scars, and she began to cry.

THREE
RICHARD

IN A WORLD filled with pain, suffering, and death, it was hard to remain an optimist. The onslaught of negativity could be overwhelming at times. And for as long as Richard could remember, he had always wanted to be a part of the solution, to help fight the affliction that ravaged the world.

He had been young then, filled with hope and energy, certain he could make a tangible difference. The odds didn't seem so insurmountable, at least not then. Thirteen years ago, when he had become a paramedic, he was ready to save the world. But he knew better now.

Experience changes people; it teaches them hard lessons. Looking back, he couldn't help but laugh at his naiveté. What did he really think he could accomplish? Did he think one more paramedic was going to make a difference in a world hell-bent on destroying itself?

What's the point of resuscitating someone after an overdose, only to find them dead on the floor a week later, killed by the same drug he had just saved them from?

And then came the constant stream of gang members. Richard had lost count of the number of gunshot wounds he had treated. He even had gotten to know some of them, or they knew him. It made him sick to the stomach when they asked him how his family was. Was it meant as a threat? He didn't want these people as his friends, or his enemies. Sometimes, after he had saved someone's life, he would later see them on the news, going to jail for first degree murder. It made him wonder whether the world would be a better place if he had never saved them.

The world is complicated, more than he had ever imagined when he was younger. Life just isn't black and white, he knew now. He had learned to keep his opinions to himself. It didn't matter what his patient might do later, what crimes they may or may not commit. What mattered is that he did his job as best as he could. The rest, well, would be what it would be.

Increasingly, though, it was becoming more and more difficult to keep his work and personal life separate. The stress and endless disappointment weighed on him, making it hard to be with his family, and for them to be with him. Admittedly, he knew he wasn't a joy to be around anymore. Especially recently, with everything that had happened. He was beginning to question himself and doubting the life choices he had made. Richard knew that his wife, Natalie, tried in her way to support him. But even she was growing weary, and he knew it. Their deteriorating relationship was affecting their children as well, and he hated himself for being the cause of that. He tried to act happy for them, to pretend nothing was wrong, but they saw through him as easily as through a layer of clean glass.

He still loved them, and he wanted to make things right. But he didn't know how. This is what he had become, and it didn't seem like he would ever change.

* * * * *

"Hey, Rick? You awake over there?"

"What? Yeah, yeah, I'm awake." Richard looked over at his partner, James, who looked back at him with annoyance.

"Really? I know it's your first day back but you gotta snap out of it. You completely missed the radio. We just got a call." He started the engine of the ambulance and flipped it into gear.

"Shit. Sorry. I didn't hear. What is it?"

James turned on the siren as he punched the gas. "Some kid got hit by a car over on Main and East Seventh."

Richard nodded. "Okay." They were about five minutes away.

The ambulance pushed through the traffic, swerving around cars that didn't move. Some drivers would be listening to music so loud that they were completely deaf to their surroundings. Other times they didn't seem to notice or care that an ambulance was trying to get by them, as if it wasn't particularly important. Obviously, their getting home in time to catch the beginning of *Survivor* was more important than someone else dying for lack of an injection of epinephrine.

James cursed as he narrowly missed another car with the music turned up to the point where Richard could feel his insides rattling. The driver glanced over to his left as they flew past. The startled look on his face as he veered to the side and slammed his brakes almost made Richard laugh. Almost.

When they arrived at the scene, a small crowd had already gathered. Richard and James grabbed their equipment and jump kits and walked quickly towards the cluster of people. They pushed their way into a clearing in the centre where two men crouched over a teenaged boy, whose exposed chest looked bruised down the left side. His breathing was steady, though laboured, and it appeared to cause him some discomfort. Richard noted with approval that the boy's chest wasn't wrapped, as wrapping the chest after a rib injury could cause pulmonary complications by restricting chest expansion.

When the two men crouched over the boy looked up, Richard realized he recognized them: Arnold and Phil, who were both paramedics with St. Paul's Hospital. Richard had worked with them in the past during his EMT training. They were good guys.

Arnold stood up and, without preamble, gave a quick rundown of the situation. "Hit and run. Kid got sideswiped by an Accord. He went up over the hood and took the mirror off. Likely has a fractured rib, but he's breathing normally, so shouldn't be too severe. Otherwise just scrapes and bruises. Phil and I were across the street having a coffee when it happened so we looked after him. Kid's name is Josh."

"Thanks," Richard said. "I'll get the cart."

He went back and pulled the stretcher out of the back of the ambulance while James examined Josh more closely. With no signs of blood or imminent death, the crowd had begun to disperse, making it easier for Richard to position the cart next to the patient. The boy winced as he was lifted off the ground but, stoically, didn't make a noise.

"I didn't know you were back," Phil said. Arnold shot him a look.

"First day," Richard replied.

"Well, it's good to have you back, buddy," Arnold said.

"Thanks."

They loaded Josh into the back of the ambulance then Richard hopped in next to him. "Hey," Arnold said as they closed the door. "We're headed to The Morrissey tonight. Why don't you two meet us after your shift?"

"Sure," James said, always happy to blow off some steam with a few drinks after work.

"Yeah, I guess."

"Good, we'll be there after eight. See you then."

Richard nodded and the door shut. He checked Josh to make sure he was comfortable, as James started the ambulance and drove away. Josh looked at him anxiously.

Richard patted his hand. "You're gonna be fine," he said. "Trust me."

* * * * *

James and Richard strolled into The Morrissey Pub just before nine, greeted by the traditional pub aroma of sweat and alcohol. A cacophonous din of talking, laughing, and clinking glasses competed with the grooves of Kings of Leon blasting over the speakers. Large, bright chandeliers covered in wax drippings lined the ceiling at the rear of the pub, while chains dangled from the rafters, and a seemingly random tricycle hung suspended in the air. Dark furnishings coupled with the ambient lighting gave everyone's face a haunting, red hue, as if they'd been pulled from a fire.

James pushed through the crowd with Richard close behind him. Across from the fireplace on the far side of the bar, they found Arnold and Phil, along with a few other people they recognized. They sat down at the table and exchanged greetings. Richard knew them all by name. Paramedics weren't exactly a large club, so most had either worked or trained together at some point in their careers. They also gossiped.

Richard shifted uncomfortably, knowing that he would have recently been a steady topic.

A curvy woman in a black, sleeveless dress appeared at his side. "What can I get you?"

Richard glanced through the drink list. "Crown Royal, double."

"Fat Tug IPA," James said.

"Great, I'll get those for you," the waitress said and walked away.

"So how've you been? How's the family?" Arnold asked.

"Good, good," Richard replied. "Happy to have me out of the house, I think."

Al laughed. "I bet! How was the first day back?"

"It was alright. Pretty easy day."

"I think he's too used to sitting at home relaxing. I swear the guy was sleepwalking for half the day," James said, then laughed as Richard leveled a glare his way.

"Hah!" Phil blurted from across the table. "Sounds just like the Rick of old then."

Richard sighed while the others laughed. He'd slept through one morning shift during EMT training and for the rest of his career he was known as the sleepy guy. And even though it was all in jest, it was something that came up during the lawsuit and probably influenced what people thought of him now. He wondered what his reputation had become since the incident. Did people think of him as a failure? Screw-up? Murderer?

"Rick? Hey!"

"Oh, sorry. What was that?"

"What did I just say?" Phil bellowed. "He's even sleeping at the table!" The group burst out in howls of laughter.

Richard smiled thinly and shook his head. He could deal with this kind of teasing because these were his friends, they'd had his back when it counted. What did it matter if they clenched a little bit too tightly to the old "sleeping in joke"? It was better than the alternative.

The waitress returned with their drinks and set them on the table. Al raised his glass for a toast. "To Rick! The streets weren't the same without you. It's good to have you back."

Richard lifted his glass with the others. "It's good to be back," he lied, then tilted his head back and drank. His body warmed, as if the alcohol was sending bursts of heat through his veins. Too soon, the glass was empty, leaving nothing but the faint hint of vanilla and caramel. He ordered another.

"Holy shit, look who crawled out of his hole!" a familiar voice called out. Richard groaned inwardly. On the short list of people Richard preferred to avoid at all costs, Lee Cleats was right near the top. It should have occurred to him that Lee might show up, since Lee was one of them, one of the group back when they all trained together and had taken the Morrissey as their favoured hangout. They had been buddies back then. But people change, and sometimes a shared profession isn't enough to overcome that. Even when they stopped actively hanging out, they still worked well together. It's not always easy, but it's important to put personal feelings aside on the job. But this was different: Lee had crossed a line that put them forever at odds with each other when he testified against Richard.

"You still suspended? How long was it for again? Eighteen, twenty weeks?" Lee asked.

"Get out of here, Lee," James said.

Richard almost spoke up, but he knew Lee was just goading him, so he ignored it. There was a saying his son tended to use: "Don't feed the trolls," in reference to gaming online. Richard thought it applied here as well.

The waitress arrived with Richard's second drink. After she put it down, Lee decided to toss out one last barb before walking away. "Hey, try not to pour that down the wrong hole."

James, who had vigorously defended Richard throughout the ordeal, jumped out of his seat. Richard couldn't hear all the words exchanged, but he could accurately guess the content from the proximity of James' face to Lee's.

Richard got up and put his hand on James' shoulder. "It's not worth it, man. Don't worry about him."

James reluctantly backed down, muttering "asshole." Lee smirked and walked away. When they sat back down, everyone muttered and looked around sheepishly, not sure what to say. Richard picked up his fresh glass of Crown Royal and raised it. "To the assholes," he said. "May they get run over by a fucking truck."

His friends roared their agreement, and they drank.

FOUR
JOEL

BOXES AND CRATES. That was Joel's life these days: unload, unpack, and crush. Then do it all over again.

Not that he particularly minded. There were a lot worse things he could be doing. It also paid better than the gas stations he'd habitually worked at in the past.

People tended to walk into grocery stores expecting shelves to be stocked, but they rarely thought about the work that went into it. The huge bins of neatly stacked produce? People would be amazed at how much got thrown out before and after their time on display. Sometimes it already had mould on it when it arrived at the loading dock and Joel would have to sort through the piles to pick out the good from the bad. On average, about fifteen percent of the produce was already bad when it arrived. Would that make people think twice before buying? Knowing their clean-looking, freshly washed apples had been in a bin with a bunch of rotten, mouldy apples could turn some people off. That's why the worst stuff was always stacked near the front: to make sure it was taken first.

The prevalence of insects and rodents might also bother people. It didn't matter how hard they tried, the annoying creatures always got in somehow. It was simply a fact of life: where there's food, there's vermin.

The bulk food could also be a problem. Joel once had to toss out a fifty-pound crate of oats because rats had eaten through the box and had a feast. Hopefully, no one ever found out how much they had sold from that bin before the rats were discovered.

Canned products were both good and bad. Joel liked that they tended to survive almost anything. He also liked the fact that they didn't stink like the fruit storage. However, the all-too-common damage around the edges could make them a nightmare to stack.

No, it wasn't a glamorous job; but it paid the bills, at least to a certain extent. It was thanks to his wife, Jenny, that he could afford to live on the seventeenth floor of a Yaletown condo. Being an art curator pays pretty well, but her rich parents also helped. They were the ones paying a hundred dollars a day for Joel and Jenny's three-year old daughter, Hayley, to go to daycare.

On this particular day, he was stacking bananas. People would assume they'd be annoying to stack but, on the contrary, the common curvature made it relatively painless; as long as there weren't any gaps in the display which would freak out the produce manager.

An old man shambled up next to him and looked over the bananas. He sniffed and looked at Joel.

"Hey," he said.

Joel kept stacking. "Can I help you?"

"Do these bananas come from Mexico?"

Joel nodded. "Yes, they do."

The old man's weathered face took on an angry countenance. Joel could tell he was used to frowning, because the wrinkles on his face were all angled downwards. "That's disgusting," the man said, spittle flying out of his mouth. The loose skin on his jowls flapped back and forth as he spoke. "What a filthy country. They grow those in human shit, you know."

"Um, I'm pretty sure that's not true, sir," Joel said.

The man scrunched his face up like he was sucking on a sour candy. He shook his reddened face and waved dismissively at Joel. "Eeehhhhhhhh," was all he said, though. Then he turned and shuffled away, presumably to find some fruit that didn't come from Mexico.

Joel watched him go. What a strange thing to be angry about, although he'd seen all manner of craziness in the produce section. Once, an old lady had attacked him with an umbrella when he came to restock the cherries. She had cordoned off a corner of the display and was going through the baskets one by one picking out the best cherries. Anyone who came near got a whack.

Working at the grocery store had been a learning experience for Joel. Ten years ago, he might have knocked the old man upside the head with one of those Mexican bananas, and then shoved it into the guy's mouth. Today, imagining it would be enough.

He was a calmer man now. Being a father had taught him a lot about patience, and he'd learned to keep his temper in check. These days, instead of flying off the handle, he'd close his eyes and take steady breaths while counting to ten. It almost always worked.

Joel saw the produce manager walking through his section inspecting the displays. He was on his way over. Joel stopped thinking about the grumpy old man and resumed stacking bananas.

"Joel," the manager called.

"Yeah?"

"What's taking you so long? We still have a truck to unload before you leave tonight. I'm not paying you overtime if you can't get it done on time."

"I'm almost done here, then I'll head back."

"Look at these bananas, they're a mess. There's singles and doubles all over the place."

"People have been breaking them off the bunches and lea—"

"I don't care. Fix it. Hey, what's wrong with you? Why are your eyes closed?"

"Nothing, a headache."

"Jesus, not you too? We're already shorthanded today."

"It's fine. I'm sure it'll be gone in a moment," Joel replied.

The manager frowned. "Just hurry up," he said and walked away.

Joel considered calling out: "See? It's gone now," but decided against it. The manager was an annoying jerk, but he wasn't completely clueless. That insult wouldn't fly over his head like it would other people.

He finished organizing the bananas and pushed his pallet jack of empty boxes to the back, doing his best to avoid the crowds of people who had no interest in letting him through. Walking time from produce to storage normally: forty-five seconds. Walking time while pushing a pump cart: four minutes. First thing to learn when dealing with customers in any work environment is that your time is worth less than theirs. That was another lesson Joel had struggled to accept.

He was half done unloading the truck when one of his coworkers flagged him down.

"Hey, Joel. Someone is outside looking for you."

"What? For me?" Joel asked, surprised. He wasn't expecting any visitors.

"Yeah, you. Said he's looking for a guy named Joel. You're the only one here."

"Who is it?"

"I dunno, man. Some guy."

Joel sighed. "Yeah, but what's he look like?"

"Bit older. Dark hair, maybe same height as you, but a bigger guy."

Joel shook his head. He had no idea who it was. "Alright, I'll be out in a minute."

"Cool, he should be wandering around the deli area."

When Joel finished stacking the boxes he had pulled off the truck, he headed out. The description didn't sound like Jenny's dad. And he couldn't think of any other older people who would visit him at work.

He walked to the deli and took a look around. Other than a few customers, he didn't see the man there. Had he left?

"Joel," came a deep voice from behind him.

That voice. Joel froze. His heart thumped once, then stopped.

He turned around to get a look at the man.

His dark eyes were level with Joel's, but they were sunken into his face, making them seem shadowed. His black hair was streaked with grey, and his weathered face was adorned with a thick, black moustache. Big, wide shoulders complemented his thick neck and large arms. Meanwhile, a medium-sized beer belly hung overtop a belt that held up a pair of worn blue jeans. His belly had grown substantially since the last time Joel had seen him. But Joel knew, belly or not, he wasn't someone to trifle with. There would still be plenty of strength left in those muscles. That's what happens when you spend your life working in a lumber mill.

The two of them stared at each other. After hesitating, the old man cracked a menacing half smile and spoke.

"Hello, son. It's been a long time, hasn't it?"

FIVE
ALEX

ALEX FELT A tap on his shoulder and turned around. His team manager, Trudy, motioned questioningly to his headset.

"I'm not on a call right now, just filling in the notes for this account and setting a follow-up."

She smiled. "When you're done with that can you come to my desk please."

"Okay, I'll just be a minute."

He watched her walk away, although in her case it was more of a waddle, then sighed. She was conducting year-end performance reviews and, if anything, he was looking forward to this one even less than usual. On the bright side, this would be the last one.

Less than five minutes later, Alex was sitting at Trudy's desk waiting for her to finish something on her computer. "Okay," she said and turned her pockmarked face to him. She opened a thick manila folder and leafed through the pages until she found the ones with his name on them.

"I know we're busy right now so I don't want to take up too much of your time," she began, then handed him the papers, keeping one copy for herself. "This is your performance review. The top section of each category is the score I've given you along with my observations. And the bottom section is where you have to fill out what you believe you were successful at and what your goals are for the next quarter. Okay?"

Alex nodded. He'd ridden this carousel before, knew how it spun.

"So we'll start off with call handling. Your Average Handle Time is nine minutes forty-two seconds. Almost two minutes of that is after-call work. Do you know what our target AHT is?" Her beady eyes looked out at him over the rim of her thick glasses.

He tried to remember. "About eight thirty?"

"Eight minutes twenty-nine seconds," she said. "You're over by a minute thirteen."

Considering how absurd these targets usually were, he didn't think that was too bad. He didn't really have anything to say to that, so he was silent.

"But your time has gone down by almost thirty seconds since we last spoke, so there is a definite improvement. We need to keep chipping away at it. Is there any way I can help you do that?"

The thought of her sitting beside his desk listening to his calls for a day offering advice sounded about as pleasant as wearing a dental dam for an afternoon while a trainee dentist drilled holes in his gums. "No, thanks," he said. "I'll keep focusing on getting my notes done while I have people on the line to cut down the after call." As far as Alex was concerned, all that would do was shuffle minutes around instead of actually improving the call time. But Trudy seemed to think it was like an acceptable answer.

"Good. So I gave you a five out of ten there. Your handle time is still below expectations but because you are improving, I gave you a boost. Does that sound good?"

It actually sounded a bit harsh. At the same time, he knew her job was to make sure people scored as low as possible. Lower scores meant smaller raises, smaller raises meant higher profit, and higher profit meant bigger management bonuses. No one on his team had a higher average review than seven, so he decided five was good enough and nodded.

"Okay."

"Next is your call resolution and escalation rates. You are taking an average of..."

He stopped paying attention. *I really don't give a shit about your stupid metrics.*

Someone a few desks back was getting frustrated. He could hear a woman's voice getting louder. "Sir! Sir! You can't talk to me like that! You need to calm down, sir. No. No. Sir, I will be forced to disconnect if you continue—" It was Lisa. Alex was pretty sure she had more escalations than anyone else. Maybe it was her annoying Fran Drescher voice, or her abrasive personality. Likely a combination of the two.

"Alex?"

"Yes."

"Does that make sense?"

He nodded. "Yep."

She frowned slightly, but didn't challenge him. "Okay, the last thing we'll talk about is attitude. Your attendance and punctuality are excellent; no complaints there. Keep it up."

That wasn't very hard, not like he had a particularly busy or interesting life.

"But you still aren't working with the team. And I think this goes back to what we were talking about before."

Oops, missed that.

She must have picked up on his confusion. She sat back, her chair squealed in protest. "Your lack of engagement."

Oh.

"On a call your quiet personality can be a great tool. It helps to keep people calm and it defuses most situations. But there is such a thing as too little emotion. It seems like you don't seem to really care, you know? You don't empathize. If customers can pick up on that over the phone, how do you think it comes off with your co-workers?"

I'm pretty sure you're the only one to notice. "I'm sorry. I'll be more involved."

She stared at him, a look of unhappy concentration on her face like she was holding back some powerful gas. After a few moments she asked, "Alex, where do you see yourself in five years?"

Either a coffin or an urn. "Umm."

She leaned forward, the chair squealing again, struggling under her weight. "Do you plan on staying with us here? Do you want to work your way into a position with Escalations? Something off the phones? Or something completely different?"

I wonder how much it costs to be cremated? Is it cheaper than a burial? I haven't really thought about it. "I don't know. I haven't really thought about it," he said.

"Well, you need to think about it, Alex. I can see you aren't passionate about what you're doing, and that is what is holding you back. I think you have real potential, but it isn't being realized right now."

He looked away. "Are you firing me?" *Wouldn't that be funny?*

"No! No of course not. I'm trying to help. I want you to be successful."

"What's the point?"

She looked genuinely confused. "What do you mean what's the point? Don't you want to be successful? Don't you—"

"No! What does it matter? Why do you care? Why does it matter what happens to me? Is my life really your concern?"

"I'm trying to help you, Alex."

"Well, don't. Just stay out of it."

For once she was at a loss for words. He saw the hurt look on her face and felt a wave of guilt. *She's not a bad person. She doesn't deserve all the shitty things I've thought and said about her behind her back.*

"I…"

"I think you should go home for the rest of the day," she said, her jaw set in a way he hadn't seen before.

"Okay." He stood up and looked around, his coworkers were watching now. *Piss off.*

He looked down at Trudy, who was facing her monitor now, back straight and studiously avoiding looking in his direction. He felt bad for her.

"I'm…" he stopped, and sighed instead. *Why bother?*

He went to his desk to grab his backpack, then left. What's one more regret amid a lifetimes worth?

* * * * *

Later that night, after he knew Trudy was no longer in the office, Alex called to request some time off. Word of their exchange must have gotten out because the manager he spoke with was rather cool towards him. When he apologized for the late notice and said he needed some time to himself, she responded: "I think that would be a good idea. You should really think about what you want to do."

Her catty attitude bothered him, but she approved his request, so he put up with it. *If only you knew, you might treat me differently.*

But different how? Would she speak softly, and meekly acquiesce to whatever he asked? Would her voice drip with honey instead of venom? *Better not upset the guy who wants to kill himself. Best be his friend, show him that life isn't all that bad.* Honestly, if he would stick it out for a bit longer, maybe he would have some sort of epiphany and everything would change.

He didn't want to hear it. Fake words from fake people trying to make sure they avoided feeling any guilt over what he did with his life.

He sighed. It was a good idea to take time off. It seemed silly that he was saving up three weeks of holidays and wouldn't use them. Might as well forget about work and do whatever last things he wanted to do before, well, before he couldn't anymore.

It was surreal thinking about it, now that it felt so close— like a companion he'd spent his entire life looking for, whose presence he could almost feel now. And if he looked over his shoulder quickly enough, he might catch it there, waiting for him, arms open wide, ready to welcome him into its embrace. The thought was comforting.

He had a nagging feeling that it was taking too long, that he was over-thinking it, preparing needlessly. *People don't do it this way. I need to stop thinking about it and just DO IT.*

It was important to do this right, though. He had to make sure.
Coward.

Not that, perhaps considerate? He had to be mindful of—
Coward!

"No!" He slammed his hand on the table. "I'm not a coward, I'm…"

Crazy. "Talking to myself." He began to laugh, quietly at first. Soon he was holding his stomach, tears spilling down his face as his body was rocked by giant sobs of laughter.

"Oh…oh." He wiped the tears from his face and tried to catch his breath. "This makes me something else entirely, doesn't it?"

SIX
MELISSA

MELISSA FINISHED ACCESSORIZING the mannequin in the window and wiped her brow. It wasn't too hot outside, but the spotlights and reflective white surfaces made the store window display feel like the inside of a furnace. She picked up the box filled with clothes she had removed from the mannequin and retreated.

Exiting the overheated display area, a soft gust of wind swirled through the open entrance, causing her body to shiver reflexively. *What strange weather.* A week ago it was so cold and windy that everyone was sure winter had arrived early. Then the cold disappeared and, suddenly, it felt like summer had returned in the middle of October. Melissa didn't mind. As far as she was concerned, any warm, sunny days at this time of year were a blessing. Best soak it up now, before November when the sun had a tendency to disappear for about four months.

Amrit was dancing and singing in front of the counter while Robin Thicke's new single *Blurred Lines* played on the stereo. "Oh, I love this song," she said to Tam, who was standing behind the counter with a bored expression.

"Oh yeah?" Tam said noncommittally. "It's ok, I guess. I like the beat."

"It's a stupid song," Melissa chimed in. "Have you listened to the lyrics?"

"Who listens to music for the lyrics?" Amrit asked. "It's all about *dancing*."

Melissa rolled her eyes and continued towards the back of the store where her manager Lynn was sitting at her desk doing paperwork.

"I finished the front," Melissa said. She stacked her box on top of a pile of similar boxes of outgoing display merchandise.

"Thanks," Lynn responded. "When you go back out, can you tell Amrit to stop singing before she scares away all our customers, please?"

"Okay," Melissa said, with a laugh.

"Hey, Amrit," Melissa said when she came back out. "Lynn says you sound like an injured cockatiel and should stop singing before animal services comes here to put you down."

Amrit made a face and gave Melissa the finger, but she stopped singing. She didn't stop dancing, however.

Ilsa came over from the cosmetic counter. She'd just finished a consult and waved goodbye to her customer. "Melissa is right," she said. "Even my customer was laughing. She said she'd love to see you on *Canadian Idol*."

"See? That means I'm entertaining and should keep singing."

Ilsa looked at Melissa with dismay. "Umm, that's not what I meant."

"Amrit!" Lynn called out from her office. "I hope you're not standing by the till instead of at the front door where you're supposed to be."

"Yep, I just had to throw something away," Amrit called back. She stuck her tongue out at the rest of the girls and went back to the front, reaching the door in time to greet a couple entering the store. "Welcome to Blackbird," she said to them.

The woman nodded and walked right past, man in tow.

Melissa approached them. "Hi, what can I help you with?" she asked.

"Um, nothing," the woman answered. "I'm just looking for my size." She dug through a rack of pants while her companion stood impatiently behind her.

"Of course, if you need anything let me know."

"Actually..." the woman said.

Melissa turned around just in time to catch the man quickly looking up. He had been staring at her ass. "Yes?"

"I'm going to need these hemmed," the woman said. She pulled out a pair of pants and held them up to her legs. "I love this brand but they're always too long."

"Not a problem. We can do that for you. Why don't you come back here and we'll get your measurements."

They walked to the till where Melissa handed the pants to Tam, who did the alterations. "She would like these hemmed."

"Of course," Tam said brightly, her earlier countenance completely displaced. "Follow me ma'am and we'll get you looked after." They disappeared into a fitting area at the back of the store.

Melissa started to organize the row of pants that had been rummaged through and caught the man looking her over again. If he thought he was being subtle, he wasn't. "Can I help you?"

"Oh, uh, no," he said, looking away.

"There's a chair over there if you would like to sit down and relax while you wait," Melissa said, pointing to a white chair near a pillar in the middle of the store.

"Thanks," he muttered and walked away.

Melissa fought off a shiver that had nothing to do with the temperature and focused on folding. She knew men, and people in general, had a tendency to let their eyes wander. But it still made her uncomfortable to catch a man staring at her. That was the main reason she worked in a women's clothing store: it reduced her chances of having to deal with members of the opposite sex. Though she knew she would never get away from it completely, at least here she felt somewhat shielded.

Tam and the woman reappeared a few minutes later. "Alright, I'll have this ready for you tomorrow afternoon," Tam said. She filled out a claim stub and handed it to the woman. "Please remember to bring this with you when you pick up your pants."

The woman nodded. "Thanks." She motioned to her male companion and they left, nearly running over a dark haired woman at the entrance, who glared at them before walking over to the cosmetics area.

Ilsa spent nearly twenty minutes helping the woman, while the rest of the girls prepped the store for closing. It brought a smile to Lynn's face when she left with a bag of expensive cosmetics. When the last customer left, Amrit closed the door and called out, "Closing time, ladies!"

"Okay," Lynn said. "Ilsa and Tam, bring your cash drawers to the back and we'll count them. Amrit and Melissa can start cleaning up. Closing meeting in fifteen."

Tam turned the music up and the girls went about their tasks.

"Hey, Melissa," Amrit said, bouncing around in tune with the in-store music. "Are you coming out with us tonight or not?"

"I don't know," Melissa said. "I haven't really thought about it." She had thought about it, and she wasn't interested.

"Aw, come oooon. You never come clubbing with us."

"It really isn't my scene, you know that," Melissa said.

As the most social one of the group, Amrit had taken it upon herself to drag Melissa out of her shell.

"But it's my birthday. Come on, it'll be so much fun. You don't have to drink, just come dance with us. We're going to Venue, it's amazing there."

Melissa had heard of Venue. It was a dance club, the kind of place she used to frequent with her friends before…"I don't think so, Amrit."

"Seriously. You're going to give me a complex here. You won't even come out on my birthday? Are we even friends?"

"We are, we are. I…" Melissa paused, not wanting to talk about her real reasons for avoiding the club scene. She didn't feel comfortable talking about what had happened to her, especially as an excuse for not doing something. She didn't want to use it as some sort of pity card, that felt *cheap*. And she didn't want to deal with the way it changed people's perception of her, the way people looked at victims, like they had a broken component in need of fixing.

Melissa didn't want, or need, to talk about it. She wanted to forget.

The other problem was that she knew how easy it would be to poke holes through her anti-club logic. Yes, she had been attacked after going to a club, but there was no evidence that those two facts were linked in any way. The man who attacked her had never been found. The police had gone over the security tapes, and every person she came into contact with at the club that night had been interviewed. All of them came away clean. The only real link between the club and her attack was the timing and proximity. A tenuous connection, but it was enough in her mind.

Melissa used to love clubbing. The chaos of the noise, dancing, and alcohol had always been such a rush. She even tried going back, once, about three months after she'd been attacked. Lindsay was celebrating a promotion at work, so Melissa went out with the old crew to party, but she never made it inside. She had stood there, foot on the threshold, unable to move. Her heart had begun to beat faster, almost in rhythm to the electronica playing inside. Someone from behind nudged her, telling her to move it. Suddenly she was back in the alley, clothes ripped, hands all over her body, the metallic tang of blood in her mouth.

She made up an excuse then too, told her friends she felt sick, like she was going to throw up. The latter was true, just not for the reasons her friends assumed.

"Hellooooo?" Amrit said, waving her hand in front of Melissa's face. "Earth to Melissa."

"Oh, sorry. Listen, I'm not feeling well right now, I think—"

"Do you think I'm dumb? Look, I'm not taking no for an answer. So here's what's going to happen. We're going to pick you up at your place tonight at nine. You're going to come with us to Venue. We'll all have a great time. We'll take you home later and you'll wonder why in the world you haven't been hanging out with us more often. Got it?"

Melissa felt trapped. She wanted to go, but she also wanted not to go. On one hand, she hadn't been to a club in years; surely she wouldn't have the same reaction as the last time. But on the other hand, she'd been feeling nervous recently and hadn't been sleeping well. The incident at Playland was still running through her mind.

"I...I guess so," Melissa said, forcing the words out as if dragging a team of horses.

"Great! This is going to be awe-sooome." The last word came out as Amrit's attempt at singing. Melissa cringed.

They finished cleaning the store and joined the other girls waiting at the tills.

"Okay, ladies," Lynn started. "We finished the day at ninety-two percent to budget. That's not bad considering we were only sixty percent at four o'clock. So, good job during the last two hours. Ilsa led the way again today, selling one hundred and fifteen percent of her budget in cosmetics. Good work!"

Everyone clapped while Ilsa smiled modestly.

Lynn continued, "I know Christmas season hasn't really started yet, but our budgets are going to start going up every day from now until January. So I need everyone focused and selling as much as they can. Always remember to match accessories. People don't just need a top or a skirt; they need an outfit. So find the accessories that finish that outfit. Always make recommendations, and don't be offended if they don't buy the product right then. They might buy it later or put it on their Christmas list. Got it?"

"Yes," the girls said in unison.

"Good. Okay, good work today. We'll see you tomorrow."

Lynn flagged Melissa down as the other girls began walking to the back office to get their belongings. She waited until they were alone: "I hear you're going to Venue tonight."

"Yeah."

"Are you okay? I know you said you were having trouble." Lynn had been a family friend for years and knew what had happened to Melissa. She was actually one of the few people Melissa had spoken to with any degree of candor about how she was feeling.

"I was. I am. But, I dunno. Maybe I shouldn't go."

"No, you should go. Amrit loves to party, but she's a good girl. They all are. You'll have fun. I think it'll be good for you."

"Yeah? I hope so."

"I'm here for you if you need anything. They will be too, if you let them."

Melissa smiled. "Thanks."

Amrit, Tam and Ilsa came out of the office together, chatting and waving at Melissa and Lynn as they walked past. "See you tonight," Amrit said.

Melissa waved back. "See you later." She turned to Lynn. "Alright, I'm gonna go."

Lynn nodded. "Go ahead. I've got some paperwork to finish. I'll see you tomorrow. Have fun tonight!"

"I'll try."

SEVEN
RICHARD

WHEN RICHARD GOT home after his first full week back at work, there was no welcome party. No cluster of happy children crying out his name. No loving wife standing watch behind them, waiting her turn to greet her husband. The kids were off playing on the Xbox or computer and, from the sound of it, Natalie was in the kitchen watching *The Ellen DeGeneres Show*.

Life, as it turns out, is far different from the way it's depicted in TV shows: There are no grand entrances, audience applauding, and everyone cheering for your return. There is only routine. And, while the blandness of everyday life stands in stark contrast to the happily dysfunctional families everyone knows and loves, it isn't necessarily a bad thing. The real problem is when people expect life to be like a TV show.

Richard hung up his jacket and put away his shoes. He went to the kitchen where his wife was sitting at the table watching Ellen on the small corner TV.

"Hey." He bent over and gave her a quick kiss.

"Hi. How was work?" She didn't take her eyes off the TV. Gerard Butler was being interviewed.

"It was fine. You?"

"Same. I defrosted some pork chops for supper. I thought we'd have them with risotto."

"That sounds good. I'm gonna go change first."

"Okay."

He climbed the stairs to the bedrooms. His twelve-year-old son, Nathan, was definitely playing Xbox, as the walls were vibrating from the sounds of the explosions. He glanced into his daughter's room as he walked past, where Sara was on her laptop Skyping with a friend. At thirteen, she had reached the stage where she was communicating with her friends all day, every day. He didn't understand, she'd told him. But he remembered being young and thinking every little thing was of world shattering importance. Kids always think their parents don't understand, even when they do.

Nathan's door was closed, so he opened it and was greeted with a blast of sound. "Hey, can you turn that down, buddy?"

"What?"

"The walls are vibrating. Turn it down, please."

"But I can't. I'm playing."

Sighing, Richard walked in and turned the sound down.

"Awww, Dad! Now I can't hear it."

"You can hear it just fine, Nathan. You don't need it that loud."

He could hear his son mumbling behind him, but he didn't really take notice. Yet another one of the things you brush off when you're a father. He wasn't really a fan of his son playing those kinds of games. They were a lot more realistic than the games he played when he was a kid, and he worried that it would warp Nathan's worldview. But with society so full of sensationalized violence, it was nearly impossible to shield him from it. Maybe getting used to it now was the best way to save him in the future.

Richard avoided thinking any further about the implications of that thought. What did it say about the world when the only emotional defence was to become numb to it all?

In any case, he had to admit that—for better or worse—the Xbox had become the more effective parent.

He changed his clothes and went back downstairs to cook dinner. The pork chops weren't fully defrosted yet, but he was hungry and didn't feel like waiting. Natalie didn't object to his impatience. She liked it when he cooked and he liked it when she cooked, but they used to like cooking together. Now, for whatever reason, one or the other would usually fly solo in the kitchen. It ought to be easier to work together after all this time, especially on something so routine, but their lack of cooperation in the kitchen had begun to feel like an analogue for the growing gap in their relationship.

When dinner was ready, Richard called out for Nathan and Sara to come downstairs. Five minutes later, when they still hadn't come down, Natalie sighed and went to round them up.

Richard poured himself a drink while he waited. He dropped a few ice cubes into a short glass and whistled lightly as he sauntered over to the liquor cabinet, swirling the ice cubes in his glass as he went.

He opened the cabinet and pulled out his bottle of Crown Royal. It was empty.

"What the hell?" he muttered. He was sure it was a new bottle.

He rifled through the cabinet, pushing around a few bottles of red wine and a half-full bottle of Sour Puss they'd bought about ten years ago and hadn't been able to finish, but he couldn't find any backup bottles.

He heard Natalie coming down the stairs with the kids.

"Hey, Nat. What happened to my rye? I thought I just opened this bottle."

"I don't know," she said, "Maybe you drank it."

"No, I just got this."

She sighed. "I don't know, dear. You aren't exactly paying attention to what's left in the bottle once you start."

Richard's eyes narrowed. He had a feeling she'd poured whatever was left down the drain, again. He walked over to the sink, dumped his ice, and slammed his glass down on the counter. He winced inwardly at the cracking sound the glass made as it contacted the granite and hoped it wasn't damaged.

Natalie's eyes smouldered as he walked back to the table and sat down.

"That's fine," Richard said, trying to make up for his outburst. "I don't need a drink anyway."

Natalie ignored him. "Nathan," she said, "get your elbows off the table."

"Awww, Mom," Nathan whined, removing his elbows.

After a few minutes Richard spoke up, trying to act normal. "So, how was school?"

Nathan shrugged. "It was okay."

Sara stared at her plate without looking up.

"Sara?" Richard asked.

"What?"

"I asked you a question."

She huffed. "I don't know."

"Really? You don't know how your day was?"

"I don't know. It was fine, I guess. Gawd." Her tone dripped with annoyance.

"Do not speak to us like that, Sara," Natalie said in her firm mother's voice.

Richard glanced at Natalie then back at Sara, who was obviously still angry at them for banning cell phones at the table last night. Richard thought letting her get one in the first place had been a horrible mistake. A cell phone at thirteen years old! He was in his mid-twenties by the time he'd gotten one.

They finished dinner in silence.

Later that night, Richard and Natalie lay in bed. Natalie was halfway through a self-improvement book she'd picked up a few days earlier. Richard had to work early the next morning, so he was trying to doze off.

"Richard?" Natalie said.

He rolled over. She had put her book away and was looking straight ahead, eyes glistening. "Hmm? What's wrong?"

"We aren't doing well, are we?"

This got his attention. He sat up. "What do you mean?"

"I mean us."

"Is this something from that book of yours? Can't we talk about it tomorrow? I've got to get up early."

"No, Richard. I've been putting this off for too long. And this isn't something from my *stupid book*." He could tell she was aggravated.

"I didn't say it was stupid." He was on the defensive; he hated being defensive. It always made him feel like he was wrong somehow, and that he had to apologize for it.

"Your tone said it was stupid. Don't you think I know what you mean when you speak that way?"

"That's not what I meant. I'm sure it's a good book."

"Jesus." She put her face in her hands then pushed them back around the side of her head and through her hair. He knew her well enough to know that meant she was trying to collect herself. It was a good sign: it meant she didn't want to fight. He could still recover from this. "Why are we talking about my book? Richard, I need to talk to you."

"Okay, okay. Speak." He winced at the look on her face. Not the best way to salvage the conversation. He pushed himself up into a sitting position. If marriage is a war, then conversations are the battles. He needed to be at his best to come out of this one.

"Things haven't been the same since...what happened. You're not the same. *We're* not the same."

He wanted to speak, but she looked like she had more to say. This was obviously going somewhere and he was sure he wasn't going to like it.

After a few moments, she continued. "I know this has been a hard time for you. A terrible time. But we have to move on with our lives."

"Geez, Nat. What do you think I'm trying to do? I'm working again—"

"I know, but—"

"But what? I just need time."

"You keep saying that. It's been months, Richard."

"I killed someone!" Richard said, almost shouting. "A little girl is dead because of something I did, a mistake I made! I have to live with that."

Natalie bit her lip and shook her head slightly. She wiped a tear off her face. "I know," she whispered. "I can't imagine what you're going through. But you can't do it alone, you have to let me help."

"You can't help me," Richard said. He clenched his fists to keep his hands from shaking. "This isn't something that will suddenly be okay if you hold my hand."

"That's why I need help. We both need help. That's why," she paused and took his hand in hers, "I signed us up for counselling."

"Are you kidding me?" Richard shouted, yanking his hand away. He got out of bed and began to pace. He felt under siege. "You can't be serious."

"We need to talk to someone, we need—"

"*We* don't need anything. This isn't your problem. And in case you forgot, I was already forced to go to a shrink. I was cleared to work."

"I know that," Natalie said, voice rising. She stood up and faced him from across the bed. "Workplace therapy. So what? They don't know anything, they aren't the ones living with you. And in case you forgot, we are married. This is a partnership, and what affects you affects me. Or are you too busy feeling sorry for yourself to realize that?"

"What I realize is that a damned shrink isn't going to change anything for anyone. What are we going to talk about? My feelings? Well how about this: I feel like shit. I feel—"

"Richard, can you not—"

"No, no. You want feelings, right? I felt them all; I was angry, depressed, and suicidal. I'm filled with regret. I'm questioning everything I do, everything I've ever done. And I can't stop thinking about it, okay? Is that what you want?"

"No, that's not what I want."

"Then what? What do you want from me?"

"I want to help. I want things to go back—"

Natalie stopped at the sound of a soft knock on their door. She took a moment to compose herself then cracked the door open. "Hey, Nathan. What's wrong?"

"I can't sleep. Why are you and Dad yelling?" his sleepy voice queried from the hallway.

"I'm so sorry, honey. We were just talking. We didn't mean to be so loud. We promise we'll be quiet, okay?"

"Okay."

"Go back to bed." She closed the door softly and stood there for a moment. When she turned around, her eyes were bright and angry. "We can't go on like this, Richard. If you won't do it for us, then do it for our children. You *need* help." Without another word she climbed back into bed and turned her lamp off.

Richard stood beside the bed, illuminated by the moonlight shining through the window, and stared at her back. He knew he couldn't say anything else. Once she went to bed with her back turned like that, it was all over. She could be awake for hours, but if he tried to talk to her, she'd pretend to be asleep.

He sighed and crawled back into bed and lay there for a long time staring at the ceiling. The idea of going to another shrink left a bad taste in his mouth. He'd already bit his tongue and pretended to be fine for one, now he needed to do it for another? What for? It wouldn't change the facts. He'd still done what he'd done, and he still had to live with it.

But it would make Natalie happy, he thought, looking at her again. How is it that a person's back can say so much? He'd been given this treatment so many times, gotten so used to the specific arrangement of freckles near her right shoulder that seemed to form a tiny face that jeered at him—judged him. At any other time, those same freckles looked completely benign.

He looked away, unable to bear the accusations any longer. Maybe she was right. Maybe he should go to this counsellor of hers, tell some stories, and get it over with. Natalie was obviously invested in the idea. It might get him back on her good side, at least. Who knows: maybe he would even feel better.

He put his hand on her shoulder. "Okay. I'll go," he said quietly.

She didn't respond with words, but rolled over and moved closer to him. Her eyes were closed. He sighed again, and went to sleep. He knew she had heard.

EIGHT
MELISSA

Entering the club was…anticlimactic. She'd felt a small degree of trepidation on the way there, but it dissipated upon arrival. Amrit and her friends were talking, laughing, and full of energy. It was infectious. It made her forget what she had been worried about.

She didn't stop outside the club, feet rooted to the ground, unsure what to do. She didn't find herself lost in a terrible memory from the past, either. Amrit's friend Priya was busy regaling them with a story about an epic night she'd had at Venue a few weeks earlier, and before Melissa even realized it, she was inside. And just like that, a mental barrier she'd been harbouring for years dissolved.

The table next to the dance floor where Melissa sat at a table covered in full, half-full, and empty plastic cups. She spent most of the evening nursing a Sprite while Amrit and her friends took turns drinking and dancing throughout the night. Although she was feeling relatively relaxed, she had absolutely no desire to get herself tangled within the mess of bodies on the dance floor. Purple, pink, yellow, orange and blue lights flashed everywhere, while the thumping bass sent vibrations up the bench and through her spine. Three of the other girls yelled at each other across the table trying to have a conversation. Eventually, Melissa gave up trying to understand what they were saying; it was impossible to decipher all of their words. And she was woefully out of practice at piecing together drunken club-speech so her inability to effectively communicate with the other girls put a slight damper on the night, making her feel out of place, like a moped trying to navigate a ten-lane freeway.

The beat stopped, replaced by a pulsing electronic rhythm. "Make some noooooooooooooise!" DJ called out over the loudspeakers, his voice accompanied by a triple-horn sound effect. Melissa was both surprised and not surprised to hear that horn. It had been overused even back when she used to frequent these places. The more things change…

"Is everybody having a good time?" the DJ asked.

"Wooo, not really," Melissa said, knowing no one would hear.

"It's time…to lower…the BOOOOOOOOOOOOOOOOOOM!" the DJ yelled, and immediately switched into a track with some of the loudest and most powerful bass Melissa had ever heard. Was it her, or were clubs a lot louder these days?

Amrit, wearing a black and white tube dress and high heels, slid out of the press of bodies and sat down beside Melissa. Her body was covered in a sheen of sweat and her hair looked decidedly crazy. She picked up Melissa's drink, took a sip, and made a face, then reached for the other cups, looking for one with alcohol in it. She found one, knocked it back in one gulp, and put the empty cup down.

She reached down and pulled off her heels. "I can't dance in these things," she said, massaging her feet.

Melissa took a moment to process the words through the music and then nodded.

Amrit leaned over and spoke into Melissa's ear. "Isn't this DJ great? You should dance with us."

Melissa looked at the press of bodies grinding against each other and then back at Amrit. She shook her head. "Nah. I don't think there's any room out there."

"Oh, come on," Amrit said, picking up another cup and downing its contents. Then, without bothering to put her heels back on, she grabbed Melissa by the arm and dragged her off the seat.

Melissa went, unwillingly, into the fray as Amrit pulled her through the press of sweaty, gyrating bodies until they reached their friends. They'd managed to create enough space to dance in, but even then, it was nearly impossible to move without bumping into someone.

Melissa started off stiffly at first, but as time wore on she relaxed and even began to enjoy herself. Why had she been so scared? It's just a bunch of people trying to have a good time. Maybe this was exactly what she needed. It had been a long time since she'd been able to go out and have some fun.

After about an hour of dancing, Melissa and Amrit went to the bar to buy some drinks. They each had a shot called Dirty Girl Scout, and then ordered drinks. Melissa stuck with Sprite, while Amrit got a Tequila Sunrise.

A tall, blonde man with an angular chin shouldered his way in beside them. He leaned in close, his red-rimmed eyes lingering on Melissa's breasts before finally making their way up to her face. "Hey, beautiful," he said. His breath smelled like booze. "Let me buy you two a shot. Whatever you just had." He signalled at the bartender, who had placed Amrit's Tequila Sunrise on the bar.

"No," Melissa said, holding a hand up and shaking her head so the bartender knew not to get anything else. "We're fine, thanks." She paid for the drinks and turned around.

"It's okay, I got it," the drunk man said. He pulled a couple of twenty-dollar bills out of his wallet. "Drinks for my lady friends," he said, waving his cash.

Melissa sighed. "Don't bother," she said. "Let's go, Amrit."

"Why didn't you let him buy our drinks? He was cute."

"He was drunk."

"So? I'm drunk too. That's kind of what people do here."

"I'm not here to hook up," Melissa said, then changed the subject. "Come on, let's go dance."

Amrit didn't need any convincing. She tilted her head back, drained her Tequila Sunrise, then raised the empty cup in the air shouting, "Woooooooo!"

Melissa laughed. She put what remained of her Sprite down on a nearby table and went back onto the chaotic dance floor with Amrit, where they met up with the group and started dancing. A few minutes later Melissa felt a bump from behind. Initially, she ignored it. It was tight quarters, and getting tighter as the night went on; bumps were expected.

Then she got bumped again, and again. It didn't feel like an accident anymore; more like the incessant buzzing of a fly that wouldn't go away. She turned to look at who it was and realized it was the blonde man from the bar. His glazed eyes looked down her shirt then made their way back up to her face. His mouth split into a wide, feral-looking grin that made her skin crawl.

She fought the urge to vomit. "Get away from me."

The music was too loud, though, and he didn't hear her. He grabbed her by the hips and pulled her towards him.

Melissa instinctively slapped him across the face. He looked stunned for a moment, then turned angry. His face went red and he started yelling. The words were completely unintelligible, but Melissa knew exactly what he meant. A small space began to open up on the dance floor as other people got out of the way, just in case things went bad.

Suddenly Amrit was beside Melissa, shouting obscenities right back at the man. The other girls stepped forward and surrounded her. The man blinked, realizing the odds had been turned against him. He raised his hands in a show of surrender and backed away, not wanting to do anything else to upset the group of angry, protective women.

Melissa pulled Amrit close. She had to shout: "Thanks."

"Don't worry. Guys here can be dicks sometimes," Amrit said, noticing that Melissa's hands were shaking.

"Are you okay?" she asked. "Do you want to leave?"

"No," Melissa said. "It's okay, I'm fine. Thanks."

They started dancing again, but Melissa had started to feel anxious, increasingly aware of every brush, bump, or tap that contacted her body; and it sent a shiver through her every time. It was like something horrible was coming, and she was tense with anticipation; but she made it through the rest of the night.

Except for Melissa and a few designated drivers, nearly everyone else either had a healthy buzz or was outright hammered by the time they stumbled out of the club around two in the morning.

"Let's get some McDonald's," Amrit said. "I could eat four quarter pounders right now."

"No way," Tam said. "You're not throwing up all over my car again."

Amrit burst out laughing. "God, how much did I have to drink that night? How much did I have tonight?" As if to illustrate the extent of her drunkenness, she tripped over herself and would have fallen over if it hadn't been for Priya's quick reaction in catching her.

"Yeah, I think we'll take you home now," Tam said.

"Awww, come on," Amrit said. "The grease helps. It sobers me up."

"So does a glass of water and a lot of sleep," Melissa said.

Amrit continued to protest, but she was overruled. The group began to disperse; Amrit, Tam, Priya, Ilsa, and Melissa walked to the parking lot and piled into Tam's Jetta.

"I'm really happy you came out with us tonight, Melissa," Amrit said, slurring her words.

"I am too," Melissa said. "Thanks for forcing me."

"You needed to be forced. You never want to do anything. And we all know something happened to—"

"Amrit!" Tam warned.

"What?" Amrit asked, oblivious. "We all know it's *something*, right? I don't understand what the big secret is. Melissa, you don't have to talk about it, but…just know that we're here for you, okay?"

"God, you're as subtle as a dump truck, you know that?" Ilsa said.

"Yep," Amrit said, seeming pleased with herself.

Melissa nodded. "Thanks," she said quietly. She didn't know she'd been so obvious. How long had they known? And they'd never said anything, or pushed for information. Had Lynn played a part in this? "How?" she asked.

"We've been working together for a few years now. We all kinda noticed something was up. We asked Lynn and she said something *had* happened, but that it wasn't her story to tell. I hope you're not mad at us. And don't be mad at her either' she's only looking out for you."

So it was Lynn who sold her out. "Oh…okay then," she said. It felt like an invasion of privacy, knowing they'd been talking behind her back, checking up on her. Is there a reason they didn't ask her? Was it because she seemed unapproachable, or were they worried she would brush them off? She probably would have, to be honest.

"You don't have to worry," Tam said. "And we don't want to put you on guard. We were concerned, you know? We're your friends, Melissa; we only wanted to make sure you were okay."

"Yeah, alright," Melissa said.

Tam and Amrit looked at each other. Ilsa and Priya, who were sharing the back seat with Melissa, looked anywhere but in her direction.

When they arrived at Melissa's condo, the other girls got out with her to say goodbye and to hug her. It was nice; it helped wash away the strain of the revelations that surfaced during the drive. She still didn't know if she should feel angry or not.

"Drink lots of water before you go to sleep," she told Amrit.

"I will," Amrit said, who was already steadier than when they'd first left the club: for a petite girl, she recovered quickly.

Melissa swiped her access card and opened the door to her building. She turned and waved to the girls, who waved back at her and waited until she was safely inside. It was a nice gesture, and something a lot of people didn't do anymore—wait to make sure the person they dropped off made it safely through their own front door. Melissa's friend Lacey had once been stranded outside her apartment for hours after her ride left without waiting until she was inside. When she discovered that she'd lost her keys, and her cell phone had long since run out of power, she'd been forced to huddle up on the front step until someone let her in. To make matters worse, it was a cold and rainy night; Lacey was sick for a week afterwards.

She wondered how Lacey was doing. They'd been good friends once. Lacey had become a terrible alcoholic, so much so that her friends and family staged an intervention, but it failed. Melissa had been invited, and she would have been there if she hadn't had to work late that day. They'd drifted apart since then, though they still spoke. She was doing better, thankfully.

She reached her unit and unlocked the door. It creaked open and she stepped inside. She stopped to put her shoes and jacket in the closet before walking past the kitchen on the way to her room, when she heard the sound of the fridge closing.

"Oh, hey Lindsay, I didn't th—" she stopped, breath catching in her throat. That wasn't Lindsay.

A tall, shirtless man turned around, looking almost as surprised as Melissa felt. Then he smiled. "Hey, Melissa, good to see you again."

"Jesus, Luke. You scared the shit out of me," Melissa said, holding a hand over her heart. It was beating so hard she thought her skin would burst. "What are you doing here?"

"Lindsay and I, uh, made up. A few times, if you know wha—"

"Okay, I don't need details. Just put a shirt on if you're going to wander around, okay?"

"Oh, right. Sorry," he said, suddenly feeling self-conscious. He, rather pointlessly, tried to cover himself with his hands, but gave up and gestured towards Lindsay's bedroom. "I'm going to go back to bed. Good night."

"Good night," Melissa said and watched him go.

Earlier that night, Lindsay had sworn she was done with Luke. She was sick of him not "getting her," not listening, and generally being an unbearable buffoon. So she'd put an end to their ongoing, tumultuous relationship.

Melissa actually thought he was a pretty nice guy, one of the few she could tolerate being around for any extended period of time; and he tried really hard to keep Lindsay happy, but she could be incredibly difficult to please. Being her roommate, Melissa knew that Lindsay had an uncanny ability to suddenly and completely change her opinion on a subject or situation, leaving her friends struggling to catch up. Unfortunately for Luke, he was usually the victim of these sudden changes. Or, as the case seemed to be tonight, the beneficiary.

Melissa had a glass of water, brushed her teeth, and changed into her pyjamas. She snuggled into her bed and checked the time: almost three in the morning, and she had to be at work in seven hours.

"Ugh," she muttered and settled in for a short night of sleep.

NINE
JOEL – FIFTEEN YEARS AGO

"HEY, UNCLE FRANK, I'm gonna head home for the night," Joel called out.

"You stock the pop machine?" the burly man behind the counter called out.

"Yes."

"Wash the floors?"

"Yes."

"Turn into a good kid?"

"Nope."

"Figures. Alright, get out of here. You coming after school tomorrow?"

"No, I have detention. I'll be in on Friday though."

"You know," his uncle said, "if you stopped getting in trouble at school and getting stuck in detention all the time you'd have enough money to buy that Camaro you keep talking about."

"I know, I know. See you later."

Uncle Frank waved as he left. Joel walked around to the back of the gas station and unlocked the door of his eighty-four Chevy Cavalier. He sat down, the aged suspension creaking in protest, and pulled a half-finished cigarette out of his pocket. He lit it and took a few pulls to get it going, then sat back in the driver's seat and relaxed. Uncle Frank would probably fire him if he ever found out Joel was stealing cigarettes; not because he really cared if Joel smoked or not, but because they were expensive.

Joel took a few more puffs and flicked the butt off into the darkness; it hit the ground with a burst of sparks like a mini-firework. Joel wondered if any ants looked up at those sparks the same way humans stared at real fireworks. The scale seemed about right.

He turned the key and his car struggled to life. He pumped the pedal a few times to make sure it wouldn't stall out, then put it into gear and pulled out. The car was in reasonably good shape for its age, with very minimal rust showing on its grey frame. The three-speed automatic transmission, on the other hand, was another story. A decade and a half of constantly running up and down the hills around Kelowna had taken its toll. It wasn't uncommon for the gears to suddenly slip when Joel drove up the final hill near his house, sending him sliding back down the way he'd come.

On this particular night, he made it up the hill without any problems. He pulled into the gravel driveway beside his dad's red Pontiac Fiero, pulled the parking brake and put the car in park. He considered lighting another cigarette before going in but changed his mind.

When he opened the front door he was struck by a blast of noise. His dad was sitting in front of the TV watching the Canucks play the Red Wings and, judging from his yelling, the game wasn't going well.

"Jesus Christ, Hirsch, you piece of shit. We'd be better off putting a PeeWee goalie in net. What the hell are you doing out there?"

Joel slipped past him and into the kitchen, where his mom was sitting at the table reading a paper.

"Hey, sweetie, how was work?" she asked.

"It was fine," he said. "Is there anything to eat?"

"There are leftovers in the fridge."

"Thanks."

He found the plate of pasta in the fridge and put it in the microwave for three minutes. While he waited, his father came into the kitchen.

"God," his dad said. "What I wouldn't give to have Bure back on the ice right now."

"Yeah," Joel said.

His dad opened the fridge and pulled out a bottle of Molson Canadian. He twisted off the top and threw it in the sink, then took a long drink. He walked over to Joel's mom and put his hands on her shoulders. She tensed up when he touched her. Joel tensed as well.

"What are you reading, honey?"

"Just the paper," she said stiffly.

"Oh yeah, anything interesting?"

"Exxon and Mobil are going to merge and become the largest company in the world."

"Assholes."

The microwave started beeping and Joel quickly pulled his food out. That turned his father's attention to him. "And what are you doing, boy?"

"Eating. I was working with Uncle Frank tonight."

"Mmm." He nodded, then looked from Joel to his mother, then back at Joel. He took another swig of beer then turned and walked back into the living room. Joel breathed a quiet sigh and looked at his mom, whose shoulders had slumped back down into their normal position.

"I'm going to go eat upstairs, okay?"

His mom nodded. "Remember to bring your plate back down when you're done, okay?"

"Yeah," he said. "Good night." He walked over and gave her a half hug with his free hand. She was shaking.

"Good night, sweetie."

* * * * *

Joel stumbled out of bed at eight in the morning. He dug around through a pile of half-dirty, half-clean clothes he'd thrown on the floor and picked out a T-shirt and pants that seemed reasonably wearable.

He cursed as he stepped on the edge of the plate of leftovers from last night and the fork went flying across the floor. He picked it up and put it on his desk, then went to the bathroom to finish getting ready. The bathroom still smelled of the powerful aftershave his father put on every morning. Joel coughed and waved his hand in an attempt to clear the air. It didn't help.

After a breakfast of buttered toast, and a quick goodbye to his mom, he was ready to go. His beater started up with a slight squeal, making Joel sigh; the Camaro seemed so far away.

A short drive later, he was at school, parked, and walking into class on time—for a change. He sat down at his desk and looked around for Andrew, who he found sitting near the back of the room with his head turned slightly to the left. Joel waved and Andrew looked his way, revealing an impressive black eye. Joel smiled and gave him the finger. Andrew mouthed something Joel couldn't figure out, no doubt an insult. It made Joel smile all the wider.

Andrew was the reason Joel would be spending the afternoon in detention. They had gotten into an argument over something; Joel couldn't actually remember what it was, but it culminated in Andrew calling him the son of a dirty ditch pig. Joel responded with a right hook. Maybe he didn't have the guts to stand up to his father when he was in one of his moods, but damned if Joel was going to let some stuck-up school kid talk like that about his mom.

The teacher walked in the room and called the class to order. Joel slid into his desk, trying to find the most comfortable position, and prepared for yet another long, boring school day.

* * * * *

Detention lasted almost three hours. Joel's school had different ideas on how to discipline wayward students: Instead of locking them in a study room with a teacher for a few hours, they'd adopted the cost-cutting measure of having them do odd jobs around the school. Joel's task that afternoon had been scrubbing the showers in the boy's washrooms, a job made worse when hockey practice ended and Joel had to sit to the side for half an hour waiting for the players to finish their showers.

As a result, he didn't get home until nearly six-thirty that day, but as soon as he opened the front door, he wished detention could have lasted all night. The first sign of trouble was the haphazard arrangement of empty beer bottles on the coffee table. His father couldn't have come home from work more than an hour ago, yet Joel counted over half a dozen empty bottles. The second sign came as a burst of noise from the kitchen.

"You shut your mouth, you stupid bitch," his father yelled, standing with hands balled into fists and breathing heavily.

Joel's mom lay on the ground, tears in her eyes, holding the side of her face. Her nose was bleeding. "I...I'm sorry." Then she saw Joel standing in the living room. "Joel, go upstairs," she said, voice unsteady.

"I said," Joel's father kicked her in the gut, "shut your mouth."

"Hey!" Joel yelled.

"What? Listen to your mother, boy. Go upstairs." He pointed at Joel, then pointed at the stairwell.

Joel stood frozen, not knowing what to do. He wanted to protect his mother, especially because he knew this was only the start of a violent night. On the other hand, his dad never had a problem turning his anger on Joel. He had the scars to prove it.

He hesitated. His mom mouthed the word go. Even now, though it meant she would continue getting pummelled, she tried to protect him.

His dad huffed and turned his attention back to his battered wife. Obviously he didn't think Joel was worth his attention anymore.

Joel turned and walked out the side door to the garage; the automatic light turned on when he walked in. He looked around for a moment then found what he was looking for. He picked up a long, black hockey stick that had Easton printed in white letters down the side of the handle.

When he went back in the house, he could hear the continued commotion from the kitchen.

His father's voice sounded amused. "What are you going to do with that? Stab me?" Then he burst out laughing.

Joel turned the corner and took in the terrifying scene. His mom stood backed against the kitchen sink, face streaked with tears and blood. She held a six-inch cutting knife in her shaking hands. "Please," she whispered. Then she saw Joel standing in the living room with the hockey stick. She opened her mouth to say something.

His father took advantage of her moment of distraction by darting forward and grabbing her hands. He spun her around and held her tight against his body. "Now, missy, let's get that out of your hands, yes? Now, how do you like it? Is it cold?" he asked, holding the knife to her throat.

Joel took a few steps forward, trying not to make any sound. He wasn't sure what to do. The situation was too dangerous, but he still had the element of surprise—if he could just find an opening.

The opening came a moment later when his dad twirled his mom out in front of him and backhanded her across the face. "What were you—"

Joel darted forward and smashed the blade of the hockey stick into the side of his father's head; his father stumbled sideways, caught himself on the side of the counter, then turned to face Joel. "Wha—"

Joel had already pulled back for a second hit, this time the blade of the stick caught his father right in the centre of his face mid-turn. The impact split his lip in a spurt of blood and he dropped to the ground in a heap. Joel stood over him with the blood-speckled hockey stick. "How does it feel, you son of a bitch?" he yelled. For the first time in his life, he felt strong— powerful, like he was the one in charge. It felt good.

"No!" his mom cried out. She crawled over to her husband and cradled her husband's head in her lap. Aside from the blood gushing from his lip, the blade had also cut a slightly curved line across his forehead that bled down his face like heavy condensation on a glass.

"Mom. Mom, we have to go."

"Look what you've done. Look what you've done!" she said, ignoring his plea. She pulled a towel off the oven door and used it to stymie the flow of blood from the wounds. "He's going to be so mad, Joel. So mad."

"No, Mom, forget him. We can leave now. He'll never hurt you again." Joel reached his hand out to her.

She looked at him with a blank expression. "Leave? Where would we go?"

"I don't know. Anywhere but here."

She smiled sadly. "This is my life, sweetie. I'm not going anywhere."

Joel crouched down and grabbed her shoulder. "Don't do this, Mom. Don't stay. Please."

She looked at him with dead eyes. "I'm sorry. But this is my life."

"Mom!"

"Just go, Joel. Go." She shrugged his hand off her shoulder and went back to tending to her disfigured husband.

Joel stood up and backed away from the scene. Why wouldn't she leave? He didn't understand. Who would choose this life on purpose?

He ran upstairs, threw some clothes in a bag and grabbed his stash of cash. Because he wasn't an official employee at the gas station, Uncle Frank had been paying him cash under the table for his time; he'd saved several thousand dollars to put towards the Camaro, but he'd need the money for other things now. He shoved the roll of bills into his pocket and went back downstairs.

His father was starting to show signs of life. "Ugh, wha—"

"You fell and hit your head. It's okay," Joel's mom said.

Joel looked at the scene with disgust: the bruised and beaten wife fawning over her abusive husband. What a crock.

Why wouldn't she leave him? She didn't deserve what he did to her. And at the same time, she had a responsibility to take care of herself, didn't she? So what was it? Was she afraid? Joel felt a pang of regret at that thought. Wouldn't that make him just as bad for abandoning her now, when she needed him most?

But he had to look out for himself too. And he was done with this. "Goodbye," he said quietly, knowing full well no one could hear him. He turned and left, leaving his bloodied parents in the kitchen. They would have to find their own way forward. Without him.

* * * * *

Joel dropped out of school and started working at Uncle Frank's gas station full-time. The hardest thing was finding somewhere to live. For whatever reason, renting an apartment to a sixteen-year-old kid with no credit history wasn't an approved business practice. So Joel spent the first few months after he left home sleeping at the gas station, in his car, or anywhere else he could crash.

Eventually he struck a deal with the proprietor of a seedy roadside motel known mainly for hookers and drug deals. Seven hundred bucks a month. Expensive considering the quality, but it was the best Joel could manage. And it felt good to finally have a shower, even if the water was cold more often than not.

At first, the local clientele looked at him with suspicion. They accused him of being an undercover cop, and no amount of denying it would change their minds. He had returned home from work at least half a dozen times to see his place had been broken into and ransacked. But over the first year they began to tolerate, if not fully accept, him. He was still a stranger here, after all. A kid from the good side of town slumming it until his parents took him back. They had no idea.

Soon enough, he became a regular customer for the local dealer: a quarter bag of weed every Friday. It helped him relax on the weekends while he sat on his creaky bed and watched TV.

By the second year, he'd gotten to know them: The dealers, the hookers, even the regular johns became familiar faces. He continued buying a quarter bag of weed every week, and every once in a while he'd experiment with something else. The first time he hooked up with Daisy, a local hooker, she'd pulled out some meth and offered him a tweak.

"You really do that shit?"

"Yeah man, feels so good. Makes me hot. You want some?"

"Why the hell not," he said, grabbing the pipe.

The feeling was hard to describe to someone who hadn't done it before. It was like a sugar rush on steroids. Everything seemed so bright, real, and powerful. Anything he felt was like a lightning bolt of sensation in his brain.

When it finally wore off he felt weak, devoid, and lonely; like all feeling had fled his body, never to return. All he had left was the memory of how amazing it had felt.

Throughout this time, he managed to maintain a tenuous connection to his mother. See, Uncle Frank wasn't really his Uncle. He was a friend of the family who Joel had been calling Uncle since he was four. Frank and Joel's father had a massive falling out years ago, so they avoided each other like the plague, but Joel's mom still came in to visit from time to time. It was nice to see her, without having to worry about dealing with his father.

Sometimes, she came in with fresh bruises and Joel felt guilty all over again for leaving. But she would reassure him that he had made the right choice.

"We all have our place in the world, Joel. This is mine."

"You can't believe that, Mom. What he's doing to you is wrong."

Then she smiled with so much pain and sadness it broke his heart. "This is my place, sweetie. I love him."

"How? How can you still love him?"

But she didn't respond. She never did.

They went on like this for years: Joel descending deeper into drug abuse, and his mom tolerating her husband's rampant violence.

And then one morning, roughly five years after he walked out, Joel was awoken by loud banging on his motel room door.

TEN
ALEX

ALEX HATED THANKSGIVING.

But not for the usual reasons. Not because it had been hijacked by retail and greeting card companies, or because people became inordinately concerned with the start of the Christmas shopping season, or even because of the parasitic customers who called him at work thinking they could get out of paying their bills because, "Hey, it's Thanksgiving! Cut a guy a break."

These were all good enough reasons to make anyone hate the holiday, but they weren't *his* reasons. Alex hated Thanksgiving for the same reason so many people loved it: family.

While most people were busy embracing their loving relatives and singing Kumbaya together, he would be sitting at a table filled with people who, for all the world, wished he would go away. Yet they invited him every year, out of some sort of respect for his dead parents, he supposed; not because he was wanted.

He knew he wouldn't be missed if he didn't go, knew they might even hope he wouldn't show up at all; but this was one occasion when he enjoyed subverting their expectations. As much as it hurt to see the disappointment on their faces when they opened the front door to see him standing there, a small part of him got a kick out of the why-is-*he*-here expression that followed.

He still hated the whole business of Thanksgiving dinner, of course; nothing was going to change that. He didn't really know why he bothered going every year. Perhaps it was some sort of emotional self-flagellation, an explicit reminder of what he couldn't tolerate about his life anymore.

The average-sized suburban bungalow-style home loomed in front of him. *Just one more.* He made his way up the steps and rang the doorbell.

Austin, one of his brother-cousins answered the door. "Oh, hey man," he said, without glancing up from his iPhone.

"Hey," Alex said and walked in. As he took his shoes off and closed the door, he could hear the conversation coming from deeper in the house. Sounded like most of the family was here already.

He walked through the living room and towards the kitchen. Austin had planted himself on the couch, fervently tapping on the screen of his phone, a half grin on his face like something funny was happening.

The reception in the kitchen was as cursory as the one at the front door. Uncle Phil and Aunt Nikki were busy cooking, while Oliver and Lance were arguing about hockey. Arguing had become a sort of ritual for them. Even if they actually agreed about something, one would take the opposite side just to frustrate the other. The arguments usually didn't turn violent. Usually.

"Ovechkin is a better sniper," Lance said.

"So what? He has more goals than Crosby, but a lower shooting percentage. Crosby is more of a playmaker anyway, he makes everyone around him better. And he's a way better defensive player too."

"Crosby is a pansy. Him and Ovi joined the league in the same year, but Crosby has played over a hundred fewer games. The guy takes a hit like a girl."

"Give me a break!" Oliver said, his eyes bulging with frustration. "Let's see you take the hits to the head he took, or a ninety-mile per hour puck to the face."

"Whatever. Tape it together and keep going. The guy has so much drama over his health, he's like a modern-day Mario Lemieux. I'll take a guy who I know can score goals and will actually survive an entire season."

"You're such an idiot."

"And yet I'm leading the hockey pool."

"Shut up."

Alex left them to their argument. He didn't follow hockey, or any sports for that matter. Not like Oliver and Lance, who were religious about it: hockey in the winter and football in the summer. It made sense; they were built like their father—both stood around six foot three, with muscular builds that they knew how to throw around on the ice or the field. They were the quintessential sports jocks. At one point, Lance had taken up cycling, claiming he would be the next Lance Armstrong; but when his idol was convicted of doping and stripped of his medals, Lance dropped the sport altogether.

At five foot eleven, Austin wasn't much smaller than his brothers, but he was more interested in electronics and computer games than sports. He was also the youngest: at twenty-three, he was four years younger than Oliver, who was a year younger than Lance. He was what his parents called a *surprise* child. *Not as big of a surprise as me*, Alex thought.

As far as Alex was concerned, the age gap was a blessing. Austin idolized his older brothers, but since he was too young to do the same things they did, he ended up on his own path. As a result, he wasn't as much of an unbearable asshole as his older brothers.

Alex was the smallest, standing a modest five foot eight. He took after his father in that respect: short and skinny. Not much of interest going on here. That's what made it so easy for Lance and Oliver to bully him around, even though they weren't much older than him. When Alex joined the family, he was already three inches shorter and twenty pounds lighter than Austin; and that gap only widened as time went on so that, by the time Alex was sixteen and Austin was thirteen, they were already the same size. It used to bother him, but not so much anymore. A guy gets used to his deficiencies, such as they are.

The elder brothers were evicted from the kitchen while Aunt Nikki and Uncle Phil prepared the table for dinner. They were still arguing. Something about bandwagon fans now. Alex continued to ignore them. He pulled out his phone instead, he didn't have a fancy smartphone to entertain himself with, but he could play Snake on his old Nokia. And it had a colour screen.

The doorbell rang. Oliver took a break from arguing to see who was there. When he opened it, a woman on the other side exclaimed, "Hi!" before jumping inside to give him a giant hug.

"Hi, Aunt Emily," Oliver said as he hugged her back, smiling.

Lance and Austin both got up to greet her at the door. She embraced them both happily. "Look at you kids. I swear you get bigger all the time! Are you ever going to stop growing?"

They laughed with her; she said that almost every time she saw them. It was a tradition.

Uncle Phil came out of the kitchen wiping his hands on a towel he had thrown over his shoulder. He gave his little sister a long hug. "Good to see you, Em," he said.

"You too," she responded, then took her turn with Aunt Nikki, who had followed Uncle Phil out of the kitchen.

What a nice reception! For a moment, a person could mistake this for a happy, loving family. They were, Alex supposed, if he were taken out of the equation.

He stood in the living room, watching the scene unfold, feeling as awkward and alone as ever. Emily had been his crush for as long as he could remember. He had thought about this for a long time. The way he looked at it, she wasn't related to him—at least, not by blood. She was only related by marriage, being his aunt's sister-in-law; surely that was enough degrees of separation to make it okay.

Emily was a little shorter than him, so that they stood almost eye to eye when she wore short heels. She kept her hair short, neck length so that it framed her soft-featured face. She was pretty, not a knockout, but it was her personality that made her beautiful. She was also one of the only people in the world who had always been kind to him, no matter what.

When Emily finally saw him, she gave him a warm smile. "Hi, Alex." He didn't go to her, the way everyone else had; he *wanted* to, but he didn't.

"Hi, Emily," he said. He didn't call her aunt. Calling her *aunt* would make their connection less real in his mind.

"Where's Rob?" Uncle Phil asked.

"Oh, you know him. He's busy with work," she said. "Out with clients."

Nikki and Phil glanced at each other, but didn't say anything. Instead, Nikki said, "Well, you arrived just in time; dinner is ready."

They all moved to the nook connected to the kitchen and each took a seat at a round table that had a Lazy Susan in the centre. Alex had Austin to his right and Uncle Phil to his left; Lance sat directly across with Emily to his right and Oliver to his left. When they were younger, Lance and Oliver would have been separated to keep their bickering to a minimum; but sitting them side-by-side was better, after all, since they tended not to yell as much when they were closer to each other.

Before they could eat, Aunt Nikki insisted on giving thanks— another tradition. Alex groaned inwardly. He always had trouble knowing what to say.

Uncle Phil started. "I'm thankful we've gone through another year without any injuries. Here's to our continued good health." He raised his glass and everyone joined him. He tended to say something along those lines every year; a bit of a cop-out, Alex thought, though he wished he could use the line himself.

Emily's turn. "I'm thankful Rob has a good job. I know it keeps him away from home sometimes but it supports us, and I appreciate that; especially when so many people are struggling these days."

Lance made a sports joke; and Oliver was thankful for his beautiful girlfriend.

Aunt Nikki was thankful to spend time with her family, and that everyone could be there to make her feel so blessed by their companionship. Interesting how she made sure to tie everything back to how good it made her feel. Conceit, perhaps.

Austin was thankful that his marks at university were improving. If he kept it up, he might even graduate with an average GPA; too much time playing games with his friends had already tanked his chances at anything higher than average grades.

That left Alex, who—even though he got to go last—still hadn't thought of anything to say. "I'm thankful for..." Everyone waited, looking at him. He shifted uncomfortably. There really wasn't much he could think of to be thankful for, other than the fact that he wouldn't have to suffer through another Thanksgiving dinner—this would be his last; so he decided to get it over with and just blend elements of the toasts the others had made. "I'm thankful for making the money I need to live, and that I don't have any health problems to worry about." Silence. "And to be here," he finished.

"Okay, then," Aunt Nikki said. "Well, everyone, go ahead." She motioned to the food and the table became engulfed in activity.

Throughout dinner, Alex watched Emily out of the corner of his eye. She was making the conversational rounds with the family, checking up on everyone. He was so focused on not being noticed that he was startled when she addressed him directly.

"So, Alex, what about you? How've you been?"

"Oh, um, fine. Okay, I guess."

"Just fine?" she gave him a half frown. "Come on, I haven't seen you in a long time. What's happening in your life?"

Alex glanced around the table. Lance, Oliver, and Austin were more interested in their food than in what anyone was saying. Aunt Nikki was looking at him with a half-bored, half-interested look on her face. "Um, nothing has changed, really," he said. "I moved to a place downtown a while ago. It's kind of expensive, and small, but it's a lot closer to work. I'm still at the call centre."

"You've been working there for a while now, haven't you?" she asked.

He did a quick count in his head. "About four years now."

"That's good, it must not be too bad if you're still there. You like it? Thinking management one day?"

It was a fair enough question, but it made Alex uncomfortable especially after what had happened at work. "It's not terrible, I guess. I had a review yesterday; I think I'll be a team lead soon." He hated the compulsion that led him to lie, as if telling the truth would be like admitting failure.

"Congratulations," Emily said, then smiled. "And any news on the romantic front? I don't think you had a girlfriend last time we talked."

"I didn't—"

Lance and Oliver whispered something to each other and cut Alex off with an eruption of laughter. Emily's eyes flickered in their direction, but didn't otherwise acknowledge them. Alex attempted to mimic her self-control.

"No, I didn't have a girlfriend last time we talked."

"Didn't you have that one— What was her name?" Oliver asked, looking as if he was trying to be thoughtful; but his amusement showed through. "Help me out here, Alex. I'm sure she's still packed up somewhere."

Lance took the cue. "Wasn't it Dolly? Because of those giant inflatable boobs."

Oliver snapped his fingers. "Yes, that was it! How's Dolly doing these days, Alex?"

"I don't know what you're talking about."

"Don't be bashful, Alex. We all remember Dolly. You don't think we didn't see her hiding under your bed? Poor girl; she deserved better treatment than that."

Austin barked out a laugh at that. Aunt Nikki had a smile on her face, not even attempting to hide her amusement; she never did. Emily seemed to accept the exchange as a normal bout of insults between brothers.

Alex decided to ignore the doll comments. "I actually do have a girlfriend now," he said. Almost everyone at the table looked surprised.

"Oh, that's wonderful Alex!" Emily said. She seemed genuinely happy for him; it made him feel good. "Tell me about her."

"Um," he said, not sure what to say. Then he had an idea. "Her name is Diamond."

Lance snorted. "Oh, come on. If you're going to make up a girlfriend, you should give her a better name than that."

"I'm not making up anything."

"Diamond? Seriously what are the odds you'd have an actual living girlfriend named Diamond?"

"I don't know, but must be higher than the odds you'll ever make it out of that mailroom, don—"

"Go fu—"

"Lance! Don't you swear at my table," Aunt Nikki finally intervened. "And Alex, show a little respect for your brother."

He's not my brother—not really.

Lance glared from across the table and mouthed asshole at Alex. He had a degree in accounting but, in spite of years of effort, hadn't been able to find a job. The closest he had come was the mailroom in an accounting firm. That was two years ago, and it didn't look like he was going to move up anytime soon. Lance was a bit prickly about it. He was prickly about a lot of things. Maybe if his mother hadn't coddled him all his life he wouldn't act like the world owed him a favour.

Emily, seeing how uncomfortable things had become, decided to steer the conversation back into safe territory. That meant leaving the boys alone to stew and engaging with her sister-in-law.

Later, after dinner was finished and everything cleaned up, Alex relaxed on the couch in the living room. The remainder of the meal had passed uneventfully: Lance very specifically didn't talk to him again; and as far as Alex was concerned, that was quite alright. Except, they still hadn't spoken when Lance and Oliver left that night; and since they would never see him again, Alex wondered if they would feel regret at leaving things in such a negative way.

He pulled out his phone and checked the time; it was past ten. He wanted to make sure he left before the buses stopped running; so he dragged himself off of the couch and made his way to the kitchen where everyone else was still gathered at the table. "I think I'm going to go now. There's a bus coming in ten minutes."

Aunt Nikki responded. "Okay. Thanks for coming. Have a good night." Nice words, but she didn't even get up from her seat.

"You said you live downtown now, right?" Emily asked.

"Yeah."

She pushed her chair back and stood up. "Why don't I drive you home then? I'm going that way anyhow."

Alex paused, surprised. He couldn't remember the last time he'd spent time alone with her. He felt nervous. What would they talk about? *Hey I know it's pretty weird and we're sorta related but I've kinda had a crush on you for years.* That would go over well.

"Um, it's okay. I don't want to be any trouble."

"Nonsense. It's no trouble at all," she smiled at him. "I should be going too."

Aunt Nikki looked up. "Oh, I thought we would open another bottle of wine. I picked up a bottle of Pinot…"

"Thank you so much, Nikki." She put her hand on Nikki's shoulder. "If we drink any more I won't be able to drive! Besides, Rob should be home by now."

"Oh, okay." Aunt Nikki looked a bit let down, but she and Uncle Phil got up to see them out. They paused at the front door to put their shoes on and say their goodbyes. Emily gave both Phil and Nikki a hug and promised to see them again soon; while Alex waited at the open door, trying to decide what to say. What do you say when you know you're never going to see someone again?

He looked at them, and they looked back at him. He wanted to speak, but his tongue had become thick and heavy, and he couldn't seem to open his mouth. He felt a tightness in his chest, like an invisible clamp slowly closing around his heart, restricting the blood flow to the rest of his body. His head hurt, and he couldn't breathe.

So he stood there, on the doorstep of the only family he had left in the world, struggling with the weight of all the things he had never said. They looked at him, totally oblivious to the torrent of emotion running through him, with looks of mild confusion. For them, this was just another night, just another moment in time, passed and soon forgotten like the millions of other moments that constituted their lives. There was no special meaning here, not for them; but for Alex, this was an important goodbye. So much so, that he couldn't even get past the lump in his throat to open his mouth and say something, anything. He wanted to cry out in frustration.

Phil broke the silence. "Well, see you later."

Alex nodded and cleared his throat. "Yeah," he said, finally. Then, with a burst of sentiment, he stepped forward and opened his arms for a hug. Both Phil and Nikki were startled by the uncharacteristic gesture; but Phil stepped into the embrace and returned it, awkwardly. Alex moved towards Nikki and completely enveloped her with his arms; he'd forgotten how small she was. After a moment they separated. He couldn't remember the last time he had hugged either of them. It wasn't something they usually did; it felt odd, foreign.

But tonight was different, even if they didn't know it yet.

He left without saying anything else, and didn't feel like he had to anymore. Sometimes, important moments don't need words.

* * * * *

Alex stared out the window of Emily's Ford Focus, still feeling unbalanced after the exchange at the house. After all the time he'd spent picturing the confrontation, rehearsing the moment in his head— how he would finally tell them how he really felt about them, how much they had hurt him with their callous neglect —he couldn't believe he had hugged them, which wasn't in any version of his imaginings. In some, they cried and apologized, desperately trying to atone for their mistakes. In others, they coldly rebuffed him, validating his suspicion of their disdain for him—the scenario he particularly liked, as it gave him the emotional fuel to take the final step.

But none of that had happened: He hadn't bared his soul, hadn't even said a word. Instead, meek as a mouse, he gave them a hug and walked away. The worst part of it was that he had *liked* it; it had made him feel *good*.

Emily broke him out of his reverie. "So how long have you lived downtown?"

"Um, I think, maybe a bit over a year now. Yeah, a little over a year."

"That long! I didn't realize. So how do you like it?"

"Well, it's easier to get to work now. It's one bus; I used to have to transfer."

She nodded her agreement, looking as though she'd had long experience with public transit and acutely felt his pain. "Yeah, that's gotta be nice. When you're stuck on those long routes it feels like you're wasting so much time, doesn't it?"

"Yeah, it kind of felt like I was slowly dying on those buses, like it was some kind of torture."

"That's awfully maudlin," she said, looking over at him and smiling.

He stared at her and slowly smiled back.

They continued to chat for the rest of the ride home. She had a nice way about her, Alex thought. A generosity of spirit that made him feel comfortable and safe with her, made him want to open up. He had noticed this about her before, her disarming friendliness that was capable of winning over even the dourest personalities. He had always admired that quality in her; now she was using it on him, her words striking like a hammer, slowly tearing a wall that had been between them all this time.

When she stopped the car in front of his apartment building, Alex was surprised at how fast the ride seemed to have passed.

"Here we are," she said.

"Yeah. Thank you for the ride."

She waved her hand dismissively. "No problem. I'm barely five minutes from here anyway."

"Okay," he said as he got out of the car. "Well, good night."

"Hey, Alex."

He felt a small shiver when she called his name. "Yea?"

"This was really nice. We should talk more often. Why don't we go for coffee sometime?"

"That— That sounds good. I would like that."

"Great! Give me your number."

He read it off to her and she typed it into her phone. She added a smiley face beside his name when she typed it. He wondered how many people were honoured with smiley faces.

"Okay, I'll give you a call and we'll work something out."

"Great." He shut the door.

"Happy Thanksgiving," she called through the open passenger window before driving off.

He turned and waved. "Happy Thanksgiving," he said. And for the first time in memory, he actually meant it.

ELEVEN
RICHARD

"RICHARD, NATALIE: THANK you so much for coming," said the woman, extending her hand. Richard shook it.

"Yeah, thanks," he said.

Natalie smiled warmly and shook the woman's hand as well. "Hi, Dr. Cox. Thank you for seeing us."

"It's so nice to see you again, Natalie, and remember, call me Jessica," she responded. "Make yourselves comfortable. Can I get you anything—tea, coffee?"

"Whiskey?" Richard asked, only half joking. Natalie slapped his shoulder. "Coffee would be great, thanks."

Natalie declined. Richard surveyed the room, the warm colours that abounded—from the wall paint to the cherry hardwood—even the shelves and chairs oozed warmth and class. The stained oak shelving was lined with reference books on psychiatry and sociology. Creases marred the spines of the leather-bound volumes, and yellow strips of paper stuck out the top, marking passages the good doctor had flagged. A large painting of a serene meadow hung on the wall between the bookshelves. On the opposite wall, in a dedicated space, hung Jessica's diplomas. Richard wasn't impressed. No matter how many diplomas she had, or how many books she'd read, there was no way she understood what he was going through. No amount of pointless talking was going to change that.

He and Natalie sat down on either end of the plush, beige couch. Richard didn't hide his glower.

"It's good to finally meet you, Richard. I've been looking forward to seeing you here with Natalie," Jessica said, returning with Richard's cup of coffee. She set it down on the coffee table, then sat down across from them.

Richard shot Natalie a look. "Oh, is that so?" Natalie looked at him sheepishly.

Jessica smiled, unperturbed by his snarky tone. "Yes, yes. I think it's great that you took the step to come here today with your wife. It's important to face your issues together and work towards a common goal."

"I wasn't aware we were having any issues," Richard said, disingenuously.

Jessica smiled again. She'd had reluctant clients before. "I want you to know that this is a safe place. I'm not here to judge, I'm here to help. We're here to talk about our feelings in an honest way and go from there. Okay? So, Natalie, why don't you begin and tell us how you feel."

Natalie turned and faced Richard. He had the distinct feeling that this whole thing had been rehearsed without him. "Richard, I feel like we've grown apart, like you've closed yourself off to me. We used to talk about everything, but now—well, you don't even talk to me at all; it's like we aren't in a partnership anymore. I wish you would let me in, let me help. I want us to move on with our lives together. But you just sit and drink, then get all withdrawn and quiet. I feel like I don't know you anymore."

"That's good, Natalie," Jessica said. "Now, Richard, how do you feel about what Natalie just said?"

"I don't think it's anything that hasn't been said before, to be honest."

"Do you think you've closed yourself off to her?"

"I don't know, I guess."

"And why would that be?"

"Because she doesn't understand."

"Then help me understand," Natalie said. "I want to understand."

Richard rolled his eyes. "You keep saying that, and then you say you want to move on. You don't get it."

"Get what? How can I get it if I don't know what I'm supposed to get?"

"Okay," Jessica intervened. "I don't think we should get caught up in who gets what right now. How about I get to know more about you, Richard? How long have you been a paramedic?"

"I finished my EMT training and became a qualified paramedic thirteen years ago."

"What made you want to be a paramedic?"

Richard shrugged. "I wanted to help people."

"Was there a specific moment? Or did you always see yourself in that role?"

Richard thought for a moment. "I guess it was a specific moment. There was an incident, a car crash."

"Were you involved?"

"No, I was a bystander."

"What happened?"

"A car crashed, people died. That's about it."

"Jesus, Richard, must you be such an ass?" Natalie burst out, glaring at him.

"It's okay," Jessica said. "It's a defense mechanism. Richard, you're deflecting. You don't need to deflect here. You can talk to us."

Richard sighed heavily and glanced at Natalie, who continued to aim her dagger-eyes in his direction. After he'd composed himself, he continued: "I was seventeen and out on a date with my girlfriend at the time; and we were walking down the street when, suddenly, this car blasted through a red light and T-boned another car. My girlfriend called 9-1-1 and I ran to see if everyone was okay. The guy who ran the light was fine—airbag saved him—but he reeked of booze and puke. The couple in the other car weren't that lucky. The driver's side had taken the brunt of the hit. The driver looked mangled; I think he was already dead. The woman in the passenger seat was still breathing; she was trying to crawl out of the car. I went over to help her. I'd never seen anything like it: every part of her was coated with blood—her head, legs, arms. But I pulled her out of the car; one of her legs flopped around and had bone sticking out. I put my hand on her head to try and stop the wound that was bleeding, and her head was soft, like a rotten apple. I felt scared sitting there, holding her, not knowing what to do. The woman kept trying to say something, but I couldn't understand her. She was coughing up blood. My girlfriend was crying and screaming. Then suddenly, the woman stopped moving—just stopped. Her lifeless eyes still staring at me. I'll never forget those eyes."

He stopped and looked at his hands, remembering how covered in blood they had been. He hadn't been scared; he'd been terrified. It was a moment that changed him forever.

"Richard...You never said." Natalie reached out and touched his leg.

"Later, I found out they had a son, just a kid. His name was Alex. I met him at the trial where I was a witness. I kept thinking about how he was going to grow up without any parents because I didn't know how to save his mom; how she died while I did nothing. And that, if I'd had only had some sort of training, then maybe..."

"You can't take responsibility for that, Richard; it isn't your fault. You were seventeen; you did what you could," Jessica said.

"I know that. Of course I know that now. No one could have saved them, but that was the moment: That's when I decided I'd become a paramedic. I would never sit there again, helpless, while someone died in my arms—never."

"But that's not a promise you can make. Sometimes there's nothing you can do," Jessica said.

"I know. I was young, stupid, and naïve; I thought I could save the world. I was idealistic," Richard said, still staring at his hands, not wanting to look at anyone.

"Is that why it hurts so much that you couldn't save that girl?"

Richard looked up, suddenly furious. "That girl didn't die because I couldn't save her. She died because I screwed up."

Jessica raised her hands. "You're right. My mistake."

Natalie grabbed Richard's hand. "Why didn't you ever tell me?"

As fast as it came, his fury died away. "What? The accident? I don't know. It never came up. We didn't meet until years after that."

She shook her head at him. "I wish you had told me."

"This is important, Richard," Jessica said. "It's an important part of who you are and helps us to understand you. Experiences like that shape people. It's impossible for us to understand what you are going through now without knowing about your past."

Richard was skeptical. "Sure."

"So, tell us about being a paramedic."

"What's to tell? You go to work and drive around answering calls. Most of them are meaningless. You'd be amazed at the number of hypochondriacs there are and how much time we waste answering their calls. And then there are the problems caused by people just being stupid. I once had a guy who was unloading a dresser from a truck. He got this idea to tie a rope around his arms and wrap it around the dresser to get a better grip, but he slipped and the rope snapped his wrist. Then the dresser fell onto him and broke his leg."

Natalie giggled. "I remember you telling me about that. He kept asking you to not tell his wife because she would yell at him."

"Yeah. Not sure how he planned to keep that a secret."

"You can't lie to us," Natalie said with mock seriousness. "We'll know."

"Sure you will," Richard said. "But anyway, it's not as dramatic as TV would have you believe. The big multi-casualty scenes are few and far between."

"That's good, right?" Jessica asked.

"Yeah, sure, but it doesn't change the stress level. Every procedure we perform, no matter how small, can always go wrong. Even the hypochondriacs might have a real problem hiding behind their neurosis; we still have to make sure they check out every time."

"What about the incident with the girl? Where does that fit in?"

Richard took a deep breath. He had hoped time would run out before this came up. He really didn't want to talk about it.

"I'm sure you saw it on the news or read about it in the paper," he said.

"The media have a tendency to sensationalize, to dramatize news to increase sales. I'd rather hear about it from you."

Richard couldn't disagree with that. "It goes in the category of real emergency. We knew before we got there it was serious."

"Okay, so what happened?"

Richard sat for a moment, then looked at the time.

Jessica smiled. "You've got lots of time."

"That's what I was afraid of," he mumbled.

"Excuse me?"

"Nothing," he said quickly. "So, we got the call about this girl suffering from an asthma attack. She had been playing soccer with her friends and forgot her inhaler. But it was also one of the hottest and most humid days of the year, and thirty-some degrees outside. So this fourteen-year-old girl had been running around in the heat all afternoon, not only suffering from asthma, but heatstroke too. By the time we got there, she was already throwing up and her oxygen levels had dropped way below normal. We gave her an IV and went to intubate, but we couldn't because she kept vomiting, so her throat was blocked. But I made the decision to do it anyway. We gave her an epinephrine mask and put her on a monitor to watch her heart. For some reason nothing helped; her oxygen kept dropping and her heart rate kept going up. Her lips turned blue and her eyes started to bulge. I knew her heart was about to give out. I checked her throat again and realized I had intubated the esophagus instead of the trachea. She hadn't been getting any air. I tried to fix it but it was too late, and she died. Her name was Gabrielle."

He shook his head slowly. "I...I think you know the rest. Her family sued, I was suspended, and here we are."

"It sounds like it was a stressful moment. Is that an easy mistake to make?"

"Easy? Of course it's an easy mistake. All mistakes are easy; that's why mistakes happen."

"That's not what I meant."

"I know what you meant. You want me to feel like: hey, that was a tough call; and it's really difficult to properly intubate a throat filled with vomit, so, don't take it so hard, okay? But that isn't going to help. My job is to do the right thing and make sure people don't die. People trust me, and I didn't live up to that trust. I had a little girl's life in my hands and I let it slip away. That's on me."

"Everyone makes mistakes; it's part of being human. We can't be perfect all the time," Jessica said.

"What kind of crap is that?" Richard asked, aghast. "The fact is that, right then and there, I needed to be perfect—and I wasn't."

"You can't fault yourself for your basic humanity. You made a mistake and someone else paid for it. But what does that mean for you?"

"What are you talking about?"

"Do you see the correlation here, between your past and your present? You became a paramedic because someone died in your arms. Now, your life is in crisis again because someone else died on your watch. You're suffering from the same feelings of helplessness and loss as you did back then, but now it's compounded by the sense of failure. It's making you question yourself, along with all of the choices you've made in your life."

"So? Yeah, I'm questioning my life. I'm feeling like a giant failure. What's the point?"

"The point is you can't turn to the bottle to answer these questions. You have to turn inwards, you have to see the worth in yourself. That's why you need your wife more than ever, to help show you that worth."

Richard began to grind his teeth. That bottle comment set him on edge. So Natalie had complained about his drinking? That was a slap in the face.

"I want you to know that I'm here for you," Natalie said. "And you're such a wonderful and amazing person who's done so much to help so many people."

"Is that so?" Richard asked.

"Yes, of course. Think of all the lives you've saved. Think how many people are still around today because of you."

Richard shook his head. "It doesn't matter how many people I help, if one person dies because of me."

"That's bullshit—total bullshit. And you know it," Natalie shot back.

Richard continued to shake his head, but didn't have a chance to respond before Jessica intervened.

"We're out of time right now, but I think we've made a great breakthrough today. I think with more time, you can overcome this situation and move forward."

Natalie stood up first. "Thank you so much, Jessica. I really appreciate it. We'll see you next week."

Richard stood and gave her a curt nod, then followed Natalie out the door.

"I'm not going back," he said when they got outside.

"What?"

"I'm not going back there next week to see that woman. I told you: I'm done with shrinks. I did this as a favour to you, but I'm done now."

"Really? A favour to me?" She stopped and faced him, crossing her arms. "What about us? What about you? You don't think that helped at all? Was it all a giant waste of time?"

"Yes! I'm glad we're on the same page here. We don't need anyone to help us through this." He grabbed her shoulders and massaged them. "We're fine on our own."

She pulled away. "I'll be here next week at the same time," she said as she walked away. "If you don't come, that's your choice."

"Oh, come on. Don't be like that."

"No, it's fine, Richard. If you don't want to go, don't go."

He knew exactly what it meant when she said it's fine. It meant if you don't go, you're in big trouble, mister. But he had no intention of caving this time. If she wanted that woman whispering platitudes in her ear then so be it; he didn't need it and wasn't interested. They hopped into their Chevy Equinox and drove home in awkward silence.

TWELVE
MELISSA

MELISSA WALKED THE streets of downtown Vancouver on a cool, foggy night. A thick white mist had blanketed the city in the days after Thanksgiving, giving the area an eerie look and feel. The fog absorbed all sound, making everything muted and less real. She felt like she was walking through the set of a horror movie and not a real city.

She thought back to Monday night and the Thanksgiving dinner she had had with her family. The holiday seemed pointless and the routine had always bugged her: the eternal Groundhog Day-like nature of it. The whole event acted out by rote for the sake of, what, showing thanks? She was having a hard time with that these days. It's not that she didn't want to be thankful. She didn't take for granted the fact that she was alive, relatively healthy, had a job, and a place to live. But what did all that mean if she found herself haunted by a past that wouldn't let go? She wasn't sleeping properly, she was always stressed, and she couldn't stop thinking about finding *him*.

In truth, Thanksgiving had become a microcosm of her life, and she was the one trapped in a loop, as if her life had become a book with no ending—only rewrites of the same chapters over and over again. And this, being out here, searching the city for a man that she'd probably never find, was just another one of those repeating chapters.

She clutched the can of pepper spray in her pocket as two guys in dark jackets approached, and she didn't let go of it, even as they walked past her without sparing a look in her direction.

These walks weren't just about finding her attacker, although that was how it started. In the beginning, she'd been so frustrated at the lack of progress the police were making. They said there was no DNA evidence, her description wasn't good enough, and there were no witnesses. In short, without a massive stroke of luck, it would be impossible to find him.

Melissa couldn't accept that. She refused to believe that someone could get away with beating and raping her, or anyone, for that matter. How many women were in the same boat as her? Had this degenerate waste of humanity attacked other women? *Probably,* she thought. How often would someone like that stop at doing it once?

So, after half a year of waiting for closure, she got fed up with waiting for the police and took matters into her own hands. She bought a gun and a few cans of pepper spray, and she started going out at night, searching the downtown streets for the man the police couldn't find. She didn't have a clear picture in her head of what he looked like, but she had a certain feeling, a gut feeling that if she ever crossed paths with him again, she would recognize him. Only this time, she would be ready for him.

But it hadn't happened yet. She had searched for the better part of a year, with no results, and against the advice of her brother and her therapist, who both thought it was a sign she was holding too tightly to her pain and letting it control her life. *Let it go*, they had said. *You have to move on.*

"Let it go, let it go, let it go. It's not so easy," she had started to sing in her head while she was out searching—a motto for her stubborn refusal to give up.

Eventually, though, she did give up, to some extent. At her therapist's insistence, she handed her gun over to the police and stopped going out multiple times a week.

She felt naked without the solid weight of the gun in her pocket. It reassured her. The feeling of security it offered was the main reason she was able to force herself to leave the house when it was dark outside. She feared that without it she would revert back to the whimpering girl who couldn't even enter a nightclub.

Over time, she began to trust in the security of her pepper spray. And the truth was that she never had any problems; people tended to just leave her alone. It was a strange feeling, always being ready for confrontation, almost hoping something would happen; but nothing had. Eventually, she began to laugh at herself for even thinking she needed a gun.

As time passed, her need to search the streets diminished, and she went out less and less: First it was down to once a week, then to once a month, and then every six months. Now, she couldn't even remember the last time she'd been out for one of these walks. It seems time was able to induce the behavioural change her therapist had tried to explain.

Time and apathy, but not a traditional sort of apathy, the kind where people don't vote because they don't think it will make a difference. Rather, she had become so used to feeling bad that it became her normal state of being. Now, instead of effectively dealing with her emotions, she buried them deep down and tried to hide from them, like she was some sort of sneak, creeping around her own head, saying: "*If this feeling can't find me, then I won't have to confront it!*"

The problem with that approach was the simple fact that nothing stays hidden forever, whether the emotions hid from her, or she hid from the emotions. There's a difference there too, though both came from the same place.

But why did this have to happen now? She'd been getting better, hadn't she? Then she let Lindsay sucker her into a trip to Playland and suddenly everything was unravelling. Her, most of all. If only—

Melissa was jolted from her reverie by a hand on her shoulder.

She let out a short, cut-off scream and, in one smooth motion, spun around, whipped the can of pepper spray out of her pocket and sprayed her attacker.

"Could you te— AAAAHHHH," a man screamed. He covered his eyes with his hands and backed away. He tripped over his feet and tumbled to the ground, rolling back and forth, screaming. "Ahhh, what the hell? What the fuck!"

A woman knelt down beside the man and cradled his head in her lap. "Oh, my God! Jake! Jake, are you okay?" She turned to Melissa and started yelling. "You bitch! What the hell did you do that for?"

"I…I'm sorry," Melissa said. "I thought…I thought he was attacking me. I thought—"

"What?" the woman asked, eyes wide in disbelief. "He was asking for directions, you stupid cow!"

"What's going on here?" a different man asked, walking up from the side.

"She pepper-sprayed my boyfriend," the woman said, pointing at Melissa.

Melissa tried to explain, "I'm sorry, he surprised me. I thought he was a mugger, or…or…"

"Are you serious?" the woman asked.

"It burns. Oh, my God, it burns so much," Jake said, weeping profusely.

"I'm calling the police," the man said.

"You don't have to do that. It was an accident."

"No, call the cops! They need to put her away."

"What happened?" someone else asked, emerging from the crowd that had formed.

"That woman pepper-sprayed this guy," someone answered.

A man calling the police spoke into his phone: "Hi, I need the police and an ambulance. I'm calling because—"

"No, no, no," Melissa said quietly. She was starting to cry too.

"Hey, are you alright?" someone asked, reaching out to her.

"Don't touch me," Melissa snapped in a high-pitched voice and raised the can of pepper spray defensively. She was starting to get a mental picture of how this must look, and it didn't look good.

"See? She's a crazy bitch," Jake's girlfriend said.

People started backing away from her, looking scared. "I have to get out of here," Melissa said. She started to push her way through the crowd, then broke free and started running.

"Don't let her go! Hey, come back here!"

She didn't stop. Didn't turn. Just kept running.

* * * * *

A knock sounded from the door. "Police," a voice called out.

Lindsay and Melissa were both sitting on the couch. Melissa had stopped crying, but her eyes were red and puffy. Lindsay looked at the door, then back at Melissa, who nodded.

Lindsay got up and went to the door. She opened it about a foot and poked her head through after recognizing Melissa's brother. Melissa could hear the conversation. "What can I do for you, Dan?"

"I need to speak to Melissa. Is she here?" a deep male voice asked.

"She doesn't want to talk to anyone right now."

The man sighed. "Come on, Lindsay. Just...Let me talk to her."

"I don't know. I think—"

"This is serious, Lindsay! She assaulted someone. You need to let me talk to her."

Lindsay looked back at Melissa and opened the door. A tall, dark-haired man in full police uniform entered. He clinked as he walked, making him sound like a giant cat toy. He picked up a chair from the dining table and sat down across from Melissa. Melissa glanced at him then looked away. Lindsay went to her bedroom, leaving them alone.

"Are you okay?" he asked, taking note of her puffy eyes.

Silence.

"I know it was you," he said.

Melissa still didn't respond. The silence stretched on. Dan shifted uncomfortably.

"The guy, Jake, he's okay, by the way; in case you were wondering."

"I wasn't," Melissa said. Dan raised his eyebrows and she instantly regretted the words.

Dan sighed. "Why do you have to make everything so difficult?"

She shrugged.

"Melissa, can you look at me?" His voice took on a firm, police-like tone that she knew well. It meant he was nearing the end of his patience.

She rolled her eyes and turned towards him. "What?"

He took a deep breath. "Look, those people wanted to press charges, Melissa. I was able to talk them down, but it wasn—"

"Oh, so I should thank you?"

"For starters, yeah, that would be nice. That would be really nice."

"I didn't ask for your help."

"I'm your brother, I'm going to help you whether you ask or not."

"Thanks." Her voice dripped with sarcasm, which offended him, but he didn't show it.

"So, do you want to talk about it?"

"Talk about what?"

"Don't— Can we have a conversation, please? What's happening with you? I haven't seen you for a while. I know I couldn't make it to Thanksgiving but—"

"Whose fault was that?" she asked.

He didn't take the bait, just sat and waited.

"I'm fine," she finally said. "I went out for a walk, and the guy caught me by surprise. And that's all."

"You always carry pepper spray when you go out for a walk?"

"Maybe. Yeah. Why shouldn't I?"

"Because it's dangerous, not to mention it's illegal to carry around in the city. I thought you had gotten rid of that stuff anyway?"

She shook her head. "Just the gun."

"Well, I'm going to have to take the spray."

"Why?"

He laughed. "Are you serious? You want to know why I'm taking the pepper-spray, right after you nearly blinded some guy with it?"

"It's for protection. You know, people are allowed to protect themselves."

"That's what the police are for."

"Yeah, lot of good that did me."

He went silent. She knew she'd hurt him.

"I...I'm sorry, Dan. I don't blame you. I—"

"We're still looking...*I'm* still looking. I haven't given up. You know I won't stop until I find him, right?"

She nodded. "I know. And neither will I."

He pursed his lips. "Melissa, I'm not sure that's a good idea. I don't think you should—"

"You just said you're still looking too!"

"I know, but that's my job. I'm supposed to find the bad guys, not you."

Great job you've done so far. How's your search going? Yeah, nowhere, she thought, but decided not to say it. Her venom was spent for the night. Instead, she said, "I...sometimes I feel like everyone has forgotten, ya know? That he's still out there. And he's going to get away with it. God, what am I even saying? It's been five years, he *did* get away with it."

Dan looked down at his hands, then back up at her. "Why now? I mean, I know why, but…I thought this wasn't…bothering you anymore." He frowned, seemingly not sure his words did justice to what he was trying to say.

Melissa lifted her shoulders, ever so slightly, then dropped them back down. Someone who didn't know her could have mistaken the motion as nothing more than an indrawn breath. It wasn't.

"I…" Did she tell him about the nightmares? About what happened at Playland? She *should* tell him. But what if it was nothing? "It comes and goes, I guess."

"Have you talked to Mom?"

"No," Melissa said. Her mom was actually the last person she wanted to talk to. Not because her mother didn't care, but because she cared too much. Her mother could be the most dangerously empathetic person Melissa had ever met. She would not just share, but amplify whatever negative feelings she came into contact with, as if she could somehow take the pain upon herself, and seal it away from the person feeling it. She was always surprised and hurt when she learned it didn't work.

"What about your therapist?"

She shook her head. "No."

"Do you think maybe you should?"

"I don't know. I guess."

They sat in silence for a few minutes, then Dan checked his watch. "I need to get back to work," he said and stood up.

She stood up and walked him to the door.

"I will need the pepper spray before I leave," he said.

"Seriously?"

"Yes, Melissa. I'm required by law."

She made a show of sighing, then pulled the can out of her jacket pocket and handed it to him. He didn't need to know she had two more stashed away in her closet.

"Jesus," he said. "You're using bear spray?" He shook his head, appalled.

"Well, I wanted something strong."

He laughed, at that. "Then I guess you got what you were looking for." He paused and fidgeted with the can. "Look, I don't want you wandering around out there by yourself. It doesn't feel right. Can you promise me you won't do it again? Or at least, call me first and we'll go together. How about that?"

"Okay, fine. I'll do that."

He forced a smile and appeared to relax. Melissa was a little surprised he accepted her lie so easily. But when she looked into his eyes, she realized he didn't believe her at all. He wanted to, obviously, but he also knew better.

She felt a twinge in her heart at that look of sad betrayal.

"Good night," he said. "Be safe."

"Good night. And Dan?"

He turned in the hallway and looked at her. "Yeah?"

"Thanks," she said. And this time she meant it.

THIRTEEN
RICHARD

"GUYS LIKE EDWARD Snowden are heroes, if you ask me," James said.

"I didn't," Richard mumbled as he chewed on a hot dog.

"No, really," James continued. "The guy had the balls to stand up to the NSA and say, hey, what you're doing is wrong. He took a stand for the people."

"Lot of good that's done. Didn't the surveillance programs get renewed anyway?"

"Well, yeah. But people are fighting against it now."

"Good luck to them. I'm pretty sure all that's going to accomplish is the NSA will go even more underground on what it's doing. Meanwhile where's your hero now? The guy is on the run with a target on his back. That's what you get for standing up for the people."

"Yeah, whistleblowers and activists tend to get screwed, but they aren't doing it for themselves. They're doing it to change the world."

"Pretty hard to change the world when it doesn't want to be changed. Why do you care about the NSA anyway? We don't even live in the States. Isn't there some sort of local news for you to rail on about?"

"Local? The only news here is where city council is going to put the next bike lane. Vancouver is boring. Anyway, it's worse for us in Canada; we're stuck with a government that's been running NSA-style programs for years and doesn't even have to hide it because no one has the power to do anything about it anyway. Besides, the NSA aren't only spying on their own people; they're spying on us too."

"You think they know about the pile of Hustler magazines you hide under your bed?" Richard asked.

"If they do, then I'll bet they know about your subscription to Just Us Boys," James replied.

"As long as no one tells my wife I think I'll be okay."

James slapped him on the shoulder. "Don't worry buddy; your secret is safe with me."

They finished eating their hot dogs in companionable silence. When they finished, as if on cue, a call came in: An elderly man had fallen down the stairs. They jumped into the ambulance and sped off.

Less than five minutes later, they were parked in front of a row of grey townhouses. They grabbed their kits and equipment and went up to the door which, fortunately, was unlocked. Stepping inside, they surveyed the unit. Richard was struck by the stale smell of molasses and sweat. On the floor, partially hidden by an ancient looking couch, he spied a pair of legs. He walked over to the man and crouched down.

"Sir," he said, loudly, "Sir, can you hear me?"

The man's eyes fluttered open. He opened his mouth and took a long, wheezing breath of air, obviously struggling. "I…fell," he said quietly.

"It's okay. Don't try to speak," James said. "I'm going to ask you some questions and all you have to do is blink once for yes, and twice for no. Do you understand?"

The man blinked once.

While James quizzed him on what had happened, Richard pulled out a pulse oximeter to measure the blood oxygen levels. The result came back as a dangerously low seventy-eight. He relayed the information to James, who nodded and said, "Likely pulmonary contusion; he'll need to be intubated." He turned back to the patient, "Sir, we're going to have to…"

Richard tuned him out and pulled his intubation equipment out of the pack. Why was it so hot in here? He felt like the sun was shining directly on his face. He turned back to the patient. For a moment, everything went fuzzy; then he saw the vomit. "Hey, we have to clear the airway. Tilt his head."

"What?"

"He's vomiting. We have to clear the airway!"

"Richard, what are you talking about?"

The heat was beginning to bother him. He felt himself sweating all over. The sun was so bright, he could barely see. "If we don't clear the airway, she'll die," he said. "I have to save her."

His name echoed around him, but he ignored it. He reached for her head but something held him back. If he could clear the airway and intubate properly, this time he could save her. She would survive, and everything would be okay.

In a blinding flash, sharp pain blossomed above his left ear and he was on the floor, holding his hand over a suddenly tender side of his head. His ears rang like someone had smashed two oversized cymbals together in front of his face. He blinked the tears out of his eyes and sat up, fighting a wave of nausea. His head throbbed. "Wha...What happened?" He looked around; James was intubating the old man.

Richard blinked again and shook his head. Where had the girl gone? He was sure there had been vomit. And a young girl who looked like Gabrielle—no, it *was* Gabrielle. But he'd been here all along, in this living room. Their patient was an elderly man with weathered skin covered in large, dark lentigines. Not a small girl suffering from heat-induced asthma. He had almost...

"James," he said.

"Go get the cart," James said without looking in his direction.

Richard nodded and struggled to stand up. He felt dizzy, but it began to pass after a couple of steps. The side of his head ached. It was hot and felt like it was covered in blood, but when he put his hand on the area it came away clean.

He brought the cart back into the house where they loaded the old man onto it before bringing him back to the ambulance.

"Can you look after him?" James asked.

"Yeah, I'm fine," Richard answered.

"Sure?"

"Yeah. I'm here. I'm okay, now."

"Alright," James said and started walking to the front.

"James."

"Yeah?" James stopped and looked back.

"Sorry. It won't happen again."

James opened the driver's side door. "Maybe I should hit you in the head more often," he said, and jumped in.

Richard climbed in back with their patient. He closed the door and James began to drive.

* * * * *

Richard checked the time, it was nearly eleven o'clock. He had skipped out on dinner with Natalie for the second straight evening without so much as a phone call. She'd be mad but, with any luck, she'd be asleep again when he got home. Maybe he should have stayed out later.

He turned a corner onto his street and groaned when he saw a white van parked in front of the house; that was the last thing he needed.

He parked his late-model Sunfire in the driveway beside the Equinox and stepped out. Almost immediately he had to shield his eyes from a bright light mounted on a large TV camera. A short Asian woman, wearing a grey pant suit and holding a microphone, stood beside the cameraman.

"Excuse me. Richard Lain? My name is Amanda Troyes and I'm with—"

"I don't care," Richard said. "I have nothing to say to you."

She stepped in front of him. "I'm doing a story on Gabrielle Anderson and I wanted to ask you a few questions."

"No comment." Richard pushed his way around her.

"Sir, are you drunk?"

"What? No." Then, in apparent contradiction, he took a step backward to steady himself. *Damn body.*

The reporter, sensing an opening, pushed forward. "You've been drinking. I can smell it. You can barely stand."

"Get off my property."

"I have you on camera," she said. "You were obviously driving while under the influence. Just answer a few questions and I'll make sure this video doesn't go public."

"Blackmail?" Richard clenched his fists. "Get off my property you worthless scum, before I force you off."

"I won't be bul— Hey!"

Richard darted forward and yanked the microphone out of her hand and threw it at the van. He pushed her out of the way and reached for the cameraman. He grabbed the camera, covering the lens with one hand, and pushed the man back. "I *told* you *to leave.*"

"Hey, you can't do that," the reporter said, her squealing voice like a nail in Richard's eardrum. She struggled to stand up again in her high heels. He hadn't realized she'd fallen; he must have pushed her harder than he intended.

"Richard," someone called from the front door. He turned his head and saw Natalie, wearing her red housecoat. "What are you doing?"

"Mrs. Lain, your husband is assaulting us."

"Shut up," Richard said to the reporter then, turning back to Natalie, "I'm dealing with some trespassers. I'll come inside in a moment."

"Richard, leave them alone. Come inside."

"If I ever see you on my property again, I'll press charges," he said, waving his finger at the retreating reporter. The cameraman had already retreated to the van and was starting the engine. After they pulled away, Richard finally went inside.

Natalie was waiting for him. "What the hell was that?"

"What?"

She hit him on the shoulder. "What do you mean, what? You know what."

"They jumped me as soon as I got out of the car. They were trespassing."

"Oh, come on. One reporter? We had over a dozen here at one point. They were a lot more forceful than that poor woman out there."

"I had a bad day at work."

"Is that why you're drunk?"

"I'm not drunk!"

"God. Don't lie: you stink of booze. And you drove home like this. What's going to happen when that footage goes on TV?"

"Umm, I don't know. They won't—"

"Of course they will. It'll be all over the news. You know how toxic the media is, you experienced it first hand, and you just threw us under the bus again."

Richard frowned. "This isn't about you. I told you I had a bad day at work, there was—"

"It's always a bad day at work," Natalie said, throwing up her arms. "Or whatever other excuse you can come up with."

"Hey," Richard shouted. He stepped forward, towering over her. She craned her neck to look up at him. He felt his chest puffing out like a gorilla trying to show its dominance. Natalie, however, kept her feet planted, refusing to move. "I don't know how many times I've told you: I'm dealing with this on my own, in my own way. This isn't so—"

"You are such a child."

She'd spoken quietly, but it stopped his rant right in its tracks. The words echoed in his head like a whip crack.

"Me me me," she mocked. "Always worried about yourself; to hell with everyone else."

"That's not—" he began.

"How can you possibly say that you are on your own? After all we've been through together?" She shook her head. "I can't believe it."

Richard took a step back. His anger drained away, leaving the same feeling of helpless failure he'd been living with for the last six months. Suddenly, he felt very small.

Natalie reached forward and put her hand on his chest. "How long are you going to punish yourself? How long are you going to punish us? We can't do this forever."

"I'm sorry."

She shook her head and walked away. When she reached the stairs, she stopped and said, "There's a pillow and blanket on the couch. Good night."

He watched her climb into the darkness of the stairwell. When she was gone, he cursed silently. He pulled his shoes off then went to the bathroom to wash his face and brush his teeth. When he came back, he stared at the couch: his bed for the night—or longer, depending on how mad Natalie was.

He lay down and rolled around a bit, searching for the best spot. At least it was comfortable, as far as couches went. His back was going to ache in the morning, something about the space between the cushions always left him sore the next day. He thought about the bed he had been exiled from and sighed. Seven hours until sunrise.

FOURTEEN
JOEL – TEN YEARS AGO

"JOEL!" *BANG, BANG, bang.* "Joel!"

Joel rolled out of bed and landed on the floor, where something hard jabbed into his ribs. The impact knocked the wind out of him. He pulled the object out from under him and realized it was his bong. He tossed it to the side and groaned.

Bang, bang, bang. "Joel!"

"I'm coming," he mumbled.

He stood up and stretched, then sauntered over to the door wearing just his underwear.

He opened the door. "Oh, hey, Uncle Frank. What—"

"Put some clothes on," Frank said and barged in. "Jesus this place is a mess. Come on, get moving."

"Ugh, what for?"

"It's your mom, Joel. She's in the hospital."

That woke him up. "What? What happened?"

"Don't know. They said she's pretty beat up. I got the call half an hour ago and I came to get you."

Joel threw on some clothes and rushed out the door with Uncle Frank. They sped to Kelowna General Hospital and tracked down his mom.

93

When they finally reached the room, Joel burst in first, with Uncle Frank and a nurse trailing behind. She lay on a bed with an IV sticking out of her arm and a breathing mask covering her mouth.

"Mom? Mom, are you okay?"

She nodded.

"What happened?"

She looked to the side and shook her head slightly. Tears welled in her eyes.

Joel looked at the nurse.

"Someone dropped her off outside; then she checked herself in this morning, said she fell down the stairs."

"Really? Does it look like she fell down the stairs?"

The nurse looked over at his mom, then looked down. "I don't know. She has two broken ribs and a fracture of her right humerus. She was having trouble breathing so we took some X-rays. The doctor is looking at them now; he'll be in to see her soon."

Joel looked over at Uncle Frank. "He did this. You know he did."

Uncle Frank nodded slowly. "Yes," he said quietly.

Joel felt his heart beating faster. "I have to stop him. I have to do something."

Uncle Frank grabbed his arm. "No, Joel. Don't. Don't do anything stupid."

He ripped his arm out of Frank's grip. "I have to." He bent over his mom and took hold of her hand. "Mom, I can't let him do this to you anymore."

She looked at him. Her eyes were wide and scared. She began to shake her head, then winced in pain.

Joel wiped a tear from his eye. "I should have done this a long time ago." He stood up.

"Joel. Think about this, what are you going to do? Let the police handle it. I'll take care of your mom."

"No. No, I've had enough."

Uncle Frank grabbed Joel's arm again, but when Joel looked at him, he saw something in his eyes that made him let go almost immediately. "Just...be careful, okay, kid?"

"Yeah, of course," Joel said, having no intention of following the advice.

* * * * *

He caught a taxi back to his motel and found Herb, the local drug dealer.

"Herb, I need a favour."

"Hey, whatever you need, man. I got it."

"I need a gun. Something small—"

"Whoa whoa! I don't do that, buddy. I'm here for—"

Joel grabbed his arms and shook violently. "Don't screw with me. You know someone. I know you do."

Herb shrugged out of Joel's grip. "Jesus, chill out man." He looked at Joel suspiciously.

"Well?"

"I might know a guy. Won't be cheap."

"How much?"

"About five bills, maybe more."

Joel cringed at the cost. "Fine. Call your guy and send him to my place. I need it today. Got it?"

"Yeah, yeah."

Joel went up to his room. His hands trembled with rage and his heart was still slamming in his chest. He rolled up the last of his weed, lit it up and took a few long pulls. He began pacing back and forth, waiting for Herb's guy to show up, and worrying about what would come next if he did show up.

He was still pacing nervously when the knock finally came late that afternoon.

He opened the door to see a shifty-looking guy wearing a blue hoodie, standing in the doorway with Herb behind him.

"Come in."

They walked in and took a look around. Joel waited as long as he could stand for them to say something, then gave up. "Well? You have it?"

"You know the rules?"

"What? This meeting never happened? All that crap? Yeah, I know the rules."

"What you need it for?" the blue-hooded man asked.

Joel's eyes narrowed. "Whatever I want."

"That's not how this works. I don't want to turn on the news and see some guy got shot by my gun."

"Then don't turn on the news," Joel said. When they stared at him he added, "It's for self-defence."

"You got someone after you?"

"No. Look, do you have it or not?"

Blue-hood looked over at Herb, who shrugged with indifference. He looked back at Joel. "Six bills."

"Fine." Joel had the cash ready. He pulled a roll out of his pocket and counted out six one-hundred dollar bills and handed them to Blue-hood.

Blue-hood shoved the money into one of his pockets and pulled a small, silver revolver out of another. "You know how to work one of these?"

"I'll figure it out."

Blue-hood laughed. "First six bullets are included. You need more?"

"No," Joel said, "that'll be enough."

"Try not to shoot yourself," Blue-hood said. He and Herb walked out, leaving Joel alone with his new gun.

He balanced it in his hand; it was lighter than he thought it would be. It was also smaller. He'd imagined them bringing something a lot larger and more intimidating; but he guessed this would work just as well.

He lifted it up and pointed it at a mirror across the room. The version of himself reflected back looked a lot more like his father than he wanted to admit. He aimed right between his eyes, his father's eyes. "Hey, Dad, you bastard!" he said, channelling Charley Bowdre from Young Guns. "It's you and I."

* * * * *

Joel stood in front of the house, a gun in his pocket and a brand new wooden baseball bat in his hand. His car was parked safely around the corner where it wouldn't be noticed. He tested his old house key in the lock—*click*— the door opened. No surprise there. He slipped inside and locked the door behind him.

The place looked exactly as he remembered. Same shaggy grey

carpet, brown fabric couch, and coffee table covered in empty beer bottles. It was like he'd never left.

He looked around for a good place to hide and eventually settled on the laundry room—the place his father would be least likely to visit after coming home from work.

Joel stood in the cramped room and waited, the only light provided by the thin gap at the bottom of the door. Half an hour later, when he heard the front door open, he jumped and tightened his grip on the bat, then took a deep, steadying breath.

The door shut, followed by barely audible footsteps that slowly grew louder as they moved closer. *He's not going to the kitchen. He's coming here!*

Joel wiped his sweaty hands on his pants and gripped the bat again. He lifted it into the air, ready to lash out as soon as the door opened. *There's not enough space here. This is bad. Shit.*

A shadow passed in front of the door and stopped. Joel's heart thumped like a giant bass drum. He swallowed and tried not to make any noise. He still had the element of surprise. He just had to—

Suddenly he heard splashing, like liquid pouring into a bowl, and he breathed a sigh of relief. Of course, he was across from the bathroom. *I'm an idiot.*

He heard the toilet flush and the tap turn on for a few seconds. The shadow passed in front of his door again, and was gone. The noise from the toilet prevented him from hearing anything else for the next minute. He strained his ears, trying to pick up something, anything. He thought he heard the fridge shut, but wasn't sure.

Eventually the toilet finished refilling with a loud hiss, then there was silence.

He cracked the door open and looked down the hall. Seeing nothing, he stepped out into the hallway.

He crept down the hallway until the living room slowly came into view. The TV was still off, and the couch empty. That left one option.

Joel took a deep breath and inched his head around the corner to take a look.

His father was standing at the table reading a newspaper, back turned towards Joel. He flipped a page nonchalantly, lifted a bottle of beer to his mouth and drank.

Joel readied himself, his blood burning through his veins. His breathing quickened and all the pent-up anger he'd been holding compressed itself into a toxic ball of fierce intent. He lifted the bat and bolted forward. He swung in a wide arc, grunting with the effort. His father heard the noise but it was too late: The bat smashed into his arm above the elbow with a loud, crunching sound. The force of the impact left Joel's arms vibrating. His father stumbled into a counter, screaming in pain.

"What the FUCK?" his father yelled, spittle flying from his mouth. With his left hand, he grabbed a knife from a drawer; his right arm hung limp at his side. "I'll kill you for that, you little piece of—"

"Shut up!" Joel yelled back. He tossed the bat to the side, pulled the gun out of his pocket and pointed it at his father. "Sit down, *Dad.*"

His father glared at him, red-faced, hatred simmering in his eyes. "Fuck you."

Joel cocked the hammer. "I said *sit down.*"

"You wouldn't dare."

Joel let out a tense, high pitched laugh. Something about the sound made his father take a step back. "Are you shitting me? Do you know how long I've wanted to do this?" Without waiting for an answer, he yelled, "Do you?"

"No," his dad said quietly.

Joel pointed the gun at the table, then back at his father. "Drop the knife. And sit."

"Fine," his dad said. He put the knife on the counter and shuffled over to the table and sat down. "So what are you gonna do now? Shoot me?"

"I don't know. Maybe." He began to pace. He didn't know what he was going to do anymore. Was he really going to kill him and spend the rest of his life in jail?

"If you do, then make sure you shoot yourself while you're at it."

"Excuse me?"

"You heard me."

"What the hell does that mean?"

"You think you can kill me and walk away?"

"Maybe. It happens all the time."

Now it was his father's turn to laugh. "Well, what are you waiting for, you righteous little bastard? You've always thought you're better than me. You think those drugs and whores lead to a better life than this?" He laughed again.

"Shut up," Joel said, still pacing. He ran his hands through his hair; they were shaking. His father kept laughing at him, heedless of Joel's growing agitation. How did he know about what Joel had been doing? Had he been watching, or was it a guess? The laughing echoed in his head.

He changed direction and walked up to his father. "I said," he pushed the barrel of the gun into his father's forehead, "Shut up!"

His dad suddenly grabbed Joel's hand. But instead of trying to disarm him, he pulled it harder into his head. "Then do it. That's what you want, right? You can end it all here, right now."

Joel tried to pull his hand away, but his father's vice-like grip held him fast. He used his free hand and tried to pry his dad's fingers loose, to no avail. "Let me go!"

"Do it! Pull the fucking trigger!"

"No!" Joel punched him in the face, the sound like a dull slap. His father grunted, but didn't let go. Joel leaned in and went to work on his head, punctuating each punch with a word: "Let. Go. Of. Me!"

Finally, his grip loosened and Joel ripped his hand free. As soon as he had control of his arm again he swiped back in, pistol-whipping his father across the head. His dad's head lolled to the side, a trail of blood running down from his temple.

"You pussy," his father said. "I'll come for you."

He grabbed his father's still-functioning hand, put it on the table and pushed the barrel of the gun up against it. "No, you won't," he said, and pulled the trigger.

The blast wasn't as loud or satisfying as he'd hoped. But the ensuing scream from his father was more than enough.

"You come after us, I'll finish this. I promise." He took a few steps back. The table had a hole in it, the floor as well. Blood was spattered all over.

His father held his maimed hand against his chest. He still couldn't move his other arm. His cheek was swollen and blood flowed freely down the side of his face. He was whimpering. "I'll kill you—one day."

Joel shoved the gun in his pocket and walked away.

"You hear me? I'll kill you!"

Joel left. The last thing he heard before he shut the door was the sound of his father moaning.

* * * * *

Joel speed-walked through the hospital, keeping his head down and his hands tucked in his pockets. He burst into his mom's room and shut the door. "Uncle Frank, are you here? Uncle Frank?"

"Shhhhh," Uncle Frank said, walking out of the bathroom. "She's sleeping."

"I did something bad," Joel whispered. "I don't know what to do."

"What did you do? Jesus, what happened to your hand? It looks like you were punching a wall."

Joel looked at his hand, the knuckles were red and bloody. "A head, more like." He took a deep breath. "I might be in trouble."

"Okay, calm down and tell me what happened."

Joel nodded and relayed the story to Uncle Frank, who became increasingly distressed as time went on. At the end, when Joel told him he decided not to kill his dad, Uncle Frank breathed a large sigh of relief. Then he cringed when Joel finished the story off with the bullet through the hand.

"I don't know what to do now. I should have killed him."

"No! Absolutely not. It's okay, you did the right thing by not killing him. But you can't stay here anymore, not now."

Joel was stunned. "What do you mean?"

"Think about it, Joel. Either the cops come for you, or he does. I can protect your mom; she's a victim in this. But I can't protect you."

"What do you mean? I'm a victim too; he didn't just hit her, you know."

"I know, I know." Uncle Frank pulled Joel into a forced embrace. "But this changes everything. You can get into big trouble for this."

"He won't go to the cops. He'd never—"

"He doesn't have to go to the cops. Even if he goes to the hospital he'll have to report the gunshot wound to the police. That would lead right back to you. Do you want to take that chance? Even if he doesn't, you know what's going to happen. He won't forget this. You need to leave; go somewhere he won't find you."

Joel pulled away and shook his head. "No, you said you'd protect her. Why not me?"

Uncle Frank looked over at Joel's mom, then down at his hands. "I…" He struggled with the words. "I just can't," he said, shoulders slumping.

Joel's lip turned up and his sorrow turned to anger. "Oh, I see how it is. You want her to yourself."

"No." Uncle Frank reached out and put his hand on Joel's shoulder. "It's not like that."

Joel shook him off. "Fuck you, Uncle Frank."

He went over to the bed where his mom lay sound asleep. He lifted her hand and held it. "I have to go, Mom," he said. "I'm so sorry—for everything. Uncle Frank's gonna look after you now. Stay away from Dad, okay? Don't let him suck you back in. You don't have to live like that. You hear me? You deserve better."

He held her hand for another minute, then gently put it down and turned back to Frank. "Don't let that asshole near her. You got that? Don't let her go back to him."

"I won't, I promise. Do you need anything? I have some money—"

"No. It's fine. Take care of her."

"Okay."

Uncle Frank extended his hand out, and after a moment's consideration, Joel accepted it, glaring at him as they shook; hoping he wasn't moving her from one prison into another, that this would make his mom's life better. He opened the door and took one last look back.

"This is for the best," Uncle Frank said.

Joel shut the door. "I hope so," he whispered.

As hard as it was for him to leave his mother in the state she was in, he knew he would never be safe if he stayed in Kelowna. Uncle Frank was right: he had to get away. So, with nothing but the clothes on his back and the roll of bills in his pocket, he boarded a half-empty bus to Vancouver.

FIFTEEN
RICHARD

"YOU KNOW YOU'RE putting us in a bad position," said the dark-skinned man sitting behind a large wood desk. He looked at Richard with steady eyes, hands steepled in front of him. "You know the top brass wanted you fired; they said you've become more trouble than you're worth."

Richard smirked. His boss, Emmanuele, was posturing. So he called him out. "I think the union would have something to say about that."

"Don't bring those assholes into it, please. Listen, this doesn't look good. You do something stupid, it reflects back on us. We can't have our employees putting other people in danger like that. Especially— "

"Especially what? Me?" Richard asked, crossing his arms and glaring across the desk.

"Especially right now," Emmanuele said levelly. "Budgets are coming up, we're trying to convince the government to give us more money instead of cutting it back. That gets a lot harder when my people are out drunk driving and fighting with the press."

"Sorry I made your job more difficult."

"You're lucky you're a good paramedic, or else I'd sign your release papers right now."

"Thanks?" he asked, sarcasm dripping from his voice. He continued to surprise himself when he spoke. It felt like he kept digging new holes for himself, but for some reason, he couldn't stop doing it. He and Emmanuele used to get along.

They stared at each other for what seemed like a long moment, then Emmanuele took a calming breath and moved on. "I'd rather not suspend you again right now. We're short-handed as it is. So, instead, I have something here for you to sign." He pushed a piece of paper and pen across the desk to Richard.

"I'm not signing anything without a union rep."

Emmanuele smiled. "He already signed it. You'll find his signature at the bottom."

Richard grabbed the paper. "What is this?"

"It's an agreement. You go to AA for ten weeks, you go back to work. Simple as that."

"What?" Richard jumped out of his seat. "AA? What the hell? One mistake doesn't make me an alcoholic. Nothing even happened."

"Sit down," Emmanuele said, iron in his voice. When Richard was back in his seat he continued. "Something did happen: you were caught on camera by a reporter. You would have been better off if it had been the police. Now your face is plastered all over the news and we can't be seen as not dealing with it. Besides, since you're not a real alcoholic, this should be a cakewalk. But it is a requirement."

"And if I don't?"

"Let me rephrase that. This is a requirement for your continued employment. Do you understand?"

Richard sighed and picked up the pen. "I understand."

"Good."

After signing the agreement and leaving the office, Richard found James in the waiting room chatting up one of the new nurses and recent target of James' romantic plotting. She twirled her long, blonde hair in her fingers and laughed at something he had said. When James saw Richard waiting, he touched her arm, smiled, and walked away.

"She's warming up to you," Richard said when James was in earshot.

"Yeah, took a while, but it'll be worth it," James said, staring longingly at her shapely hips as she walked down the hall. "I'd like to see her in some exiguous clothing."

"Exiguous?"

"Yeah, like scanty or very small."

"Word of the day?"

"Yup," James said, proud smile on his face.

Richard shook his head ruefully and walked away.

"Hey, how did the meeting with Emmanuele go?" James asked, falling into stride beside Richard.

Richard shrugged. "I'm still here. But they're making me go to AA meetings."

"Awww, man, seriously? That's bullshit."

"Gotta do something so the media don't think I'm getting away with it, or some crap."

"Whatever, they're being dicks. You gonna go?"

"I have to; I can't work if I don't go."

"I'll be your sponsor. I'll tell them you're hitting up the meetings and that it's all good."

"Thanks," Richard said, "but somehow I don't think that'll fly."

James looked dejected for a moment, then brightened up. "When's your first meeting?"

Richard pulled a folded paper out of his pocket and opened it up. "He gave me a list of some meetings in the area. Looks like the closest one is tomorrow night at nine."

"Perfect, that means we have one more night."

"For what?"

"To turn you into an alcoholic," James said happily.

Richard laughed. "Sounds good to me. Meet you at The Morrissey?"

"Nah, leave your car here and come with me; better not let you drive drunk again."

"Asshole," Richard said, but he wasn't angry. He was looking forward to a drink.

* * * * *

Richard stepped into the sparsely furnished room. A foldout table was set up in the corner, where a coffee machine and box of Tim Hortons donuts sat next to a bag of styrofoam cups. In the centre a dozen chairs were arranged in a circle, their white plastic coverings reflected the light from the fluorescent lamps overhead. A few people were already sitting, while the rest milled about the room in pairs, chatting quietly.

Richard tapped an extremely tall, lanky-looking fellow on the shoulder. "Hey, sorry, I'm looking for Jeff."

He looked down at Richard for a moment, then smiled. "No problem. I'm Mandeep. Jeff is over there." He pointed towards the chairs at a short, bald-headed man with glasses who was reading over some notes.

"Thanks," Richard said, then walked over and sat down beside Jeff.

"Hi, I'm Richard," he said, extending his hand.

Jeff shook it and nodded. "Welcome, Richard. What can I do for you?"

"I'm here for work. I need you to sign this paper here saying that I attended the meeting. I've already filled out the date and location." Richard handed him the sheet.

Jeff took a look at it, then handed it back to Richard. "I'll be happy to sign it for you, after the meeting."

"I thought it would be easier—" He stopped at Jeff's raised hand.

"I don't sign anything before or during the meeting. If you stay for the whole time, you'll get your signature."

Richard sighed. It was the same response he had received from the work-mandated therapist he had been sent to. He wondered why these people were so intent on wasting their time. "So how does this work?" he asked. "Do I tell everyone a sad story about my life and shed a few tears?"

"No," Jeff replied without looking at him. "Tonight you listen."

With nothing else to say, Richard got up and walked over to the table to grab a coffee. He had a feeling he was going to need it.

A brunette woman was stirring a cube of sugar into her coffee when he arrived. As he filled his cup she leaned over and said, "The coffee is pretty terrible. You might want to mix in some extra cream and sugar."

"Thanks for the heads-up," Richard said. "But I usually drink it black."

"Your funeral," she said, crossing her arms. Richard tried not to get caught looking at her suddenly very obvious cleavage.

He took a sip and almost spit it back out. It tasted like tar. The woman chuckled at his expression. "In this case, I think I'll make an exception," he said.

She laughed again as he dropped three cubes of sugar and poured a liberal helping of cream into his cup. This time, he took a cautious sip to see if the additions had helped. It did, at least now the drink was palatable, if not good. "Can't you guys afford some decent coffee here?"

"It's free; what do you expect. By the way, my name is Lacey."

"Richard."

"Welcome to the club, Richard," she said, then walked towards the circle and sat down. Richard wasn't sure if it was because she was the only girl in the room or not, but she definitely had an alluring sexuality.

He realized he was the only one still standing and quickly took a seat three spots over from Lacey.

When everyone was settled, Jeff began: "My name is Jeff, and I'm an alcoholic."

"Hi, Jeff," came the predictable, robotic sounding chorus.

"First, I'd like to welcome Richard to the group." He gestured in Richard's direction. Richard nodded uncomfortably at the smattering of clapping and half-hearted greetings. Lacey had a knowing look on her face as she clapped her hands, like she knew a secret about him that no one else had figured out.

"Second, do we have any anniversaries today?"

A ragged looking man put up his hand; Jeff nodded and the man began to talk; and Richard realized his mistake: "My name is Mona, and I am an alcoholic." He, no, *she* stopped for a moment while everyone uttered the obligatory response. Richard chided himself for not realizing her gender earlier. A big part of his job was being able to observe things that weren't immediately obvious. But he had to admit, this woman looked spent.

"Last weekend was six years since I had a drink," she continued in her raspy voice.

Everyone clapped.

"I didn't like who I was, back then; but with your help and God's blessing, I'll stay strong and keep it going, twenty-four hours at a time."

"Thanks, Mona," everyone said in unison when she finished. Richard was starting to realize these people were really big on saying things together. It was a lot like church.

Jeff took over again. "Today I'd like us to read a section of chapter five." He lifted his copy of the Big Book, and opened it to a pre-marked page: "Chapter Five - How It Works," he began.

Richard tuned him out and looked around at the other people in the room. There were some he'd already met, but about six others he hadn't: as a group, they ranged in age from about twenty-five to sixty, and ran the gamut of racial distribution. It wasn't a prototypical group of drunks, either. Sure, a couple of people looked rough, but you got that everywhere these days. Overall, they seemed like normal people, not the sort you'd find stumbling around the Downtown Eastside. They could just as easily have been mistaken for students in a cooking class. Richard realized he'd had this image in his head of what these people would be like, and the reality didn't match.

"Richard."

"Oh, yeah? Sorry." Richard looked over at Jeff, who was pointing at the person beside him.

"It's your turn to read. Carl has the book beside you."

"Right. Um, where were we?" He took the book from Carl and looked around the page. Jeff narrowed his eyes, but didn't say anything. Carl, thankfully, pointed out where he had left off. Richard thanked him and began to read.

"Here are the steps we took, which are suggested as a program of recovery: 'One, we admitted we were powerless over alcohol - that our lives had become unmanageable. Two, came to believe that a power greater than ourselves could restore us to sanity. Three, made a decision to turn our will and our lives over to the care of God as we understood Him.' "

"Thank you, Richard," Jeff said. "You can pass the book to Heng."

Richard passed the book. *This really is like church,* he thought, listening to Heng read out the rest of the steps. He hadn't known a lot about AA before. Chalk that up to poor representation on TV, or a general lack of interest on his part. He'd always imagined it as a group who focused on sponsors and telling stories as a means of catharsis. But the religious aspect was a complete surprise; though, maybe it shouldn't have been. Didn't support groups always run on some sort of faith?

After everyone had taken turns reading sections of the chapter, Jeff put the book away and asked if anyone had anything they wanted to share. He prefaced with the reminder that everything is confidential, what happens in AA stays in AA, or something along those lines.

Lacey put up her hand and was given the floor. "My name is Lacey, and I'm an alcoholic," she said. "I would like to talk about the fifth step: admitting to ourselves, God, and another human being the exact nature of our wrongs.

"I started drinking when I was a teenager. It was always social, but I was a very social person, so I drank almost every night. Eventually, I started to drink when I was alone because it made me feel like I wasn't. I didn't know it, but alcohol had become my companion. I thought it was my friend, instead of the enemy that it is. The first time my friends staged an intervention, I cursed them. I told them they didn't know anything and they should leave me alone. I told them lies to convince them I would stop, but I never did. After a while, I realized that alcohol hadn't just become my friend: it had tricked me into driving away my real friends, and it was all I had left.

"Then my Dad died, and I missed his funeral because I was passed out in some guy's apartment who I didn't even know. That was when I finally knew that I had a problem. But even then, it was still so hard. To say it, you know? The day I decided to quit, I went to my father's grave. The ground was still fresh, and I could smell the wreath of daisies sitting against his gravestone. He used to grow all different types of daisies in the backyard. He used to call me his favourite little daisy. I could smell myself as I sat there; I smelled like stale booze. I still remember that. Even the flowers couldn't cover it up.

"I put my hand over his name, and speaking to both him and God, I said 'Dad, I'm an alcoholic. I'm so sorry.' And then I cried."

She stopped for a moment to wipe the tears that had begun to form in her eyes. Everyone watched her, silent, waiting.

She let out a strangled laugh. "That was eight hundred and twelve days ago, the same number of days I've been sober."

"Thank you, Lacey," Jeff said, and everyone echoed him. Richard was surprised to find himself joining in. He looked at her as he said the words and it seemed she was looking at him as well.

A few others shared their stories, and Richard found he was paying a lot more attention to them than he had expected. Before long, it was past ten o'clock and Jeff was calling an end to the meeting.

"Okay, everyone, let's join hands for the Serenity Prayer."

Richard hesitated for a moment, then grabbed onto the offered hands from Carl and Heng, then listened as they all spoke in unison: "God, grant me the serenity to accept the things I cannot change; the courage to change the things I can; and the wisdom to know the difference."

After the group had begun to disperse, Richard found Jeff in the corner eating a donut. "Hi, would you mind—"

"Oh yes, your form, of course." Jeff pulled a pen out and took the paper. As he was signing, he said "So, will I see you next week?"

"Yeah, I'll be back," Richard said, then, "Thanks," as he took the paper back from Jeff and put it in his pocket.

"You should think about finding a sponsor," Jeff said.

"I don't know if—"

"I'll be his sponsor," said a woman from behind them. Richard turned to see Lacey standing by the door. She smiled and waved at his startled expression.

"You haven't sponsored anyone before, Lacey. Are you sure you're ready?"

"Oh, I can handle this one, Jeff. I know his type."

Richard frowned. "And what type is that?"

Instead of responding, she smiled all the wider.

"Do I have your blessing?" she asked Jeff.

Jeff looked from one to the other, then shrugged. "You do. Good luck."

Richard thanked Jeff and walked over to Lacey, who was loitering outside the door. "Listen, I appreciate your interest, but I really don't need a sponsor."

"Mmhmm. Hey, you want to go out for a drink?"

"Excuse me?"

"Coffee, Richard, just coffee," Lacey said, barely repressing her amusement. "There's a Tim Hortons down the road."

He was tempted, very tempted. "I should head home; my wife will be waiting." He wasn't sure why he added that last part; Natalie would likely be in bed by the time he got home.

"Alright, let's meet tomorrow then. Give me your phone."

He passed her his phone and she put her number in it, then texted herself so that his number showed up on hers. She gave him his phone back and winked. "Okay, see you tomorrow. Give your wife a kiss for me."

What did that mean? "Um, sure," he said.

He continued staring down the empty hallway long after she left, her scent still lingering in his nose.

It smelled like daisies.

SIXTEEN
ALEX

"WHAT ABOUT AVATAR?" Emily asked.

"Yes. Didn't like it," Alex answered.

"What? How could you not like it? It looked amazing; it was filled with action for the guys, and had a love story for the girls. I thought everyone liked that movie."

He shrugged. "I guess it was alright, but it didn't really do it for me. It didn't seem realistic. Seriously, what was with those floating mountains with the waterfalls? How did they have an infinite source of water up in the air like that? It doesn't make sense. And the entire evolutionary chain on that planet was wrong."

She looked blandly at him. "We're talking about a world populated by giant blue people, and you're complaining about realism?"

He opened his mouth to respond, then changed his mind and laughed instead. "Okay, you're right."

"Of course I am." She smiled widely, her eyes glittering in the afternoon sun. She took a sip of her latte and set it down.

"The ending was lame though. Everything tied off too nicely. I'm not a fan of endings that are happy just for the sake of it. Life doesn't work like that; it's more complicated."

"Oh, you're such a sceptic!" she said. "You know happy endings are good once in awhile, right? Every story doesn't have to end on a downer. Maybe life is more complicated, but people usually watch movies to get away from reality, you know? Sometimes people need those happy endings in their lives, even if they aren't real. Everybody should have a happy ending sometime, Alex. Even you."

"Hmm, I guess," he conceded, "but I still prefer the sad ones."

She rolled her eyes and laughed. "You can be such a sad nelly sometimes."

Normally a comment like that would have hurt his feelings. *Who says sad nelly, anyway?* But coming from Emily, with her sparkling green eyes and songbird laughter, it didn't bother him. When he talked her, he didn't feel defensive, as if every word was a knife he had to be armored against; he could be open, exposed like he couldn't be with anyone else. It was liberating.

But it hadn't come easy. Even after that revelatory ride home on Thanksgiving, he hadn't believed there was a chance of anything happening between them. It was a one off, he thought, a fluke. She wasn't going to call.

Yet she had, the next day, in fact. He had been sitting on his couch wallowing in a ball of depression, thinking about all the things he had done wrong the night before, and how she would never call someone like him. Why would she? He was such a pathetic mess, hardly worth the effort. No doubt the night before had been a mirage, some sort of cosmic joke meant to taunt him, cause him even more pain.

Then the phone rang, and her voice was on the other end. He was so shocked she had to ask for him three times before he could speak.

"Oh, uh, hello."

"There you are! Hi, it's Emily."

"Hi," he said cautiously.

"How are you? I hope I didn't interrupt anything—"

"It's okay, I was just watching TV. I'm okay, I guess."

"Oh good."

"Yeah. Um, how are you?"

"I'm great! I was actually thinking of going for a coffee and thought I'd give you a call and see if you wanted to join me."

"Really?" He hadn't meant to say that, but he was too surprised to hold back.

"Yeah, there's a nice cafe not far from either of us; I like to go there to relax. You said you're on holiday, right? So I thought we could hang."

"Yeah, um, I am. I guess then, yeah, if you want…I could meet you there."

"Great!"

That was all it took: one incredibly awkward conversation and suddenly his day had changed, his entire vacation had changed. They had met up multiple times before, always at the quaint little Roca Cafe.

It was during these coffee dates that Alex got to know more about Emily, and why she had so much free time: she was between jobs. She had been working at Sears when rounds of layoffs began to hit. She survived the first round, but the second was targeted at management, and even she wasn't able to escape the relentless march of corporate austerity. She was sad to go; but fortunately, she had worked her way up to a high enough position that she walked away with a fair severance package.

The economy being what it was, finding a new job hadn't been easy. So she and Rob decided to take advantage of the paid time off and started trying for a baby, almost a year ago, but the proposed fetus had yet to make an appearance. They certainly hadn't expected it to take this long, but they were okay with it; sometimes these things take time. Although, her voice was strained when she told him about it, so he could tell the situation was tough on her. He didn't know quite what to say, but he was happy when she changed the subject.

And so, here they sat—meeting for the fifth time in less than three weeks—in amicable silence on the patio of the Roca Cafe on a sunny fall afternoon. If anyone had asked Alex before Thanksgiving what he thought his vacation would be like, the answer would never have matched the reality. Truthfully, he likely would have been gone from the world by this time. He'd been in that deep of a depression, with no hope of ever coming out.

Had this woman, this stunning woman sitting across from him, somehow managed to save his life? It was still too early to say for sure. But she had extended it, no doubt. He had a light now, something to reach towards and guide him out of his darkness.

It was almost like one of the daydreams he'd had when he was younger. Not the same as the inevitable carnal daydreams teenagers are bound to have. It was better, actually. He had never imagined them taking the time to really get to know one another, to become friends. Then, maybe, one day, something even more. It was incredibly fulfilling, far more so than any lewd fantasy.

"So tell me about your girlfriend. We still haven't talked about her," Emily said.

"Hmm?"

"Your girlfriend; you mentioned her at Thanksgiving."

Shit. "Um, right, yeah. Diamond." Suddenly, he felt uncomfortable. Diamond wasn't a lie, but she wasn't really the truth either.

"That's it! What an interesting name. Is that actually her real name or a nickname?"

"Um, I think it's her real name. I haven't actually asked her."

"Really? That's funny. So what does she do?"

Alex didn't like it when he had to think fast; he needed time to consider his words and always worried that if he spoke too quickly, he would say something stupid, or get himself dumped in the frying pan. And right then and there, he felt like he was in the frying pan, all because of a thoughtless burst of annoyance he'd had weeks ago. "She's, uh, she's in the service industry."

"Oh, yeah. So like a waitress or something?"

"She's a...masseuse, a massage therapist." That sounded good. The best lies always contain a grain of truth.

"Ooooooh," Emily winked at him. "I bet that's nice to have in the relationship."

Alex smiled back at her. "You bet it is." He felt a twinge of guilt. Emily always accepted whatever he said without question. He hated to abuse her trust.

"I wish Rob still gave massages. He used to give me wonderful foot rubs years ago, but it was always so hard to convince him to do it. Then he bought me one of those foot massage tubs and he hasn't touched my feet since. I'm telling you, if you give Diamond a foot massage every once in awhile, she will love you for it."

"I'll have to remember that."

"Have you two been together for long?"

He sat and thought. This was the kind of question he could take some time on, it was expected. "Um, well, we've known each other for a while. I've been seeing her for years now. But we didn't really, we didn't really sort of, hook up, I guess, until recently."

"I see," she said. "Well, that's nice anyway. It's good to be with someone you've known for a while."

Alex looked her straight in the eyes. "Yeah, you're right."

"Wait a second. Aren't massage therapists forbidden from relations with their clients? Isn't that some sort of professional code of conduct?"

Alex froze.

She looked at him shrewdly. "Must have been some pretty special massage sessions to convince her to put herself in that position, hmm?" She finished off with a wink and started to giggle.

Alex breathed a sigh of relief. He took a sip of his now-cool latte and tried to concentrate on keeping his hands from shaking. He laughed with her. His voice may have been a slightly higher pitch than usual but, thankfully, she didn't notice.

"Look at you. Your face is all red! You get embarrassed so easily."

"Yeah, um…"

"Fine," she said, laughing. "I'll leave you alone." She had a broad smile now and her eyes sparkled mischievously, as though she had learned a naughty secret. "But I want to meet her one day."

"I dunno. We're not, like, very formal or anything. But, yeah, maybe. Maybe one day." *I hope not.*

"You should— " She tilted her head and looked towards the door. Alex tried not to stare at the curve of her neck, but it wasn't easy, with the light reflecting off her skin just so. "Hey! Is that Rob?"

She stood up and waved at the man standing near the entrance. He waved back and made his way to their table.

"Hey, I thought you might be here," Rob said. He was tall, dressed in a dark suit and wearing—in Alex's opinion—a rather staid-looking tie. He had short, black hair and a clean shaven face with angular cheekbones. He reminded Alex of a better looking version of his older siblings. The guy looked like he'd been cut out of a magazine. Alex hated him immediately.

Emily gave Rob a hug and kiss, then turned to face Alex. They were holding hands. "Rob, this is my cousin Alex. Alex this is my husband Rob."

"Nice to meet you," Rob said, reaching out his free hand.

Alex shook his hand; the grip was business-like, strong, confident, and blessedly brief. Alex felt limp-wristed in comparison. "Hi."

"What are you doing here? I thought you'd be at work," Emily asked.

"I was able to get out early today," Rob said. "I thought I would surprise you at home but you weren't there, so I knew I would find you here."

"Aw, that's so sweet," Emily said.

Alex tried to keep his face neutral. He was happy he didn't have to talk about Diamond anymore, but he wasn't happy Rob had intruded upon their afternoon.

Rob, for his part, had pulled out his BlackBerry as soon as he sat down and seemed more interested in that than in anything else.

"We were talking about Alex's girlfriend," Emily said.

"Oh yeah?" Rob responded absently, typing into his phone.

"Yeah, I was just saying...oh, I just had a great idea!" Emily said.

Oh no. Given their topic of conversation before Rob interposed himself, Alex didn't like the sound of that at all. He was worried about where this was going.

Emily continued, "Why don't we all go for dinner? It can be a double date!" She looked incredibly pleased with herself.

"Um, I dunno. I'm not sure."

"Oh, come on. It'll be fun!"

Although Alex usually enjoyed Emily's enthusiasm, he felt it working against him now, and he didn't know how to counter it. But he needed to; this couldn't possibly work out. "I don't think we're really at that stage, you know? We, um, we're...it's still early."

"That's okay," Emily said, ever so helpful. "Rob and I will help you! Right, Rob?"

She elbowed him and he looked up from his phone. "What? Yeah, of course."

"See? It'll be great," Emily said, smiling brightly. She and Rob looked at him expectantly. It made him uncomfortable.

"I'm not sure. She doesn't like going out, really. So we just hang out."

"Come on. You're too shy for your own good, Alex. She'll love it."

"Listen, kid, here's what we'll do," Rob said, taking control of the conversation. It seemed he'd had enough of Alex trying to get out of the idea. "I'll make a reservation at *La Pentola della Quercia* for Friday night; you tell her that. It's one of the best places in the city. Trust me, she'll be happy to go."

He didn't like Rob's big-shot attitude. It reeked of conceit. Alex had no idea what restaurant Rob was talking about; he wasn't even sure he could pronounce the name. But it sounded expensive, snobby, and totally out of his league. He also had zero interest in spending an evening with Rob and Emily together. In his mind, he and Emily had a real connection, a burgeoning relationship. The more time they spent with Rob around, the harder it would be to maintain that illusion, and he didn't want to let that go.

There weren't many excuses left, though, other than the truth. But that wasn't really an option. "I think she works Friday," he said as a last ditch effort.

Emily sighed, Rob looked frustrated. "Geez, kid. Saturday night, then. I'll make it for seven o'clock. We'll meet you there." Instead of waiting for Alex to answer, he turned to Emily. "I have some work I need to get done at home. You coming?"

She nodded and the two of them stood to leave. Rob waved dismissively and walked away. "I'll see you on Saturday," Emily said to Alex. "I'm so excited!"

"Yeah, see you then," Alex responded, defeated.

He watched them walk out of the cafe together, and stewed in his chair over what to do about the double date. He could cancel, but he didn't want to get Emily mad at him, not when his status in her life seemed so fragile. She might take it personally and then he'd be back where he started: alone and miserable. He could say that he and Diamond had broken up, but the timing might sound suspect. He also worried that part of the reason she was so comfortable spending time with him was because she thought he had a girlfriend. If he were suddenly single, would Emily trust him as much and still spend time alone with him? Would Rob allow it? He didn't want to take that chance.

Technically, it was possible to bring Diamond to dinner. It would be an expensive night, but he was pretty sure she would do it if she were available. It was the best option.

He pulled out his Nokia and dialed her number. He was surprised when she answered, he usually didn't get through the first time.

"Hello, this is Diamond."

"Hi, it's Alex."

"Hey, Alex. How are you?"

"Good good. Um, I was wondering if I could see you tonight."

A brief pause on the other end. "I'm free at eleven."

"That works."

"One hour?"

"Yeah."

"Okay. I'll see you then."

"'Kay, thanks."

He ended the call and heaved a sigh of relief. He'd been worried that she might not be available. Eleven was later than usual, but he didn't mind. Now he needed to secure her for Saturday night. It was a longshot, but it might work. It needed to work.

* * * * *

That night Alex walked along the deserted sidewalk amid towering residential high-rises. The occasional buzzing street lamp lit his way, birthing shadows that raced along with him, slowly pulling ahead and out of reach only to appear at his side once more. At times, as he passed the lobby of a building, he could see dim shadows all around him. He was never alone here.

When he neared his destination, he pulled out his phone and dialed. Diamond answered.

"Hello."

"Hey, I'm outside."

"Dial two-nine-one-four on the pad. Floor twenty-three, room four. The door will be unlocked. Come in, don't knock."

"Okay," Alex said, and hung up. He already knew the numbers, of course, but it was all procedure, part of the dance; he could no more cut out those words than he could the whistle at the beginning of a hockey game. It gave the whole exercise a feeling of formality, and that was important.

He dialed the numbers into the pad; no one spoke back to him over the intercom, but the buzzer for the door sounded immediately. He went inside and waited for the elevator. He didn't have to wait long.

As he got off the elevator, Alex checked his watch: one minute after eleven. To his left was a door, slightly ajar, with an ornate number four on it, right above a peephole. He pushed the door open and stepped inside. It was a short, dimly lit entryway leading to a room beyond. He shut the door behind him, when it clicked shut he heard a sound from the living room, followed by the soft sound of feet on carpet.

She came around the corner and without hesitation reached behind his head, pulling him down into a long, deep kiss. When they separated, she had a playful smile on her face, bright red lips turned up at one corner. This wasn't the kind of smile Emily gave, where she imparted joy and happiness. Diamond's smile was suggestive and knowing. Emily projected herself out with her expressions. Diamond drew you in.

"It's been a while. I missed you," she said.

"Sorry, I haven't had time," Alex said as he bent down and took off his shoes. When he stood back up, he made sure to get a good look at her. She was shorter than him by some six or seven inches, and her body was well-toned; she barely weighed a hundred and five pounds soaking wet. In the escort business, she was what people called a spinner. She was wearing a hip-length black see-through negligee with slight frills at the edges. It was open up the middle, hitched between her smallish breasts, making an upside down 'V' that exposed most of her stomach and the matching lace panties she was wearing.

"We'll have to make up for that, won't we?" She reached behind him and flipped the lock on the door. Making sure her body pressed on him as she reached past. She turned around and started walking towards the bedroom, hips swaying seductively. He followed.

When they reached the bedroom, Alex pulled out his wallet and counted out twelve twenty-dollar bills. He handed it to Diamond, who quickly made it disappear into the bedside table.

Payment complete, she came back and put her hands on his waist. "Why don't we get you out of those clothes," she cooed. "Maybe I'll join you in the shower."

Alex took a deep breath. "That sounds great. But I have a question for you first."

"What's that?" she asked, unbuttoning his pants.

"If you're free on Saturday, I'd like you for the evening."

"Really? How many hours?" She slowly pulled down the zipper.

"Yeah, um, about three hours. Ah. It's for dinner. Starting at seven." It was getting hard to concentrate.

"I can do that," she said. "For you, seven hundred."

"That's, ah, okay. It's dinner with, ah, my cousin. I need you to be my...girlfriend."

She smiled. "Let's talk about that later," she grabbed his hands and started pulling him towards the bathroom. He let himself be pulled along.

She wasn't his girlfriend, not really. It doesn't exactly count when you're paying for it, does it? He held no illusions that her interest in him extended outside of these transactions. But he imagined he might get away with a semantic argument: Are you seeing someone? Yes I am seeing someone; Or maybe: Do you have a girlfriend? I do (for an hour once every month or so). But he would only be playing with the truth, not offering it.

He didn't feel guilty paying for companionship. In his opinion, it was a lot more honest than trying to pick up a girl at a club. At least here they both knew the rules and the outcome was never in doubt.

Since Alex started seeing Diamond two years ago, she had been a better friend to him than anyone else he knew. She listened to him when he talked, really listened. She even shared stories from her own life. And yes, they had sex.

Maybe it wasn't anything more than that. Maybe someone paid to be your friend isn't really a friend at all.

But sometimes it was enough.

SEVENTEEN
JOEL – FIVE YEARS AGO

JOEL OPENED HIS eyes, winced at the sunlight and closed them again. His head pounded. He felt sick, weak. His body shook.

He heard a sound behind him and he rolled over, holding a hand out in front of his face to block the glare. A wrinkled, half-naked woman shuffled about the room; her bare, saggy breasts swaying back and forth as she moved. Her arms were covered in large, red marks. She looked at him with dark, hooded eyes and grinned, baring her few remaining yellow teeth.

Joel struggled to sit up and perched himself on the edge of the couch. He reached into his pants pockets. Nothing. He started patting down his body, feeling for any lumps. Nothing. Where was his shirt? Frantic, he dug through the couch pulling out cushions and tossing them to the side. Still nothing.

In the adjacent room the woman now sat at a table, staring at the wall while humming tunelessly.

He grabbed her shoulder. "Where is it?" When she didn't respond he shook her and repeated the question.

She looked at him, reached out and grabbed for his manhood. "You want to go again?" she asked, licking her lips and grinning.

Joel slapped her hand away. "Where is it? Where's my stuff?"

She tried to pull away. "I don't know, I don't know."

He shook her again, harder this time. "Did you steal it?"

She covered her ears and let out a high pitched keening. "Aaaeeeeeeeeeee."

Joel let her go and backed away. She stopped squealing, but kept her ears covered and started rocking back and forth.

He started searching the tiny apartment. He dug through a pile of dirty clothes in a corner of the room and found his shirt. He reached into the inside pocket and pulled out a small plastic bag filled with white powder. He shook it and smiled.

He opened the bag and stuck his finger in, scooping out a small mound of powder. Holding it up to his nose, he sniffed it in.

"Aaaahhh," he moaned and sat back. He heard footsteps and looked around. The woman stood, watching him. She looked hungry. He shoved the bag into his pants pocket, put his shirt on and stood up.

She shuffled towards him. "Can I have a bit?" she asked.

"No," he said.

"I can pay, let me pay." She grabbed his pants and started pulling them down. "I can pay."

"No," he said again, pushing her away. She stumbled and fell on the floor, where she sat looking at him, her expression one of desperate, pained hunger. It was an expression he recognized from the last time he'd looked in a mirror. He looked away, suddenly desperate to get out of there.

He fled the rank apartment and went downstairs, trying not to step on any used needles. Outside, a man on a bench sat smoking in front of the door. Joel reached out and the man passed him the cigarette. He took a drag and passed it back.

Joel started walking with no real destination in mind, just walking for the sake of walking. Down the street a shirtless man stood in front of a shop window, screaming at his own reflection. Watching as the man started punching at the air and delivering spinning karate kicks, Joel wondered who was winning the fight.

Eventually Joel's haphazard wandering took him to a park or, more accurately, a square trash-covered green-space mostly abandoned by the city. He found a relatively clean section of yellow grass and decided to lay down, try to relax, and forget about the pit in his stomach. When was the last time he had eaten anything? It felt like days. He pulled out his plastic bag and had another sniff. After a few minutes of peace, someone sat down beside him. The smell of piss and shit permeated the air. Joel knew he stunk and hadn't showered in weeks, but this stench was on another level entirely.

Joel knew the man who had joined him. He went by the name Blue, mainly because of the colour of his teeth, but also because he was almost always crying. He was one of the mainstay personalities of the Downtown Eastside, a middle-aged man with a mangled right arm. He'd been there long before Joel arrived, and would likely still be there long after Joel left. Assuming Joel ever left.

Blue was struggling to get the lid off a Listerine bottle. Joel helped him, then watched as he knocked the bottle back.

When it was almost half empty, Blue stopped for a breath and offered Joel the bottle. Joel shook his head. He hated the taste of mouthwash, and couldn't fathom how the 'Listerine drunks' could drink it. Not that he was in a position to judge others.

Blue stared down at his misshapen arm. "It was the accident, man."

Joel said nothing.

"I had a wife, kids. I haven't seen them in so long. It's my daughter's birthday today, you know. She's nine years old now."

Joel nodded. It was always her birthday. Blue didn't know one day from the next anymore, and he cried every day because he was missing his daughter's birthday. She had been turning nine for as long as Joel had known him.

Blue started crying. "It wasn't my fault. I swear. I didn't do nothing wrong." He sobbed for a few more minutes, muttering unintelligibly, before drinking the rest of the Listerine. He looked over at Joel, vertical smears down his face where his tears had fallen, like water drops on a dirty window. "I just want to see them again, that's all."

"I know, Blue, I know."

* * * * *

Joel used the last of his cocaine that night. When he'd gotten all he could sniff, he flipped the bag inside out and rubbed it over his gums to get every last bit of powder off the inside.

The next two hours flashed by like a series of dioramas: running down the sidewalk pushing people out of the way; foraging through a trash bin and fighting someone over food scraps; trying to climb a brick wall to get at a naked woman in a window three floors above; falling on pavement and crying from the pain.

Being high felt both real and unreal. Like an unseen force had control of his body. It was both liberating and intoxicating, not feeling responsible for his actions. Not caring what happened. He had never hurt anyone when he was high, at least not that he knew of.

He became a different person when he was high. A *better* person. A person who lived in the moment, who didn't obsess over problems or worry about the past. A person who didn't feel guilt or shame. The complete opposite of the guilt-ridden mess the *normal* him had become.

When it wore off, he felt like he was waking from a dream. He never knew for sure whether the blurred images remaining in his head were real or not, and he rarely knew how he'd gotten to whatever location he'd found himself in.

All he knew was that he needed more.

* * * * *

Joel spent the next weeks feeling like he was on the edge of a cliff.

He was out of drugs, and his money was gone. Welfare Wednesday, the day the government deposited monthly welfare payments directly into people's accounts, was still weeks away. He'd burned through his entire payment in just over a week.

The longer he went without a hit, the more desperate he became. As he became more desperate and his withdrawal got worse, he turned into yet another version of himself. If the high version of him was the man in the spotlight, then the version of him going through withdrawal was the long shadow that stretched out behind.

He became angry and depressed. He was in constant pain. Gone was the happy thoughtlessness of his high self. Instead he was driven by an unflinching desire to obtain more, regardless of how it might harm him or anyone else. He simply lost control of himself, like a devil had been unleashed inside of him, and all he could do was sit and watch helplessly while it destroyed what was left of his life. And he had done things in the past to get another hit—horrible things.

* * * * *

Joel had gone for a week and a half without a hit. The night before he'd let himself be used by a dealer with certain...tendencies...in exchange for an eight-ball. Unfortunately, it turned out to be pure bunk. Instead of running off on a euphoric high he spent the night dry heaving into a gutter.

He was angry. Not just about the bunk and what he'd done to earn it, but because he still hadn't been able to score a hit.

So he branched out. There were good areas nearby filled with crowds of straight-edge people. He wouldn't find any coke on them, but they had money. He had to be careful though; the cops weren't as tolerant when a junkie strayed outside of the Downtown Eastside.

He kept to the alleys to avoid being seen and before long he was in a *clean* area downtown. He stopped in an alley near a night-club. Thumping bass echoed off the glass high-rises that lined the street while drunken twenty-somethings stumbled around on the street with their friends. Too many people were around for Joel to do anything, but they had money, that much was obvious. So he sat back and waited. His chance would come, he knew. He just had to be patient.

* * * * *

The club closed, and a mass of people discharged into the clear August night. Joel watched and waited while the crowd slowly dispersed. Foot traffic was minimal where he hid because the Skytrain was in the other direction. But a few people walked his way. A threesome of men strolled past, one of them laughed about how he "totally could have banged that chick." Joel wanted to laugh, but kept quiet.

A minute later he spied a woman walking alone up the street. She was pretty, with bright, red hair flowing down her back. She stared up at the sky, not paying any attention to her surroundings. Joel's eyes latched on the purse hanging off her shoulder. There'd be cash in there. There had to be.

She walked past the alley with a silly smile on her face and Joel grabbed her. He missed her coat but got a good grip on her long, red locks, and yanked. She began to scream but he covered her mouth with his free hand. He let go of her hair and reached around her, locking her arm in place and giving himself a better grip to drag her deeper into the alley.

She struggled, but couldn't break free of his hold. Then her head whipped back and caught him on the cheekbone. The move caught him so off guard that she was able to pull his hand free from her mouth and scream. He quickly covered her mouth again, and she chomped down hard on his hand. *Ow! God dammit!*

He ripped his hand free, spun her around and backhanded her in the face. Then, while she was dazed, he grabbed her again. "Don't fight it. This doesn't have to hurt," he said and reached for her purse.

She flew into a rage, attacking him with heels, knees, nails and teeth. It was all he could do to hold her off. She almost got away after a particularly surprising elbow to his stomach, but he wasn't letting her go so easy—not now. Not when he was so close to what he needed. He finally backed her into a corner. She stood there, breathing heavily, hands held out defensively, and hair sticking out at wild angles. She looked like a feral animal. He couldn't help but laugh. "You're a feisty bitch, aren't you?"

But enough was enough. As he stepped towards her, she fired off a right-handed haymaker that he easily sidestepped. He slugged her in the gut and threw her against the wall. Her head made a sickening sound when it hit the brick, like a bowling ball landing in a tub of pudding. He punched her in the gut again and threw her on the ground.

She tried feebly to crawl away from him, but she wasn't going anywhere. He was amazed she hadn't blacked out. A stream of blood ran down her neck.

He rolled her onto her back and sat down on her midsection. She raised her hands and he slapped them away.

"Please," she said, so quietly he could hardly hear.

He leaned in. "What was that, missy?"

"Please don't."

He picked up her purse and dug through it: a cheap cell phone, lipstick, makeup, gum, and a small wallet.

"I told you not to fight, didn't I? But you did anyway." He shook his head. "You earned this. You deserve it."

She struggled to stay conscious; tears rolled down the side of her face. "No," she said.

He opened the wallet: credit cards, driver's licence, Starbucks card, health card—no cash. *Shit. Where's the money? Who doesn't carry cash? Fuck!*

He grabbed her purse and shook it out on the ground: no money— just crap. *Who goes to a club without any money?* A black rage began to take hold of him. His hands balled into fists and he fought a powerful urge to start hitting her again. What had he accomplished here? Nothing! All this work, and still he hadn't gotten what he needed. Why didn't she have what he needed?

All he wanted was a little money. Enough for a hit, a real hit. Not that bunk shit he'd been sold the night before: something good, something to take the edge off. Instead, he had a Starbucks card and some credit cards he'd never get away with using—useless.

The woman groaned and tried to push him away again. He pinned her hands and grabbed her throat. She really *was* pretty. He hadn't been with a girl like her since…well, he couldn't remember; probably never. He licked his lips and looked back toward the street, then back at her. Maybe she had something for him after all. He ripped her shirt open, then reached down and lifted up her skirt. Her thighs were warm.

Joel had been on the other end of this before. It was how the world worked. If you couldn't pay with cash, you paid with your body. Simple.

"You deserve this," he said again. Then he leaned in and bit the exposed skin of her breast. His teeth broke through her soft skin and he tasted blood. She stiffened and arched her back, her mouth opened in a silent scream. *You always have to pay,* he thought. *Always.* He licked his bloody lips.

He began to have his way with her, when an image of his father came unbidden to his mind. *No.* He closed his eyes and tried to focus on what he was doing, but it was no use; the image wouldn't go away.

He saw his parents standing in the kitchen: His dad holding his mom by the throat while backhanding her back and forth. Again and again, screaming: "You deserve this."

You deserve this.

Joel's rage dissipated. He stopped and pulled away. *Oh my god.*

What am I doing?

He realized with a shock that he hadn't just become his father; he'd taken that ball and found an entirely new playing field. Tears trickled down his face. He was worse than his father, so much worse.

He crouched over the battered woman and touched her face. "I'm sorry," he said. "I'm so sorry." He covered her back up as best he could and stood up. She would be okay. She would wake up soon and it would all seem like a bad dream.

But even he couldn't lie to himself about that. She would be scarred for life because of him. He shook his head and fought off a wave of nausea.

The woman groaned and Joel knew he had to leave before it was too late. He turned and ran.

* * * * *

For the first time in what felt like years, Joel was thinking clearly, and he knew what he had to do. He had to change. The incident the night before was a giant wake-up call telling him his life had gotten out of control.

The Downtown Eastside was filled with outreach programs. As a rule, he always avoided these places like the plague. Since his arrival, whether through luck or folly, he'd managed to avoid contact with both the police and the social workers. He'd come to Vancouver to hide and, as far as he knew, he'd been one hundred percent successful.

But that was over now. He had to admit that he couldn't stop himself from doing awful things and, if he ever wanted to stop, he would need help.

He went to the supervised injection facility, but not to inject; he went to take advantage of the various outreach programs, and signed up for everything he could: addictions counselling, housing, and any other support service he could find.

Over the following months, they looked after him on the long road to recovery. He knew he could never make up for what he'd done to that woman in the alley; and he still cried when he thought about it. But no matter how bad he felt, he couldn't face turning himself in.

The incident had been on the news: woman beaten and raped in downtown Vancouver. There had been a manhunt. Somehow he'd managed to escape without leaving any useful evidence. People questioned their safety. "What is happening on Vancouver streets?" they asked, and "Are we really safe?"

But it died down soon enough, as stories do in the twenty-four-hour news cycle. The media found another darling story to follow and, *poof*, the poor woman was yesterday's news.

Joel only learned all this later, though. While police searched for him, Joel had been so deep in the throes of withdrawal that the only thing on his mind was his excruciating pain. And a rapacious desire to find more drugs.

He had only made it through the program because of one person: a volunteer with the social housing group he'd been set up with. She'd been a single pillar of strength and goodness in his otherwise shattered existence. Her name was Jenny, and he knew—just *knew*—that she would be the one to save him.

Whether he deserved it or not.

EIGHTEEN
RICHARD

RICHARD HELD OUT at first but Lacey, it turned out, was very persistent.

She had been texting Richard for three days trying to arrange a meeting, and for three days he'd successfully invented excuses as to why he couldn't go.

Eventually, he ran out of excuses and couldn't escape it any longer.

"Who's that waving at you?" James asked, indicating the woman sitting on a bench outside the front entrance to the hospital.

"Oh, that's Lacey," Richard replied.

"Buddy, wow, you've been holding out on me."

"She's my sponsor."

"Great! I like them damaged."

"You really are a terrible person."

Lacey stood up when they arrived, and James wasted no time introducing himself. "Hi, I'm James. I'm told you're Lacey. What a fittingly beautiful name."

"Thank you. Nice to meet you."

She held out her hand and James took it, then bent down and kissed it on the back. "The pleasure is all mine."

Richard groaned.

"Your friend is quite the charmer," Lacey said.

"He seems to think so," Richard said.

James put on his most dashing smile. "I know so."

Richard shook his head. "So, what can I do for you?"

"Well," Lacey said, "since you're too busy to meet me for coffee, I decided to bring the coffee to you." She lifted up a large Tim Hortons cup. "Black, the way you like it."

Richard took the proffered drink. "Thanks. So, how'd you figure out where I work?"

"It wasn't that hard. You mentioned you're a paramedic, and I saw the logo for Vancouver General on that paper you had Jeff sign. I put two and two together."

"I see. So that's it? You don't know me from anywhere else?"

"No." She looked confused. "Why would I?"

"Nothing. Forget about it."

"Okay then. Sorry, James. I hope you don't mind if I steal Richard from you."

"Not at all," James said. "You two go ahead. I'll talk to you tomorrow, Richard."

"Yeah, see ya," he said and waved as James walked away. He turned back to Lacey: "You know, you didn't need to track me down at work."

"Really? Because you didn't seem interested in meeting me otherwise."

Richard sipped at his coffee as they began to walk. "It's not that. It's just that I don't really need a sponsor. I'm only doing this for work."

Lacey gave him a sidelong look. "In my experience, employers don't force their employees to go to AA without a reason."

"No, there was…an incident. Public relations and all that, you know."

"I don't know. Why don't you tell me?"

Richard sipped his coffee again. He didn't really want to share this stuff with her, but he already knew she wasn't the type to give up. "I had an altercation with a reporter and it showed up on the news."

"So? People fight with reporters all the time."

"I had been drinking."

"That's it? So, how was that newsworthy? Did you hurt

somebody?"

"No, no one was hurt. I pushed her, but she wasn't hurt. The real problem was that I had been driving."

"I see," Lacey said. She took a drink from her own cup of coffee. "Have you done this before?"

"What? Push a reporter? No."

"I'm not talking about the reporter."

Richard knew what she was talking about. He didn't answer.

"I see," she said again.

The knowing look on her face irked him. "So what; it's not like I was so blasted that I couldn't see straight. Maybe I was a drink or two over the limit, but I can still drive better than most people in this city."

"You remember the first step?"

Richard began to grind his teeth. "I don't have a problem."

"Okay. That's fine, if you're not ready—"

Richard stopped walking and turned to face her. "I do not have a problem. And you know what? Screw these stupid steps. And why is everything about God? What about people who don't believe in God? What about other religions? It seems pretty insulting that AA assumes everyone is a Christian."

"We aren't assuming anything. Step three says 'God as we understand Him.' That means it's open to interpretation. It doesn't have to be the Christian God. In all honestly, it doesn't even have to be God. People interpret the steps in different ways. Some people may replace God with the group. The important thing is recognizing that you need help from someone, or something, greater than yourself."

"Oh yeah? And the spiritual awakening in step twelve, or the prayer and meditation in step eleven? We need *Him* to remove our shortcomings, and then we need to carry out *His* will. That sounds like a cult to me."

Lacey shook her head. "There are so many different people in the world, Richard. These steps will make sense to a lot of people who are already part of a faith. But even then, they're meant as a guide. Something to help you along in your journey." She put her hand on his chest. "What's important is how you interpret them, how you make them your own. You don't need to suddenly switch religions, or turn into a bible-thumping Christian."

He smiled at the image of her running door to door with a bible; it didn't fit. He turned away from her and her hand fell down to her side.

"But you will need faith. What you put it in is your choice. But you can't do this without it."

They walked in silence for a few minutes. They passed a recycle bin and threw their empty cups in it.

"What is your sponsor like?" Richard asked.

"He was a good man. He helped me through a lot of really tough times. He loved Stanley Park. We used to meet by the totem poles and then walk around the seawall. Something about the ocean helped me relax, you know? We would find a bench and sit there watching the cruise ships and the freighters going in and out. Sometimes a seal would go by, or an otter. Once we even saw a whale. It didn't matter how badly I needed a drink, I could always go there and the urge would go away." She looked at him with a slight smile. "His name was Richard too."

Of course it was. He filed that information away for another time. "That sounds nice. Do you still go there?"

"I jog along the seawall whenever I can."

"How come you say he *was* a good man? Why was?" Richard asked.

She smiled slightly, face layered with regret. "Can't slip anything past you, hey?"

He didn't say anything, just watched her.

"He fell off the wagon a few months ago. Ex-wife remarried and moved to Toronto with his two kids. They were such a big part of his life, he couldn't live without them. He said he was going to move there to be with them. But one day I called him, and I knew he had been drinking. After that, he fell off the face of the earth, disappeared without a word."

"Maybe he made it to Toronto."

"I hope so," she said. "Don't say anything to Jeff; he doesn't know Richard is gone."

"Okay, I won't."

They came around the corner to the front of the hospital and stopped.

"Well, thanks for the coffee," Richard said.

"No problem."

They stared at each other for a few awkward seconds.

Lacey broke the silence. "I want you to know that if you ever need anyone to talk to, about anything, I'm here. Any time, okay?"

"Okay. Thanks. Same here."

She stood up on her tip-toes and surprised him with a kiss on the cheek, then turned and left without another word.

He rubbed his cheek, hoping she wasn't wearing the kind of lipstick that left a mark. He still wasn't quite sure what to make of her, but she had successfully gotten under his skin, and now he was looking forward to their next meeting.

* * * * *

The following Saturday, Richard found himself standing at Third Beach in Stanley Park. A light breeze swirled through the air, bringing with it the fresh smell of salt from the ocean. The wind had a bit of a chill to it, but that didn't seem to bother the forty or so people playing in the water or reclining on the beach.

Richard leaned against the rock face beside the stairs facing the seawall, waiting for Lacey. A biker rode past, followed by a pair of female joggers. He looked up and down the path, then back up the stairs; still no sign of her.

He muttered and pulled out his phone to re-read their text message conversation from the morning.

Hey, are you free this afternoon? 1:00? she'd said.

Yes, he'd replied.

Okay, meet me at Third Beach. Bottom of the steps.

Where's that?

Stanley Park, she said.

Is that near the totem poles?

LOL. I thought you've lived here all your life? It's on the other side of the park.

Never heard of it, he said. He wondered if there was a way to display annoyance via a emoticon.

Just Google it. See you soon.

He checked the time: quarter after one. He sighed, and hoped she wasn't always late like this.

"Hey, Richard!" a female voice called out.

Richard looked over and had to catch his breath for a second. Lacey had been jogging. Her long, brunette hair was tied back in a ponytail, and her tanned skin—which she was showing a lot of—had a sheen of sweat over it. She wore tiny, black yoga shorts and a tight, green tank top that left nothing to the imagination.

He swallowed the lump in his throat. "Uh, hi," he said. "You've been jogging." Pointing out the obvious. Way to be composed.

"Yeah," she said and smiled, completely oblivious to the long looks she was getting from the men walking by. "Come on, let's go."

"I'm not exactly dressed for jogging," Richard said, indicating his pants and button-up shirt.

"We don't need to jog, silly. Come on." She gestured and started walking.

Richard obliged and fell in step beside her.

"Did you have any trouble finding the beach?" Lacey asked.

"Not too much. I drove past once by accident and had to turn around."

Lacey laughed. "You're so funny," she said, leaning in and bumping him. Richard glanced towards her and was forced to quickly look away when he realized his height advantage, along with their proximity, gave him an uncomfortably expansive view of her cleavage. He looked forward and resolved to keep his eyes where they belonged.

"I love coming here. It's so beautiful, isn't it?"

He nodded. "Yeah, it is."

They came to a curve in the path and stopped. About ten metres off the path, surrounded by water, stood a tall rock outcrop topped by a Douglas fir.

"Siwash Rock," Lacey said.

"I've never seen it before. I can't believe there's a tree on top of it. How does it even survive?"

Lacey shrugged. "Sometimes life can thrive in the most unlikely circumstances."

Richard looked at her and she smiled.

They continued walking for a few more minutes, then stopped at a shaded semi-circular rest area lined with benches. They sat down and admired the scenery. Siwash Rock stood to their left; a seagull sat atop the proud Douglas fir, then lifted off, shrieking at them as it flew past. The bay was littered with at least a dozen tankers, by Richard's count. All waiting their turn to travel beneath the Lions Gate Bridge into Burrard Inlet, to Vancouver Harbour. To their right, the city of West Vancouver nestled in at the foot of the North Shore Mountains. The city's high-rises were dwarfed by the tree-covered mountains behind them.

A cold gust of wind swept over them, making Lacey shiver. She leaned against him. Her skin was covered in goose bumps, making Richard wish he'd brought a jacket to share.

"Maybe we should go somewhere where the sun isn't blocked," Richard said.

"No, it's okay," Lacey said. She slid one of her arms under his and rested her head on his shoulder. "I like it here."

Richard shifted slightly, but didn't pull his arm away. What was the harm?

He closed his eyes and listened to the waves gently lapping against the rocky base of the seawall. There *was* something peaceful about this place. It made him feel closer to nature than he'd felt since, well, for as long as he could remember.

Lacey broke the silence. "The first time I ever saw an orca was from this bench."

"Oh?"

"Just over there," she pointed in the direction of West Vancouver. "It breached over and over again, putting on a show for us. It looked...happy, you know?"

"I guess. Though I'm not sure whales experience happiness the same way we do."

"I think they do. You don't give them enough credit. Watch a video of an orca breaching, or being saved from nets. They're thankful afterwards. They have feelings."

"Hmm," Richard said, not totally convinced.

"It must be so nice," Lacey said, longing in her voice.

"What?"

"Living like that, the entire ocean as your playground. Free: no job, no money, no drugs, no alcohol; no family judging you for every bad choice you've ever made. Just a simple life."

The last comment made Richard think of Natalie. Nothing was ever simple with her. It had been once, but that was a long time ago. "Oh, I wouldn't be so sure. How do you know orcas don't have jobs? Maybe the one you saw was actually a scout," Richard said.

"A scout?"

"Yeah. That's why it was breaching so much: to get a better look at you. Then he went back to report to his orca military overlords. They're probably planning an invasion of the mainland right now."

Lacey laughed, loud and full. "You are ridiculous. You know that?"

"Yes, I've been told."

"I like it."

They sat on the bench for the rest of the afternoon: comfortable, relaxed, easy.

* * * * *

Over the next two weeks, Richard and Lacey continued to meet in Stanley Park. Some days they walked along the seawall, others they took lesser used paths through the dense forest.

Their relationship blossomed into something stronger and closer than Richard had ever expected. Lacey didn't judge him, or make him feel bad about his choices. With her, he felt good in a way he hadn't felt in years.

Richard was starting to love the seawall as well. It amazed him that after living in Vancouver his entire life, he had never done the walk around Stanley Park. It made him realize that, in some ways, he was a stranger in his own city. He'd spent so much of his life wrapped up in the chaos of being a paramedic that he'd never truly grasped the beauty and peace that the city offered. For the first time, he began to appreciate why people loved spending time at Stanley Park.

He held hands with Lacey as they walked. She was a very physical person, loved to touch, hug, and hold. It felt strange to Richard at first, but he got used to it, as he did to many of the things she did. She was a tough person to deny.

The sun broke through the clouds, shining down on them through the trees. Richard was thankful for the good weather. November could be a dreary month in Vancouver, but this year it hadn't been bad. It was definitely warmer than usual, as evidenced by the array of skirts and muscle shirts worn by the majority of people around the park.

They were near Lost Lagoon, taking a side trip deeper into the forest that Lacey said would lead them somewhere special. At one point on the trail, she suddenly veered left and away from the path, dragging him with her. They weaved through the trees until they reached a small clearing.

Lacey put her hands in the air and spun around, hair flying out behind her. "Isn't this beautiful?" she asked, as she jumped and spun herself around in the clearing.

"Yeah," Richard said, laughing at her jubilance.

"This was our secret place. We used to come here to be alone," she said.

"That's nice. It's very peaceful."

"Whew, I'm dizzy now," she said, then lay on the grass in the middle of the clearing, chest rising and falling as she caught her breath. She looked like a picture out of a magazine. Perfect. She patted the ground beside her. "Come, lay down with me."

Richard shrugged and complied. The cool grass on his back made him shiver. A light breeze stirred the towering Douglas fir, cedar, and Western hemlock surrounding them.

"This was our favourite spot," Lacey said. "We would lay here for hours until it was dark. Then we would make love under the stars."

Make love? "What?" Richard asked. "I don't think you should have been doing that."

Lacey laughed at him. "It was beautiful. I've never felt so close to anyone in my life. It made everything—better."

"No, Lacey, I really don't think that's right. That's not in the Big Book. He shouldn't have been doing that with you."

She looked at him, now frowning slightly. "There's nothing wrong with what we did, Richard. Everyone communicates with God in their own way."

"I'm not sure that's communicating with God."

"Of course it is. What better way to seek enlightenment than in the moment of ecstasy? That's why I brought you here today."

Wait...what? "What are you talking about?" He was starting to worry. Had the other Richard fed her this line of crap to get in her pants? Had he done this to other women?

Lacey turned, then in one smooth motion, reached her leg across his body and used it to propel the rest of herself on top of him. Then she sat there, straddling him, face barely a foot from his, her hair hanging down, tickling his nose. She flipped her hair away, but a dozen strands remained. Then she leaned forward and kissed him. Hard at first, then soft, lingering. He wanted to pull away. He really did, but where would he go? It seemed easier to take it.

When she finally pulled away, Richard needed a moment to catch his breath. "This isn't right, Lacey. We shouldn't be doing this."

"Why are you so afraid? Are you worried you'll find God? Or are you scared you'll find yourself, and you won't like what you find?"

"No, no, it's not that at all. There are other ways to beat an addiction."

"This is the way!" she said, looking fierce. Desperate, even.

For the first time Richard saw her not as a successfully rehabilitated alcoholic, but as a young girl still struggling with addiction. The difference was that this time, it wasn't alcohol she was addicted to. Suddenly her interest in being his sponsor made perfect sense.

"I can't do this," he said, contrary to what the rest of his body indicated.

She had tears in her eyes. "Isn't this what you're looking for? Isn't this what we're all looking for? To connect with each other."

"No. Well, yes. But—"

She put her hand on the side of his face. "Then be here with me. Let everything go, Richard. Imagine the breeze is pulling your problems out of you and taking them away. Imagine it is just you and me here and, in this moment, we are the only people in the world."

"I—"

She leaned forward and kissed him again. "We are the only people in the world."

NINETEEN
MELISSA

AFTER HE BIT her, Melissa went limp, but didn't black out. She wasn't that fortunate.

It was like she was in some sort of dream, or nightmare, and she had no control over her body. Like a recurring dream she had where she was relaxing on a beach, watching the waves rolling towards shore in their rhythmic fashion; then suddenly, the water drains away, leaving detritus scattered across the wet sand. And it builds, builds, and builds into a towering wave, blotting out the sun and casting a cold shadow across the beach, where she stands watching as it advances again: an unmoveable, unstoppable force of destruction. She knows she should run, because there would be a shelter somewhere, built for this moment, and all she would have to do is get to it. She could even hear people calling out to her: "Melissa, over here. Melissa!" But she could no more move than she could take her eyes off the monstrous wave bearing down on her. She was stuck, like a concrete piling, destined to face the wave by herself. Destined to die on this beach. Then it reached her, and she was surrounded by chaos and a deafening roar that spoke to her of terrible things. And just as it was about to all come crashing down she would wake up.

This was like that dream, but it also wasn't. She felt the same helplessness, the same feeling of being destined to die, but this time it was worse. Because this time she knew there would be no waking up.

She lay there, fully aware of his movements, feeling his hands all over her body: lifting her skirt, pulling down her underwear, squeezing her breasts. She felt his hot breath on her neck as he exerted himself.

She'd heard stories of operations gone wrong; where the anesthetic paralyses, but doesn't put the patient under, leaving them fully conscious while the doctor cuts them open and rifles around in their innards. That's how she felt right now. She wanted so much to scream, to fight, to do something—anything. But she couldn't move, couldn't speak, all she *could* do was lie there and suffer. And suffer. And suffer.

* * * * *

Melissa woke with a start. She tossed her sweaty sheets to the side and sat up. Her heart thumped and her hands shook. She took a deep breath, put on her robe, and went to the kitchen. She poured herself a glass of orange juice and sat down at the table.

About fifteen minutes later she heard the padding of bare feet on the floor and Lindsay's bedroom door opened. Lindsay stepped out of her room wearing a white tank top and shiny pink shorts, hand held in front of her mouth as she yawned. Her eyes were still half closed and her semi-short hair stuck out in wild angles.

"Morning," Melissa said.

"Mmmhmmngg," Lindsay mumbled in response. She turned on the coffee maker, pulled out a cup, and waited. When it was ready she sat down at the table with Melissa, cradling her hot cup of coffee like it was a precious baby. She took a few sips then finally looked at Melissa. "You look bagged," she said.

Really? That, coming from her, was a laugh. "You don't look so great either."

Lindsay smiled slightly, "I was up late."

"Oh."

"What's your excuse?"

Melissa shrugged, "I didn't sleep well."

"Again? Shouldn't you—"

"Yeah. I'm going to see my doctor today. Hopefully, she'll give me some sleeping pills."

"Good," Lindsay said. They sat in silence and sipped at their drinks. Then Lindsay spoke again. "So I need to talk to you," she said. She was coming to life as the coffee worked its way through her body. Her face had regained its usual pallor.

"What's up?"

"Well, you know my birthday is coming up soon."

"Yeah."

"Jeff was supposed to book a room for my party next week, but because he's an idiot he forgot. Sooooo, I was thinking of having the party here."

"I don't know, Lindsay. We don't have a lot of room."

"I know, but it wouldn't be a lot of people; just a few close friends."

A few close friends for Lindsay meant at least twenty people. Melissa thought about a bunch of strangers in their condo, likely even going into her room, and she shuddered. "I'm not sure, Lins."

"I know you don't like having a lot of people here. I wouldn't be asking if I had any other options. Promise me you'll think about it, okay?"

"Alright, I'll think about it," Melissa said.

Lindsay smiled. "Great!" She drank the rest of her coffee and stood up. "I need to get ready for work."

"Okay."

Lindsay left her cup on the counter and went back into her bedroom, leaving Melissa alone in the kitchen.

Melissa put her head in her hands. Great. A party. Just what she wanted.

* * * * *

"Melissa. It's so good to see you again. It's been so long."

"Yeah, it's been a while." Melissa said. She shook the doctor's hand. Her grip was strong, but not uncomfortably so.

"Have a seat. You still take your coffee black with two sugars?"

"I do, thanks."

Melissa took a circuitous route to the couch, refamiliarizing herself with the room she'd spent so much time in. She stopped between two bookshelves and admired a large painting of a meadow. Before, the spot was occupied with a painting of a lake surrounded by mountains. "You got a new painting."

The doctor finished stirring Melissa's coffee and walked over to the painting. "Yes, about a year ago. I love the brush strokes in this one."

Melissa nodded. "It's nice." She didn't miss the subtle reminder of how long it had been since she'd made an appointment.

Dr. Jessica Cox was actually a family therapist, spending most of her time working with couples or full households. She had, however, worked with Melissa's parents in the past with great success, so Melissa's mom recommended her, instead of a crisis therapist. It hadn't been a terrible decision; she was easy to talk to and Melissa liked her. But there were times when she wondered how a different therapist would have handled her case.

They sat down across from each other. Melissa put her coffee on the table and sunk into the couch. It enveloped her, like the comforting arms of a long lost lover. She resisted the urge to lie down and snuggle in like she used to. This wasn't going to be one of those sessions.

Jessica took note of Melissa's position and began. "So, how've you been?"

"Good. Well, okay, I guess. I'm still working at the same place."

"Mmhmm."

"I...haven't been sleeping well. That's actually why I'm here. I've been having dreams again, the nightmares, about what happened. Almost every night."

"How long has this been going on?"

"A few months now."

"Tell me more about the dreams."

"Mostly they're the same ones as before. I still have the dream about the tidal wave. And the quicksand one. But most are about him. Sometimes it's exactly what happened, other times it starts out differently. Like, I'll walk past the alley and nothing happens, then I get home and he's there...waiting. It doesn't seem to matter how the dream starts; it always ends the same."

Jessica nodded. "And why do you think this has started happening again?"

"I don't know," Melissa said.

Jessica sensed Melissa was holding something back. "I think you do know."

Melissa sighed. "I know what you're going to say about it."

"Really? Then tell me how it goes."

"I really need something to help me sleep, that's all. If I could get that—"

"Come now, we don't have to start this from the beginning. We know each other, Melissa. You don't have to be so guarded."

"I know. I just don't want to hear about the faces-in-the-crowd theory again."

"Look, Melissa, I only brought that up because at the time you were still seeing threats everywhere. You thought you saw him almost every day. That relates to the brain's difficulty in recognizing happy faces over threatening ones. But if you've seen him now, this is different. So, is that what this is about? Did you see him somewhere?"

Melissa picked at a phantom hangnail before answering. "Yes, I think so. I'm not sure." she said, quietly.

"What happened?"

Melissa took a deep breath. "I was at Playland with Lindsay and a few friends. We were in line for a ride, AtmosFear, when I heard a man's voice nearby. It was so familiar, I couldn't place it, but I shivered as soon as I heard it. Then he said *little missy*, and I knew it was him. I've never heard anyone else call someone missy before, so I turned and looked at him, and he looked at me. I know he recognized me too. He must have because he picked up this little girl and ran away. And I...just stood there. I didn't know what to do."

"That must have been stressful. Did you tell anyone? Your brother, perhaps."

"No. I thought about it. But I didn't know if he would believe me."

"You believe it," Jessica said.

"I think so. I mean, I don't really know. I don't know if it's what he said, or the way he said it, but it scared me. Bad." She picked up her coffee and took a sip; it was cool. Had she been here that long already?

"Well, I believe this may be what caused your dreams to return. Have any of your other behaviours changed?"

Melissa narrowed her eyes. "How did...? Did you talk to Dan? Did he call you?"

"No, Melissa, I haven't talked to your brother."

"Then how did you know?"

"Know what?"

"That I've been going out at night again. That's obviously what you're referring to."

"Would it surprise you to learn that I have a pretty good understanding of who you are? We've been talking for five years now," Jessica said. She smiled in an attempt to soften the sting of the rebuke.

Melissa stared down into her coffee cup and said nothing.

"Look," Jessica said, "I'm not judging. I brought it up because I think it hits on something really important."

"Oh? And what's that?" Melissa asked.

"This confrontation you're searching for. What do you think will happen? What do you *want* to happen?"

"I don't know. I guess I would, um…"

"See? It's hard to imagine, isn't it? You want to picture yourself fighting back, right? Getting revenge, hurting him the way he hurt you. Maybe some yelling? What would you say?"

"I think I would say I hate you."

"That's it? There must be more."

Melissa closed her eyes and pictured the scene. She imagined herself standing over him with a gun pointed at his head. "You ruined my life! I hope you die, you awful, disgusting excuse of a human being. I want your balls shoved into a vat of boiling oil then shoved down your throat so you can gag on them, YOU PIECE OF SHIT! I WAN—"

"Melissa. Melissa!"

Only then did Melissa realize she was yelling. She sat back in her chair, face red and breathing heavily. "Sorry."

"Don't be. I asked," Jessica said. "But do you see the point I'm trying to make here?"

"No."

"You're still angry. Understandably, of course. In your mind, you've built it into something that reality can never satisfy. Look at what happened at Playland. You said you were stunned, right? You stood there while he ran away. Now, maybe this really was him, and maybe it wasn't. But the truth is that I don't believe you're ready to see him again."

"Why? What do you mean?"

"Melissa, nothing will ever change what happened to you. It was a horrible, horrible crime that no one should ever have to experience. But it's a part of you now. That means you have to learn to live with it."

"I have," Melissa said. "What do you think I've been doing for the last five years?"

"No, you're not living with it. You're living in spite of it. This thing that happened, it still controls you, even now. You have to take your life back, Melissa. Take it back!"

Melissa wiped a tear from her eye. "It's not that easy," she said in a halting voice.

"Of course it isn't, but you can do it."

"How?" Melissa asked, feeling as helpless as a desperate puppy treading water in a huge, freezing lake.

"Engage," Jessica said. "With your friends and family. Stop pushing them away. Let them help you get past this. Get out. Do things with people. Put yourself in uncomfortable situations and stop shielding yourself. You can't live in a bubble forever."

"I went to a club a few weeks ago with some friends."

"Great! Do more of that, then."

She shook her head and laughed, then pulled a tissue from a box on the counter and used it to wipe her eyes and blow her nose. "You really did talk to Dan, didn't you? He put you up to this."

Jessica laughed. "No, your brother did not put me up to this."

"Okay, but it sure sounds like you've spoken with him."

"Well, I haven't," Jessica said with a half smile. "And besides, I wouldn't tell you even if I had."

* * * * *

Melissa walked outside and took a deep breath, taking in the crisp November air. She thought about what Dr. Cox had said about pulling away from her friends and family. It shamed her to know that that was exactly what she'd been doing, without even realizing it.

She pulled out her phone and dialed Lindsay's number.

It rang a couple times before Lindsay answered: "Hello?"

"Hey, Lins, I was calling to say I thought about what you said, about the party, and I think we should do it."

"That's great! I'm so happy you came around."

"Nothing too big, okay? I don't want to be cleaning the place for the next week. And we can't be too loud or strata will fine us."

"Oh, don't worry, it'll just be close friends. And we'll behave, I promise."

"Alright. Let's do this, then."

"Thanks, Melissa. You're not gonna regret this. It's going to be *awesome*."

TWENTY
ALEX

ALEX BECAME INCREASINGLY nervous as they neared the restaurant. What exactly was his plan here? Was he going to play up his relationship with Diamond? Because that certainly wasn't sustainable over the long term. He wasn't a wealthy man, not like hotshot Rob with his hotshot marketing job.

In the days leading up to Saturday, Alex had begun falling back into his depression once again. How could he ever compete with someone like Rob? The guy had money, looks, confidence, basically anything a woman could ask for. Meanwhile the only way a woman would go out to dinner with Alex was if he paid for it. What did that say about him?

Emily was a beautiful, kind, and generous woman; too good for him. She deserved better than some scrub who could barely afford his own rent and spent all his extra money on an escort. She deserved someone like Rob.

Which brought him back to the dinner he was going to. The only real justification for going through with the evening was to covering up a lie, a lie that he had created out of embarrassment. And for whatever reason, when he had the chance to come clean, he didn't.

So now he had to follow through, and hope that no one saw through the facade. If he could pull off the evening, he and Diamond could break up afterwards, and no one would be the wiser.

He looked over at Diamond. Starting above the knees, her thighs, hips and torso were tightly wrapped in a folded black dress that left absolutely no doubt about the curves of her body. The built-in push-up bra forced her breasts upward and together, making them look much larger than he knew they were. The plunging neckline was held up by thin, black straps that wrapped around behind her neck. Her long, dark hair cascaded in shimmering waves down her back. Overall, she looked stunning.

And here he was, plain white button-up shirt and khakis. He had bought the clothes for work back when he thought they actually cared about the dress code. It was the best he had, and he was hopelessly outclassed by the woman beside him. She looked so far beyond his means, their breakup would seem the most natural and believable part of this entire charade. Unless he was some sort of dot-com billionaire, how could a guy who looked like him keep a girl who looked like her? Maybe he was being shallow, but that's how the world worked.

Diamond linked her arm around his as they entered the restaurant; there were glass cabinets on the left, and an opening to the right looking towards several dining tables. More than a few of the men stared at Diamond. Alex found their jealousy amusing.

The hostess greeted them as they walked up. "*Buona sera!* Do you have a reservation?"

"We're meeting someone, it should be under Rob Moore," Alex said.

"Yes, right this way."

The hostess led them around the corner, past an opulent bar stocked with expensive alcohol, to a table near the window. Rob and Emily both stood up when they saw Alex and Diamond. Emily was wearing an elegant purple dress that wrapped around her body like an incredibly long silk scarf. Rob, unsurprisingly, was wearing a suit very much like the one he had worn the day he came to the cafe. Diamond gave Alex's arm a quick squeeze before they separated.

"I'm so happy to meet you!" Emily said before enveloping Diamond in an embrace.

She hugged Alex next while Rob greeted Diamond. She whispered in his ear: "Wow, she's beautiful! Good job!" then pulled away with a wink. She looked so genuinely happy it hurt.

Rob, on the other hand, looked like someone had wiped their ass with his favourite tie. His jaw flexed like he was grinding his teeth and when he shook Alex's hand he squeezed a lot harder than last time. The first thing he did when they sat down was wave the waiter over. When the waiter arrived, he simply said "Scotch, neat," without taking his eyes off of Diamond.

"Yes, sir," the waiter said. "Anything else?"

The rest of them asked for water. The waiter nodded and left.

"So, sorry, I didn't catch your name," Rob said.

Emily answered first, "It's Diamond, Rob. I told you that already."

"Aha. I see. That's different. I can't imagine that's your birth name," Rob continued. He was still staring.

Diamond ignored Rob's intense regard. "No, it's actually a nickname I picked up in high school. My birth name is Mary, but there were so many other Mary's in my school I wanted something different. I chose Diamond, and it stuck."

"Oh, I asked Alex that and he didn't know. He thought Diamond was your real name!" Emily said.

"Well, the only people who call me Mary are my parents. To the rest of the world, Diamond is my real name."

The waiter returned with their drinks. Rob dipped into his scotch immediately. "Well, isn't that interesting," he said, "and what about work? What do you do for a living, Diamond?"

Alex had already filled Diamond in on the backstory he had created for her; he expected the conversation would turn to her employment at some point.

"I'm a self-employed massage therapist," Diamond answered. "I operate out of my condo. That way I don't have to pay a clinic for the space."

"Is that so? You must be expensive. What's the going rate for a massage these days?" Rob sipped his scotch. It was beginning to seem more like an interrogation than a conversation.

"One hundred dollars an hour," Diamond replied without hesitation. She was a good actress. She would have to be, in her business. It made Alex wonder how much acting she did with him. "A little more than a clinic masseuse. But I'm worth it."

"I'm sure you are," Rob said.

The questions and tone were starting to worry Alex. It seemed like Rob had already seen through their lie.

"Oh, be nice, Rob," Emily said. She looked at Rob disapprovingly and picked up her menu. "We should order."

Diamond put her hand on Alex's shoulder and leaned in. "The rabbit lumache sounds lovely, doesn't it? I think I'll have that."

"Okay. I haven't decided what I want yet," Alex said, looking through the menu. The options were as expensive as he had expected.

Eventually he settled on the linguine vongole. After he decided, the waiter returned to the table to take their order. When they were done, Emily pushed her chair out.

"I'm going to the ladies room. Would you like to join me?" she asked Diamond.

"Of course," Diamond responded. They both got up and walked away.

As soon as they were out of earshot, Rob turned a ferocious glare on Alex. "What are you playing at, kid?"

Alex blinked. "Um, what?"

"You know what. What the hell are you doing?"

"I...I don't know what you mean."

"Diamond! I'm talking about your so-called girlfriend."

Alex's shoulders slumped. Rob had figured it out. He wasn't sure how, but he'd somehow seen through their relationship.

"Well—"

"I can't believe you would bring her here, in front of my wife!"

"I had to—"

Rob leaned forward, veins popping out of his forehead, pointing his finger at Alex. "Listen, you little shit. I don't know what sort of plan you think you have, but if you and that whore are planning to blackmail me, it's not going to work. "

Blackmail?

Alex sat, stunned. Rob hadn't seen through Alex because of a problem with her invented backstory, or even because Alex and Diamond seemed like an unlikely couple. Rob saw through Alex because he *knew* Diamond. Judging from his spitting rage, he knew her because he was one of her customers.

"I...I'm not trying to blackmail you," Alex said.

Rob's eyes narrowed. "Bullshit. What else...wait a minute. I know what this is," he started to laugh. "You want Emily. I saw it in that shitty café the other day, the way you stared at her. The way you've been looking at her tonight. She's your fucking cousin."

"No she isn't."

Rob laughed louder. "Unbelieveable. And you think bringing her here is going to break us up? You think that will make her yours? You think you're going to ride off into the sunset together, little incestual lovers?"

"No, I—"

"How did you find out about her anyway?"

Alex felt helpless, he didn't know what to do anymore. The situation was too complicated. "I didn't," he said quietly.

Rob downed the rest of his scotch, then realization slowly dawned on his face. "Jesus Christ, you really didn't know. Shit. Okay, listen. Do not say anything. Got that? Not one word; and this will go over just fine. Got it?"

Alex nodded. What else could he do? Rob knew he had lied to Emily about Diamond. Rob had also inadvertently admitted to cheating on Emily with an escort.

Rob looked behind Alex. "Okay, the girls are coming back." He looked at Alex with a carefully neutral expression. "Do not fuck me, kid," he said in a threatening growl.

"We're ba-ack," Emily said, returning to the table with Diamond. When she saw Alex's ashen face, her jovial expression changed to concern. "Are you okay, Alex?"

"Um, yeah. Fine," he said.

"He's fine, I know what'll help him," Rob said, then waved down the passing waiter. "Two more scotches, for my friend and me." He gestured at Alex.

"Coming right up, sir."

Alex began to protest, "No tha—"

Rob raised his hand to silence him. "Don't worry. My treat."

Diamond put her arm around Alex and rested her head on his shoulder. The kind of thing a real girlfriend would do. Any other time, Alex would have enjoyed it.

The drinks arrived. Rob lifted his glass to Alex. "Cheers," he said, teeth showing through a wolfish grin.

"Cheers," Alex said. They clinked glasses and drank.

* * * * *

Alex and Diamond waved at Rob and Emily from their cab. As the cab pulled away, Alex watched Rob put his arm around Emily and pull her close. It made him feel sick. But that could also be the alcohol. He had never been much of a drinker, and the four or five glasses of scotch were hitting him hard. For the first ten minutes of the cab ride he kept his eyes closed, hoping the spinning would stop.

"Alex."

Something in the voice was off. He opened his eyes and looked at Diamond. It was hard to tell for sure, because it took so long to focus, but she was different: head down, hands in her lap, thoughtful expression on her face. It was the first time he saw her as a person, instead of an escort. She had never broken character before, not for a single moment in the years he had been seeing her. It was enough to help shake off the worst of the alcoholic fog coating his mind.

He blinked and opened his mouth to respond. She suddenly came back together, any hint of the vulnerable girl simply vanished. As if her mask had come loose for a moment, just enough to see a crack of the person beneath; but it was back on now, tighter than ever.

She looked at him. "What happened tonight?" she asked, voice controlled and business-like.

He sighed. "You've seen him before," he said.

Her eyes narrowed. "My clients are my business, not yours."

"But you've seen him before. How many times have you seen him?"

"That is none of your business, Alex." Now he was seeing something else he hadn't seen from her before: anger. She continued, "Maybe you've forgotten how this works. We are not a couple. There is nothing exclusive here. This is a business relationship, nothing more. Do you understand?"

"Yes, I understand, but—"

"So what happened tonight?"

"I…I don't know. I had no idea, I swear. I wanted to impress Emily. Then suddenly Rob is accusing me of blackmail. I just…I…," he stopped. He wasn't sure what else to say about it. He still felt blindsided by the situation.

Diamond's anger dissipated. She shook her head sadly at him. "I'm afraid we can't see each other anymore"

Alex felt like his stomach had been cinched shut in a vice grip. "Wha…what do you mean?"

"I can't get involved with clients in this way. I'm sorry, but it's for the best."

A sense of dread settled over him. The one person he always thought he could never screw things up with. As long as he had money, he had her. Even he couldn't ruin that. Or so he thought.

"No, no. You don't understand. I didn't know, it was an accident. I swear I didn't mean to put you in that situation," he said, more than a little desperation in his voice.

She reached out and put a hand on his lap. "I believe you," she said softly, "but that doesn't change anything."

He knew she was right. Good escorts had a very specific professional code of conduct that was rarely, if ever, broken—for their client's safety, and far more importantly, for their own. After what had happened tonight, she had no choice but to cut him loose.

"I think I love her," he said, surprising himself.

"I know." She moved closer to him and rested her head on his shoulder. "I know."

The rest of the ride passed in silence. The streets flicked by like the seconds of a giant watch, block by block, counting down to their departure. Alex tried to enjoy the time he had left, but it was over far too soon.

The driver stopped the cab in front of Diamond's building. The meter showed twenty-six dollars; Alex gave him thirty. He decided he would walk home instead of riding the rest of the way. It was only a half-hour walk, and he was in no real rush to get home.

He got out first, then held Diamond's hand as she stepped out. The taxi drove away, leaving them alone in front of the large glass doors of her building entrance. He was still holding her hand.

"Diamond, I…," he struggled with the words. "Thank you—for

everything." For just a *business relationship*, this was really hard.

She smiled, stood up on her toes, and gave him a kiss. When she pulled away he could have sworn he saw a hint of sadness in her eyes. She started walking towards the doors, but stopped and turned around. "It's not only me."

Alex didn't know what she was talking about.

She bit her lip, then went on: "He sees others, too; a lot of others. We all talk. He's not always alone, either. He brings his business clients too."

Alex stared, mouth agape, dumbfounded that she was telling him this. He knew that escorts often worked in teams, often offering two-girl service for men with far too much money. He had even met Diamond's partner Vixen once. It never occurred to him that the system would be used in such a way, but of course it made sense. Businesses adapt to meet the needs of their clientele. So, of course, escorts didn't work in teams just to service the occasional horndog who wanted a threesome.

"Goodbye, Alex." She turned and walked the rest of the way to the door.

He watched, wordlessly, as she went inside, and pressed the button to call an elevator. When the doors opened, she stepped inside and turned around, keeping her head down, so that their eyes didn't meet again before the elevator doors closed.

* * * * *

It was a cool, still night with a bright moon. The cloudless sky overhead was littered with stars; nowhere near the quality of a night out in the country, far from the polluting brightness of city lights. But it was still pleasant and as clear as the sky ever was in the city. The fresh air had helped to clear out the remainder of the scotch-fueled cobwebs that had clouded his mind.

Alex watched the sky for signs of falling stars, or as his co-worker, Zane, referred to them: chunks of space debris caught by the Earth's gravity burning up in the atmosphere. Sadly, there was no such debris for him to watch that night; just the distant, unreachable stars far overhead. The light from those stars had travelled millions of miles, taking—tens, sometimes hundreds or even thousands of years to be seen from here, this pale blue dot called Earth. Some of those stars may not even exist anymore, they may have burnt out or even gone supernova. It could have happened years ago, but because of the massive distance it hadn't been seen yet. Looking in the sky was, quite literally, looking at the past. Even the sun, at its relatively close distance, was still in the past. It could suddenly blow up and, here on Earth, humanity wouldn't even know for about eight minutes.

It made Alex feel insignificant. How could anything he ever did or said have any meaning in a universe so large?

His phone rang, cutting off his train of thought. He looked at the call display: it was Emily. He answered.

"Hello?"

"Hi, Alex, it's Emily." He was getting to know her voice; he could tell something was wrong.

"Yeah. Hi."

"Listen, I won't be able to, um, go for coffee for a few days," she said.

"Oh, well, if it's the time, then that's okay. My vacation is over, actually. I have to go back to work on Monday. But I'm still free in the evenings if you are. Or next Saturday."

"No, it's not that."

She paused, seeming to consider her words. When she spoke again it was quiet, hardly a whisper. Alex had to stop and cover his other ear to catch her words. "Alex, is there something you're not telling me?"

"What? No! Of course not!" He tried to sound indignant, but he probably came off as scared. He wasn't good at lying. "Why?"

"Rob said I couldn't trust you. Why would he say that, Alex?"

Alex felt the vice grip tighten on his stomach again. "I…I don't know. I have no idea!"

"Alex?"

"I swear, Emily, I don't know! I don't know why he would say that."

He heard her sigh. "He wouldn't say that without a reason; there must be something you did, or—"

"Honestly, Emily, I don't know what I did. I don't know what I *could* have done." He did know, of course, but he couldn't tell her that, not now. Rob had already managed to poison any faith she'd had in him.

He had suspected that Rob might move against him; he just hadn't expected it to be so soon. "Why would he buy me drinks all night if he had a problem with me?"

"He says you're a good kid, just…" *A liar.* "Maybe we shouldn't hang out anymore."

"What!"

"I don't know, Alex. I don't understand."

"Emily, you have to believe me, there's no reason for this, there—"

"I can't talk about this anymore. I have to go."

"Emily, Emily! You believe me, don't you?"

"Goodbye." She hung up.

Alex stood on the sidewalk, shaking. He couldn't believe this had happened. He couldn't believe he hadn't seen it coming. Of course Rob would discredit him, in case he tried to say anything to Emily. Now, if he ever had the chance to speak to her again, any word he said would be tainted by Rob's warning: *Do not trust him.*

He wanted to throw his phone down, smash it on the ground and watch it explode into pieces. But he didn't. He took a deep breath, put it back in his pocket, and started walking again.

It seemed like the last three weeks had been some sort of dream. But now it had ended, and here he was, right back where he started. Worse, actually. He'd lost Emily, but he had also lost Diamond. Now he truly had nothing.

For the first time since Thanksgiving, he started to think about suicide again. He could feel the depression reaching out to him, soft laughter echoing in his ears as it wrapped its familiar arms around his body.

He didn't have the energy or the desire to fight it anymore.

TWENTY-ONE
JOEL – FOUR MONTHS AGO

"DADDY, LOOK AT that one! Can I have it?" Hayley pointed up at a large pink bear hanging from the top of the game stall. It was one of the water games where you fire a stream of water at a target to win a race.

The attendant saw Hayley and smiled. "Step right up, little girl. Five dollars, first place, and that bear is yours!"

"Can I play, Daddy?" She pulled at Joel's arm.

"No, you don't need another stuffed animal."

"Pleeeeeeeease," she said, looking up at him with big, round eyes.

"Okay, but just one game," he said. Trips to Playland always cost him more than he wanted to spend.

"Yay!" she squealed and ran up to a seat that had a bar of transparent plastic in front of it with the number six pasted on.

"Hold on," Joel said. He sat down first and set Hayley on his lap. He handed the attendant a five-dollar bill. After waiting a few minutes for more people to sit down, the game was about to start. Hayley took hold of the two handles that controlled the water cannon and started aiming it all directions.

"Okay, sweetie, you need to keep it still," Joel said. He put his hands over hers and re-aimed.

The buzzer went off and loud music began to play.

Hayley and Joel pulled the trigger and the water came gushing out of the nozzle, flying right into the middle of the target. A horse with a black number six stuck on it burst into motion on the back wall.

The attendant called out a play-by-play of the race: "Number Six is off to a quick lead, followed by Eight and Two. Twelve is bringing up the rear but it's gaining fast! Oh, it looks like number Four stumbled; there it goes again. Six is still ahead by a hair; number Two is right on its tail. It's going to be a close one. Number One has taken over third place but it's a race to the finish between Six and Two. Who's it gonna be? They're neck and neck in the home stretch. Two inches ahead but Six brings it level. We're near the finish, it looks like Two has...no, it's number Six! Number Six is the winner!"

Hayley screamed over the sound of the buzzer. "We won! Daddy, we won!"

"We did. Good job, kiddo."

The attendant walked up to them. "Congratulations!" he said. "Now, normally I wouldn't be able to give you that big pink bear you wanted because there weren't enough people for a full race." He watched Hayley's happy smile disappear before continuing. "But since you're so adorable I'm going to give it to you anyway."

And suddenly her smile was back, bigger than ever. "Really?"

"What do you say?" Joel asked.

"Thaaaaank you," Hayley called out.

The attendant pulled the bear down from the roof and handed it to Hayley. It was almost the same size as her. She wrapped her arms around it as far as she could and squeezed tightly, rubbing her face in the soft fur.

Joel nodded at the attendant. "Thanks," he said, then "Okay Hayley, let's go."

They walked through the rest of the gaming area, Hayley continually bumping into everyone in her path because she couldn't see over the large, pink bear head she was holding.

"Maybe I should carry your bear," Joel said.

"No, I want to carry Fluffy."

"Fluffy? Is that its name?"

"*Her* name."

"Don't you already have a stuffed animal named Fluffy? Why don't you call this one something else, like, Pinky."

Hayley looked at him with a vaguely confused expression.

"Never mind," he said.

"You're silly, Daddy," she said, smiling again, while nearly running over a kid carrying a large, blue elephant doll. The path was turning into a bumper-dolls arena.

"Watch where you're going, Hayley."

Eventually they extricated themselves from the confines of the thin avenue through the gaming area and entered the slightly wider paths between rides.

Hayley stopped and stared at the Corkscrew rollercoaster. Riders screamed as the cars went through the loops. "Daddy, that looks scary."

"Yes, it does. That ride is for bigger kids."

"Have you been on it?"

"No, I haven't."

"Why? Are you scared?"

"No, I'm not."

"Then why?"

Joel sighed. She was at the age where she was constantly asking questions.

"Because it makes my stomach feel bad."

She made a face. "I don't like that feeling."

"Me neither," Joel said.

They were about to turn into the Kids Playce when Hayley pointed at the Westcoast Wheel. "Daddy, can we go on that now?"

They had only been to Playland twice before, and both times Hayley had been below the height requirement for the Wheel. She was short for her age and, most recently, when they had come back in April for her third birthday, she was still an inch and a half under the limit; so the stodgy operator refused to let her on, citing liability reasons. Joel had been pumping her up by reminding her she'd finally be big enough to ride the Wheel.

"Yes, we can go on it."

"Yay!"

She started pulling Joel along towards the Westcoast Wheel, but before they got there they stopped to look at Atmosfear, Playland's new ride. It was much like the spinning swing rides of old, but this one rose over two hundred feet in the air, making it a much more exhilarating experience.

"Daddy, look at this one."

"Yeah, it's pretty cool."

"Do you think I can go on it? Or is it for big kids?"

"It's for big kids. But don't worry, little missy, you'll be big enough soon."

"How soon?"

"Soon, in a few years. Come on, let's go." Joel took her by the shoulder and they turned towards the Westcoast Wheel. As he turned, he caught sight of a woman with short, blonde hair standing in the line-up for Atmosfear, staring at him. Their eyes met.

Oh shit!

It was her: The girl he'd attacked in the alley five years ago. Her hair was different now, she'd shorn her long, red locks; but he had no doubt it was her.

One of her friends noticed something was wrong. "Hey Melissa, you alright? Hello? Melissa."

Melissa didn't respond. Her mouth opened and closed, but nothing came out. She kept staring at Joel, a look of intense anxiety on her face.

"We have to go," Joel said to Hayley.

"What? We just got here!"

"Now." He picked Hayley up and started speed-walking towards the park exit, all the while fighting a powerful urge to look back—at her.

"Where are we going? Daddy?"

"We're going home."

"No! You said we could go on the Wheel. You said!" She started to cry. People were looking at them; Joel ignored their stares and tried to calm Hayley down.

"Ssshhhhh. I know, sweetie, I know. I'm sorry. But we can't go on it now."

"Why not?"

"Because…I just realized what time it is. We have to get home for dinner; your mom will be waiting for us."

"Can't she wait? I really wanted to go on it, Daddy."

"I'm sorry," Joel said. He kept walking, his speed barely under a run. His back tingled, like a thousand daggers were being aimed at it, and it felt like they were going to strike at any second. "I promise we'll go on it next time, okay? As many times as you want."

"You promise?" Hayley asked, wiping the tears from her eyes.

"I promise."

They walked out the front gate and stopped at the crosswalk. Joel waited impatiently for the lights to change. He looked back, half expecting to see an army of police running after him, ready to capture and expose him for the horrible criminal he really was. But the path behind him was empty.

The light finally changed and he jogged across the street, weaving through the parking lot until he reached his car, a sensible-looking grey Volkswagen. After strapping Hayley into the car seat in the back, he sat down in the driver's seat and took a deep breath.

No one was coming. It was okay. She hadn't recognized him, he hoped.

But then, why was she staring at him with that shocked expression on her face? She must have recognized *something*.

He thought back to the initial search. The media had posted composite sketches of what the police thought he looked like and, though they had achieved a passing resemblance, they'd come nowhere near his real face. The alley had been too dark, their encounter too fast and violent for her to see him properly.

Then it clicked.

"Don't worry, little missy," he had said to Hayley.

"What was that, missy?" he had said to the girl named Melissa.

The combination of that word *missy* and his voice must have set off an alarm bell in her mind. She didn't even need to see his face to recognize him.

He put his face in his hands and wept.

"Daddy, what's wrong?" Hayley asked. Joel found it sweet that she asked about him, even though she still had tears of disappointment in her own eyes.

"Nothing," he said. He wiped his eyes and looked back, giving Hayley his best fake smile. "Nothing. We're going home now."

* * * * *

"Mommy!"

"Hayley! Hi!" Jenny said, as Hayley ran into her arms. "You're home early."

"Daddy said you were waiting for us."

Jenny looked at Joel questioningly. He shook his head slightly in response.

"Well, I missed you too much," Jenny said to Hayley. "And I couldn't wait to see you."

"Daddy said I could go on the big Wheel but then he said we had to go. I was really sad," Hayley said, then frowned and dropped her head down so that her chin rested on top of her chest. She puffed her cheeks out and looked up at her mom with sad eyes. It was her go-to expression when she was pouting and wanted someone to feel bad for her, which was almost every day. It would have been aggravating if it wasn't so damned cute.

"Awww, I'm sorry, sweetie," Jenny said, and hugged Hayley tighter.

"Okay, kiddo," Joel said. "Go upstairs and wash up for dinner."

Hayley broke away from her mom and looked up at Joel, eyes glistening. It was hard to tell in these situations if the tears were sincere or just for effect.

"I told you we'll go next time. Now go wash up."

Hayley wiped her eyes and stomped away. Joel sighed.

"So you want to tell me the real reason you came home early?" Jenny asked when Hayley was out of earshot.

"I…" he started. "I saw someone that I recognized. I couldn't stay." He couldn't lie to her; she knew him too well for that. He hoped a few well-placed half-truths would get him out of it.

Jenny's voice took on a compassionate tone. "Was it someone from the Eastside? Or before?"

"From the Eastside."

Jenny took his hand and held it between both of hers. "Was it someone who hurt you?"

"No. I…stole something from her."

"Then you should have stayed and talked to her. You could have apologized, showed her how you've changed. You're a different person now."

Joel shook his head. "No, I can't...I can't just apologize to her. Not for—"

"Joel, you can't keep running from your past. It has a power over you, and the only way to overcome it is to face it."

"I couldn't do it." *There is no atoning for what I've done*, he thought.

She lifted one of her hands to his face and ran it through his hair and back around his ear. She'd been using that gesture for years to calm him down when he felt stressed. He leaned his head into her hand and closed his eyes.

"Listen to me. You're not that man anymore. I know you think you can't move on, but you have to, for our sake—Hayley and me. But most of all for yourself."

So many different things went through Joel's mind: denials, deflections, admissions. But he couldn't bring himself to say any of them. Finally, he simply said, "I know," because he couldn't decide on anything else.

Jenny smiled thinly, as if she suspected he wasn't being completely honest. "I'm always here for you."

"I know," he said. This time, he didn't hesitate. "I know."

* * * * *

That night, Joel put Hayley to bed in spite of her protests and insistence that she wanted her mommy. She was still mad at him.

After he'd finished tucking her in, he began to speak. "I wanted to talk to you about what happened today."

Hayley pretended to sleep. Joel sighed.

"I'm sorry for not letting you get on the Wheel. I know you've been waiting a really long time."

No response.

He continued, "It wasn't fair, I know. And I promise next time we'll go, okay?"

"That's what you said before," she said, finally acknowledging him.

Last time, when she'd been too short, he had promised to take her again this summer so she could ride the Wheel. That's what today's trip had been meant to fulfill. He hated to break his word to her.

"I know. I made a mistake." He ran his hands through her hair; there were tears in her eyes. Seeing that, knowing he was the cause, felt as if someone had stuck a needle in his eye and was siphoning the water out. Hayley's tears always had that effect on him.

"I was a bad person, a long time ago. And today I saw someone who reminded me of what a bad person I was. That's why we had to go. Because I was scared."

"Why were you scared?"

"Because I did bad things in the past."

"Didn't someone tell you to stop?"

Joel smiled at the last question. "Eventually. Your mom helped me stop."

"Mommy is a good person."

"Yes, she is."

"Am I?"

"Of course you are, sweetie," he said. He leaned in and gave her a kiss on the forehead. "You're better than good. You're the best little girl in the world."

Hayley giggled. Then, after a few moments of thinking, asked, "Why were you bad, Daddy?"

Joel thought about it for a while. It was a simple question; however, the answer was anything but. How can he explain his life to a three-year-old? It wouldn't make sense. It hardly made sense to him.

"When I was a boy," he began, latching onto one of the first memories that popped into his head. And even though it didn't seem like an appropriate memory to share with a three-year-old, it was all he had: "My Daddy was very mean. If he had a bad day at work, he would make me stand on the stairs and choose how I wanted to get hurt. One hundred normal punches or one really, really hard punch. I always chose the one, because I knew it was better to get it over with as fast as possible. He would hit me so hard that I couldn't breathe and wanted to throw up. I cried too."

"That's not very nice," Hayley said.

"No, it wasn't. But I got so used to it, that I started to do bad things too. Because I didn't know any better."

Hayley looked like she was having trouble making the connection between his story and the end result.

"What I mean to say is: my life had been bad for a very long time. It became a part of who I was, and it was really hard to get past it. That's why it's so important for me to be a good dad to you. I don't want you or your mom to ever hurt because of something I did. I wouldn't be able to live with myself. You and your mom are the most important people in the world to me. You understand?"

Hayley nodded. She still seemed overwhelmed, but at least she got the gist of what he was saying.

"Okay," Joel said, and kissed her on the forehead again. "Good night."

TWENTY-TWO
RICHARD

LACEY HAD BECOME a problem: She was constantly on Richard's mind, and not just because she was texting him every hour. He couldn't shake the image of her above him, searching for a connection, desperate to fill the void created by Evil Richard.

That's what Richard called her previous sponsor. The man had used her and then abandoned her. He took advantage of her while she was most vulnerable, managed to convince her that they needed to have sex to help her overcome her alcoholism; then when he was done, invented an excuse to leave. Richard had no doubt the story about his ex-wife and kids was fabricated, a way to get out when he was bored with her.

Evil Richard was a sexual predator, plain and simple. The sex may have been consensual when it happened, but no doubt he'd mentally abused Lacey to get what he wanted. And the thought that had done this to her—and that he may have done it to other women as well—made Richard seethe with rage.

Now Richard was dealing with the fallout. Lacey was obviously in trouble. If Richard pushed her away now, she would just rush to someone else; someone who might take advantage of her the same way Evil Richard had. He had to help her.

So Richard waited outside the Tim Hortons behind the hospital before his shift, fidgeting with his phone and repeatedly checking the time. After a few minutes, he spotted Lacey coming towards him. He waved, and she returned the wave with a bright smile.

She sprinted the last few steps and jumped towards him. He was caught so off guard, they both nearly tumbled onto the pavement.

"Oooph," he said. "Careful."

She laughed and caught him off guard again by darting her head forward and giving him a quick kiss.

"Okay, okay," he said, pulling away. "We need to talk."

"About what?" she asked, slipping her hand into his.

Richard looked down at their hands. He had gotten used to her touchy-feely mannerisms over the last few weeks, and he'd accepted that she liked to hold hands, so he'd put up with it; but now he realized that he had been enabling her by going along with it. He pulled his hand away slowly, not wanting to seem rude.

"Walk with me," he said. He put his hands in his pockets to keep her from grabbing one; so instead, she latched her arm around his at the elbow like they were on their way to a ball. Richard sighed and began walking. They turned on Laurel Street and went down the hill toward Charleson Park.

They crossed a pedestrian bridge onto a tree-lined path. False Creek, and its accompanying litter of yachts, lay directly ahead. The highrises of downtown Vancouver enclosed the calm waters of the inlet. The North Shore Mountains loomed in the distance. "Lacey," Richard began, "I want you to know that I appreciate your company, and you really have helped me."

"Awww, thanks," Lacey said.

"And the last thing I want to do is hurt you."

"O...kay," she said, with a quizzical look on her face.

"But what happened at the park the other day, that can never happen again."

"Why? It was beautiful, Richard. God was with us; He—"

"No, don't say that. It creeps me out."

"How does God creep you out?"

"The idea that someone is watching me while— It's creepy." He shook his head, this was off topic. "That's not the problem though. The problem is that it's wrong. We can't be together, Lacey. I'm married, I have kids. I love them."

"So? The idea that a person can only love a couple of people at a time is silly."

"That's not the point. Look, I know the other Richard told you that this is okay; but it's not. Sponsors shouldn't be sleeping with their, um--"

"Sponsee," Lacey said.

"Yeah. That isn't supposed to happen. See this? Your arm in mine? That shouldn't happen either. It's not right; it shouldn't be a physical relationship." To illustrate his point, he pulled his arm out of Lacey's grip and moved an extra foot away from her.

Lacey smiled indulgently, like she was arguing with a child. "I told you, the rules are more like guidelines. They aren't set in stone. People can interpret them in different ways."

"I know, but they weren't meant to be twisted like this. The other Richard, he used you, Lacey. He used you for sex. He should be put behind bars for—"

"Don't say that!" Lacey burst out. "Richard helped me, he saved me. You have no idea what I was like before he became my sponsor."

"You're right, I don't know. But he took advantage of you, don't you see that?"

"And what were we doing? What, are you suddenly taking the high road?"

"That was a mistake, I shouldn't have allowed it to happen. But it doesn't change anything. He wasn't helping you, he was hurting you."

"How can you say that? I haven't had a drink in over two years. Two years!"

"I know, and you should be proud of that," he said, then stopped to collect his thoughts. "Look, I talked to Jeff, and—"

"What? What do you mean you talked to Jeff?"

"I told him what was happening, and I asked for his advice so that-"

"No no no no no! You shouldn't have done that; this was supposed to be a secret, our special connection. Why would you do that? Why would you ruin it?" She began to back away from him, tears streamed down her face.

Richard reached out and she batted his hand away. "I'm trying to help."

"I don't need your help," she said, continuing to move away.

"Please don't go."

She stopped and looked at him. "I just wanted to feel something," she said, then turned and ran towards the trees.

"Wait," he called out. But the only response was the sighing of the wind and the rustling of the leaves.

* * * * *

It was almost midnight when Richard got home from work. The lights were out, indicating everyone was asleep. He shut the front door quietly, like he was sneaking in from an illicit meeting. He put his shoes away and started towards to kitchen to get a glass of water.

"Richard."

"Holy!" Richard said, his voice rising a few more octaves than he would have liked. He looked in the living room and saw the dark outline of a body sitting in the corner seat. "Nat? Jesus, you scared me. What are you doing?"

"I've been thinking."

Richard sat down on the couch across from where she was sitting in front of the window. The dim light from outside made a sort of halo around her body; it also made it impossible to see the expression on her face. "So, what's on your mind?"

"I had an interesting talk with Jenny today," she said.

Jenny was one of her friends, but Richard couldn't remember the last time they had talked. "Okay. And what did Jenny have to say?"

"Well, she was at Pekoe Tea today with a friend of hers. You know the one, on Broadway?"

"Um, no, never heard of it." His heart started to beat faster, he had a bad feeling. It felt like this confrontation had been staged.

"It's really close to the hospital. I'm surprised you've never seen it. She says you walked right past her today."

Oh no. "Is she sure it was me? I don't—"

"Oh, she's positive. The only thing she couldn't figure out was the other woman jumping into your arms, kissing you; then hanging off of you while you two went for a lovely walk, because it certainly wasn't me. So she was a bit confused."

"Nat, I—"

"She called me to see what was wrong and I said nothing's wrong, but I guess I was wrong, wasn't I?"

Richard cringed. "She's my sponsor."

Natalie laughed. "Your sponsor? You have got to be kidding me. I don't think you're supposed to screw your sponsor."

"No…it's not like that," he said, leaning forward. "She's…troubled. I was trying to help her."

"Isn't she supposed to help you? Or maybe she has been, in a *special* way. Is that it?"

"No, you don't understand, I—"

"What am I supposed to understand, Richard? You were with another woman. She kissed you!"

"I swear, nothing happened."

"How can I believe that? You're always gone, you won't tell me anything. At least before I could assume you were off getting drunk. Now I have no idea what you're doing."

"I know. I'm sorry."

She leaned forward and Richard was finally able to make out her features. He realized that she had been crying. He hated knowing he had made both Natalie and Lacey cry on the same day. But this one hurt more, a lot more.

"I took the kids to my parents' place. We're going to stay there for a while."

"Natalie, honey, you don't have to do this. I'm done with her, I promise. I met her today to tell her that."

"I'm sure you did, Richard." The grandfather clock in the hallway began to go off, signalling midnight: *dong…dong…dong…*

"That's my cue," Natalie said, then stood up and started walking to the door.

"Hold on. We can work this out," Richard said, standing up as well. He reached for her arm and she twisted away.

Natalie stopped in front of the door. "You know, you've been clear from the start that you don't want my help. You want to deal with this alone, well, now you can be alone." She opened the door and walked out, slamming it behind her.

Richard stood in the living room by himself, hand half raised.

Dong…dong…dong.

TWENTY-THREE
MELISSA

MELISSA WEAVED THROUGH a group of bodies and found a tiny space on the couch. She slid in, careful not to spill her glass of vodka and cranberry juice. Luke had brought a laptop and hooked it up to the stereo via the TV, so they could listen to the music playlist he put together on YouTube. It took less than an hour for the music to get switched off in favour of cat videos.

A cat jumped off a bed and flew head first into a wall, and everyone burst out laughing; then someone's arm bumped Melissa, spilling her drink.

"Dammit," she muttered.

"Shit, I'm sorry," a man beside her said. "Hold on a sec." He stood up and hustled off to the kitchen; then pushed his way back through the crowd with a handful of tissues. He handed her most of them, then used the rest to wipe the drips off the hardwood floor. "Sorry again," he said.

"No worries," Melissa said. "It was an accident, no big deal."

"You probably don't want me to sit here anymore; it's not safe," he said.

Melissa glanced at him. Was that meant as a joke? "What's not safe?"

"Um, I mean it's not safe for you...with me here."

"Yeah, maybe you're right," she said without any inflection.

He stared at her, looking anxious and confused at the same time. Then he looked away.

She left the couch and went to the kitchen to get a refill. Lindsay was there talking with some of her friends, waving an empty glass in the air to illustrate some point. Luke stood beside her, nodding enthusiastically at whatever she said. She finished and everyone laughed. Then she tried to drink from her glass, realized it was empty, and passed it off to Luke, who set to work getting her a refill.

Lindsay saw Melissa enter the kitchen and ran to give her a hug. "Melisssaaaaaaaa," she said, with only a hint of slurring. "Let's do some shots!"

Melissa almost said no, but reconsidered. Why not? It is Lindsay's birthday; and they are supposed to be having fun. "Sure, what do we have left?"

"Um, I think we drank the Baja Rosa. Luke," she called out, "What do we have left for shots?"

"There's still this butterscotch Schnapps stuff," he said.

"Okay, pour us a round."

Luke set out a row of shot glasses and filled them up. They lifted the glasses and clinked them together. "Happy birthday, Lindsay," they said in unison; then they drank. Melissa pushed away an unpleasant feeling of déjà vu.

Lindsay put her glass on the table and shouted, "Another!"

Luke was happy to oblige, refilling her glass, then everyone else's.

They clinked glasses again and drank; then again, and again, until the bottle of Schnapps was empty.

Lindsay leaned on Melissa's shoulder. "I saw you talking to Mark over there."

"Who?"

"Mark, the guy who was sitting beside you."

"Oh him. Yeah, he spilt my drink on me."

Lindsay laughed. "He's a klutz at work too."

"Ooooh, that's where I know him from. I thought he looked familiar."

"Yeah, you should know him. He definitely knows you."

"What does that mean?"

Lindsay whispered in Melissa's ear. "It means he's had a crush on you for almost as long as I've known him."

"Seriously?"

"Yes! He always asks how you're doing. Every day. Literally."

"Strange," Melissa said. "I don't know why."

"Gee, I dunno Melissa, maybe because you're kinda hot?"

Melissa's face turned red. "Well, that's a shitty reason to like someone." She pulled away from Lindsay and went to make herself another drink.

"Be nice," Lindsay said, following Melissa around the kitchen. "He's a nice guy, it wouldn't hurt to talk to him for a bit."

"He seems kind of…awkward."

"Well yeah, you probably make him nervous."

"I dunno, Lins. I'm not sure I'm ready."

"Will you ever be ready? You told me you were trying to put yourself out there. Well, now is as good a time as any."

Melissa thought about it for a minute then sighed. "Fine, I'll talk to him. But I think I'll need some liquid courage."

Lindsay smiled. "That can be arranged."

* * * * *

"I know most of the people here think I'm a bitch— "

"I don't think you are," Mark said, lounging beside Melissa on the couch.

Melissa continued without missing a beat. "And I don't mean to be. But I think we're all different people now, ya know? We aren't into the same scenes anymore. I'm not out looking for excitement every weekend; I like to relax at home with a good book, or movie."

"I'm the same way," Mark said.

Melissa nodded. "That doesn't mean I don't want to go out and have fun. I just don't feel the need to do it every, single, weekend. Does that make me an ice queen?"

"I don't think so. I think you're one of the nicest people I've ever met."

Melissa looked at him and smiled, knowing full well he was trying to be charming, even though it came across as sycophantic. But she didn't mind; in fact, she was enjoying it. For the last few years, people were usually nice to her out of pity. This was different, and it made her feel good. Was that such a bad thing?

She patted him on the leg. "Thanks," she said. His face turned red and he smiled.

Melissa went to take a sip from her glass and realized it was empty. "I think I need another drink."

"I'll get it for you," Mark said. He jumped up and took her glass; then stopped and balanced himself as he appeared to fight off a wave of dizziness. "Ooooh."

"Slow down, Speedy. It's not a race," Melissa said.

"Yeah," he said, shaking his head as if he expected that would force the dizziness out. He took a few trial steps, and when he seemed stable he left.

"Hey, we're leaving," someone called out from the front.

Melissa pushed herself up from the couch and fought off her own wave of dizziness. "Maybe I shouldn't have another drink," she mumbled to herself.

Lindsay was at the door saying goodbye to a group of women.

Melissa waved. "Bye, thanks for coming."

They waved back. "Thanks for having us."

When they were gone, Lindsay walked up to Melissa and leaned on her shoulder. "I'm drunk," she said.

"I think I am, too," Melissa said.

"I don't think I've seen you drink this much since...I can't even remember the last time."

"Me neither."

"You and Mark seem to have hit it off. You've been sitting on the couch with him for a couple of hours."

"Really? I didn't realize it had been that long." She yawned. "I think I might go lie down. How long are they staying?" Melissa asked, gesturing towards the kitchen table, where Luke was playing poker with a few people she didn't recognize.

"Who knows," Lindsay said. "But if they're staying, we're gonna play something that I want to play. It's *my* birthday, dammit."

"You tell them, Lins," Melissa said with a laugh.

Lindsay stomped up to the table and demanded they play something fun, while Melissa retreated to her bedroom. She laid down on the bed and, a few minutes later, heard a knock at her door. She ignored it at first, but it kept coming, like a fly that keeps bouncing off a car window because it doesn't know how else to get outside.

"Hello?" she asked.

The door cracked open and Mark stuck his head in. "Hey, I got your drink."

"Oh, thanks." She felt bad for forgetting about him. She must have had more to drink than she realized. "I don't think I'm going to drink anymore tonight, though. I've had enough."

"I thought you might say that, so I brought you a glass of water too."

"Thanks," she said, motioning him in.

He put the glasses on her nightstand and sat down on the edge of the bed near her feet. He looked like he desperately wanted to lie down but was terrified of doing so. An annoying buzzing sound ran through her head, so she hardly noticed when he rested his arm on her leg. "Can you turn the light off? It's giving me a headache."

"No problem," he said. He stood up and flipped the switch, then sat back down. This time he was higher up the bed, and much closer.

"That's better," she said, referring to the blackness in the room.

"You should drink some water, it'll make you feel better. It'll help with the hangover too."

"Yeah, you're right," she said. It took her a minute to find the glass. A little bit of light came through the window, but nowhere near enough to make out any details. Mark looked like a black blob on the bed beside her.

She finished the water and put the empty glass on the nightstand, then lay on her back. She rubbed her temples. "I don't feel good."

"Here, let me help. Roll over."

"What? Why?"

"Come on, roll over. It'll help."

"Fine," she said. She rolled onto her belly and felt him adjust his position beside her; then she felt the first tentative touch of his hands on her shoulders. When she didn't immediately protest, he gained confidence, and began massaging her back, neck, and shoulders. He was considerate, and kept his hands on top of her shirt. Though, when her shirt rode up and left the small of her back exposed, he didn't shy away from the contact.

He was actually really good. At one point he found a knot in her lower back and was able to rub it out, prompting her to moan in a mixture of pleasure and pain. That had been bugging her for a few weeks and it felt good to have it gone.

Mark, emboldened by her response, started working his way under her shirt and up her back. "You have amazing skin."

"Mmmmph," she said, the pillow muffled her words, turning them into an unintelligible mess.

His hands ran up the side of her body, getting uncomfortably close to her breasts. He began to fiddle with the clasp on her bra.

She felt the first cool prickles of perspiration forming on her skin. She knew where this was going. But was it what she really wanted? It had been so long, but…

She rolled over at the exact moment he finally undid the clasp on her bra. His shirt was off. She tried to speak, "Mark, I— ," but she barely spoke before his mouth was on hers. They kissed for what felt like hours, and when they finally broke apart she needed a few moments to catch her breath.

Mark needed no such break. He started working his way down. His hot breath left a warm, tingling sensation on her skin wherever his lips touched her: her neck, her chest, her stomach.

He slipped her bra straps off her shoulders and tossed it to the side.

"Mark, I don't know if I can do this," she said, through gasps.

He looked up, breathing heavily. Her eyes had adjusted enough that she could make out his features. The light filtering through the window glinted off his eyes.

"It's so good to feel you again, missy," he said.

She stiffened. "What? What did you say?"

"I said if you're sure. It's okay if you want to stop.'"

"No, that's not what you said. I heard you. I heard you!"

"I don't understand. What are you talking about?"

She pushed him off the bed. "Just…just go."

"But…What did I do?"

"Go. Leave me alone. Please."

The door opened and the light flipped on. Luke stood in the

doorway with Lindsay right behind him. "What's going on?" He took in the scene, saw Melissa, then quickly looked away. Melissa grabbed the sheet to cover herself.

"I don't know. She started freaking out," Mark said. His eyes lingered on the still-exposed top of her left breast. His eyes narrowed and he opened his mouth, then closed it.

Her scar. Melissa pulled the sheet up higher, making sure she was fully covered this time. "Please. I can't do this. I can't."

"Alright," Luke said. "Time to go."

"Okay, I'm going," Mark said. He picked up his shirt, then looked at Melissa; she looked away. "I'm sorry."

Lindsay pushed her way in and shut the door after Mark left. She sat down on the bed and hugged Melissa. "Are you okay?"

Melissa buried her head in Lindsay's shoulder and began to cry. "No," she said between sobs.

"Do you want to talk about it?"

"No."

They sat there for a few minutes, until Melissa's breathing was under control. She grabbed a tissue and blew her nose. "I...I wasn't ready. I thought I was. But I wasn't."

"It's okay. I'm sorry; I shouldn't have pushed you."

"It's not your fault. I was pushing myself." She took a deep breath. "I think I'm going to have a shower."

"Okay," Lindsay said. She hugged Melissa again, then stood up. "Call if you need anything."

"Thanks."

After Lindsay left, Melissa grabbed her robe and went to the bathroom. She turned the shower on to let the water heat up and stripped the rest of her clothes off. She surveyed her naked body in the mirror and ran her shaking hands over the angry, red scars on her breast. Initially, her doctor had said they would heal, but over time it became apparent that they weren't going away; so he suggested a plastic surgeon to repair the damage.

Melissa had considered surgery. Her parents even offered to pay for it. But she couldn't bring herself to do it. Yes, the scar was a reminder of what happened. And maybe that was too much for her mom, who teared up every time she saw it. But removing it wasn't going to change anything. The real damage wasn't what was done to her skin. The real damage was done to her being, her spirit, her…soul, for lack of a better term.

She felt the water to check the temperature, then opened the glass door to the shower and stepped in. She scrubbed her body everywhere; she could still felt the tingle of Mark's touch. She knew he wasn't really her attacker, that the whole thing was nothing more than a trick of the mind. But it didn't matter. She needed to feel clean.

And when she was done scrubbing her skin raw, she sat down on the tile floor, leaned against the wall, and cried.

TWENTY-FOUR
ALEX

THE FOLLOWING WEEK passed like a commercial break directly following a cliffhanger ending on a TV drama: Each day passed as yet another mostly ignored thirty second ad; background noise, nothing more. Notable only for the slow ticking of wasted time.

Alex felt like he had been lifted up and given a glimpse of the life he had always imagined. It had begun to change him, change his perspective. For a little while, the skeptic wasn't the only voice driving his thoughts.

But all good things, as they say, must come to an end. As rapid as the rise had been, he had been tossed aside even faster. And it hurt. It hurt more than he had ever expected. Not having someone was one thing; but having someone and then losing her was so much worse. The skeptic in him had been right all along.

Work had been even more onerous than usual. He didn't want to go. He wasn't actually sure *why* he went, other than out of pure habit. His boss Trudy was still sore at him for the outburst he had at his performance review meeting; on the rare occasion when the job forced her to speak to Alex, she was always terse and mercifully brief. Even Zane, his usually chipper and talkative co-worker, noticed Alex's foul mood. They had worked together long enough that he knew when Alex wanted him to *shut up*.

He felt like he was in limbo: Unsure of what to do, or where to go. Like he was waiting, waiting for something to happen. For what, he didn't know.

It was Friday afternoon. Alex was in the midst of dealing with yet another billing dispute when his phone began to ring. Normally he wouldn't have heard it; he always left it in his jacket with the ringer turned off. It was company policy: all employee cell phones had to be put on silent before they were brought into the call centre. But today, with his jacket casually tossed next to the computer monitor, Alex happened to hear the slight vibration of the phone against the table.

He reached over and pulled the phone out; the call display showed Emily. He checked the time: three-thirty, he still had an hour of work left.

"Excuse me, are you listening?" came a woman's voice from his headset.

He hadn't been. "Yes, yes, I'm still listening. I'm going to put you on hold a moment while I look into this for you."

"About ti— "

Alex pressed the hold button, cutting her off; then quickly answered his phone.

"Hello."

"Hi, it's Emily."

"Hey, what's up?" he said, trying to sound calm and collected.

"I was wondering if we could meet tonight."

"Yeah, sure, of course. What time?"

"Um, how about nine, at the cafe."

"Yeah, that works. I'll see you then."

"'Kay, bye."

He hung up the phone and took a deep breath. She wanted to see him. Did this mean she had changed her mind about what Rob said? Or had something else happened?

The beeping from his headpiece reminded him that he still had someone on hold. He looked at the time again: three thirty-five. He smiled, mood suddenly changed, and pressed the hold button again. "Hi, thanks so much for holding. I've gone through your account here, and even though this is technically not our policy to refund these charges, I was able to get approval to give you a one-time credit for the amount. How does that sound?"

"Oh, thank you! I really appreciate that," the woman said, sounding genuinely surprised. She should be; these types of overage charges weren't usually refunded. It was her fault for not understanding the service, but since he was in a good mood now he was willing to give her a break.

"Great, I'm going to put you on hold again for a minute while I get this put through, okay?"

"Okay!" she said.

Alex put her on hold again to work on the account. Of course, he hadn't exactly been honest with her when he implied that he had to fight for approval to credit her account. It was a tactic people used in call centres to make customers feel like they were on the same team: A customer who thought an agent was on their side—working *for* them, as opposed to *against* them—was less likely to freak out if bad news was delivered. It also helped excuse long absences. Alex had seen employees put customers on hold, go to the bathroom, then come back and say, hi, thanks for holding. I spoke with my manager and unfortunately.... They'd be in trouble if they ever got caught, of course, but it rarely happened.

He finished off the call with Kayla; then powered through five more customers before his shift finished. He logged out of the computer and packed his work headset into his backpack along with his lunch bag. As he put his coat on, he noticed that Zane was finishing up too. "Hey, have a good weekend dude," he said.

Zane perked up, catching Alex's changed mood. "Yeah, you too, man! Hey, some of us are going to the Alibi Room tonight. You interested in coming?"

Zane had been inviting Alex to hang out with his group of work buddies for years now. He wasn't sure if it was a real attempt at friendship, or if he felt the need to build a good working relationship since they worked side-by-side, forty hours a week. Alex had gone a couple of times. They were decent enough people, but they'd never really hit it off. He always felt like the odd man out. Likely a result of his own dismal social skills.

"Can't tonight, I've got plans. What about next week?"

"Sure, sounds good."

"Alright, see ya."

"Later."

Alex caught the elevator just before the doors closed, squeezing himself into the confined space with seven other people. He was the first one out of the elevator and, within moments, stepped out of the building, bravely pushing into the throng of pedestrians moving along the sidewalk. He made it to his bus stop a block down the road and ducked into the shelter. It was a five-minute wait until his bus arrived. He flashed his bus pass to the driver and sat down at an empty seat, setting his backpack down beside him. The other regular commuters, who he'd dubbed Cliff, Bill, Will, Jane and Mitch, all filtered in after him, spreading across the bus into different spots.

The doors shut just as the commuter he had dubbed Kate came running alongside the bus. Fortunately, the driver noticed her and opened the door. She looked around for an empty seat, her eyes stopping at the seat beside Alex for a moment before moving on. Alex realized his backpack was taking up the last seat, so he lifted it onto his lap and gestured for her to sit.

She looked at him, their eyes meeting for the briefest moment, then she turned away. She was cute, in a feline sort of way, with a thin neck, small mouth and big eyes. They had been riding the bus together for nearly two years, but had never sat together. She rarely sat with anyone; and when she did, it was always next to a female passenger.

Alex smiled, trying to look friendly. She had a look on her face like a stray cat, suspicious of its surroundings, ready to bolt at any moment. She didn't seem like the kind of person who trusted people. She shook her head slightly, her hands gripping her purse as if she thought Alex was planning to make a grab for it; then walked back to the front of the bus, where she latched onto a pole and stared studiously forward, ignoring the rest of the passengers.

Alex tried not to feel hurt, tried not to take it personally. He'd observed her for a long time, long enough to know she was a careful, private person. But for some reason it still bothered him. He had tried to be friendly, offered her a seat, smiled, and didn't do anything offensive; yet he still wasn't good enough. Was he really so horrible that a girl on a bus wouldn't even sit beside him? It reminded him of all the years of loneliness he'd suffered through.

He shook his head: That would all change soon. Tonight, he was going to fix things with Emily. And then…who knows?

The rest of the ride was uneventful as they passed tall buildings lined up like rows of dominoes, the bright sun glinting off their glass facades. He rang the bell for his stop and walked up to the door, bumping into Kate as he passed. He apologized, but she was in the middle of a phone call and completely ignored him. Five minutes later he was inside his apartment, tossing his dirty lunch dishes in the sink and searching the fridge for something to eat. In the end, he decided to go with the old faithful macaroni and cheese.

After eating, he cleaned up and went for a long shower. He brushed his teeth, did his hair, and dressed, determined to be as presentable as possible. He looked at the time: seven thirty. Still a long way to go, but he was already getting fidgety; so he left early, walked down to the Roca Cafe, ordered a coffee, and waited.

* * * * *

He didn't have to sit alone too long: At twenty to nine, he saw her blue Ford Focus park down the street from his window seat inside the cafe. He ordered a second coffee—medium with two creams, just the way she liked it—and met her out front.

"Hey. Oh, thanks," Emily said as Alex passed her the steaming cardboard cup. She nodded towards a bench down the street. Far enough from the cafe's outdoor seating so that none of the patrons there would overhear their conversation. "Let's sit over there."

Alex followed her to the bench and they sat down. They turned toward each other, knees almost touching, and sipped their drinks in silence. Alex fought back the fountain of words trying to spill from his mouth. He wanted to apologize, to explain himself, and beg for her forgiveness. But something told him he needed to wait. She had called him. This was her meeting, he needed to be patient.

She sat for a bit longer, shooting glances his way and chewing her lip. Alex had never seen her so nervous before; it was making *him* nervous.

"You know," she began, "when I married Rob, I never expected my life to turn out like this."

"What do you mean?" Alex asked.

She took a deep breath. "We've been together so long, I didn't realize things were changing. All my friends have either moved away, or we've drifted apart. I had friends at Sears too, but not good friends, you know? We lost touch after the layoffs, and that was it. Now…"

She paused to take another sip of coffee. "When you base your entire life around one person, how can you be surprised when you suddenly realize you've lost all your friends?"

Alex watched her struggle to put her thoughts into words. He had always imagined Emily as the kind of girl with a huge circle of close friends. She was the most likeable person he'd ever met! But right then, she looked lost and alone. His heart went out to her, he knew how that felt.

"I don't even talk to Phil very much anymore," she said. "A couple of times a year and that's it. He wasn't happy with the marriage; he and Nikki never liked Rob. They always said he was an asshole." She laughed.

Alex agreed with that assessment one hundred percent, but decided to keep his thoughts to himself for the time being.

She looked at Alex. "I'm sorry, Alex. I don't mean to lay all this on you, but I don't have anyone else to talk to."

"No, no. It's okay. You can talk to me."

She smiled. "Thank you. That means a lot to me."

She stopped to take a few more sips of the coffee. "Things haven't been great between Rob and me," she said. "We never talk anymore. We barely spend any time together. And he's always working late, out doing who knows what? It's like he's bored of me. He could be cheating for all I know. I think about that a lot. I even asked him, once, if he was. He got so mad; I spent the rest of the night crying. I just…I don't know what to do. I don't know how to make him happy anymore."

"That isn't your fault, though," Alex said. "That's his problem. You can't blame yourself."

Emily shook her head. Her eyes were wet. "I was worried because I haven't gotten pregnant yet, so I went to the doctor. They said there's something wrong with me. They said I can't have children. So you see: it *is* my fault." Her body began to shake. Glistening tears began to stream down her face. She pulled a tissue out of her purse and blew her nose.

Alex stared, afraid to make a move, but wanting so much to comfort her. He reached out slowly and placed his hand on her nearest shoulder; she grabbed it with one of her hands and leaned her head on it. Emboldened, Alex slid across the bench, feeling more self-conscious than he had at any other time in his life. Once he was beside her, he lifted his hand over her head and rested it on her far shoulder. It felt like the kind of move a guy would pull on his date at a movie theatre.

She leaned into him, still shaking, and rested her head on his shoulder. He caught a scent of rose and jasmine. It made him shiver. He felt guilty, but he couldn't help feeling aroused. He hoped she wouldn't notice.

It took a few minutes for her to calm down. When she spoke again, her voice was raw: "I haven't told Rob; I don't know what to say. I'm so worried he's going to leave me."

"No, no, you shouldn't be. Emily, you're such an amazing person. If he doesn't see that, then he really is an asshole."

She laughed, but her raw voice made it sound more like a forced croak. She sat up and wiped her eyes. Regretfully, Alex pulled his arm away and rested his hand in his lap. They were still very close; their legs were still touching. He didn't move.

"Thank you, Alex," she said. "But— "

"No buts," he said. "You're a beautiful, amazing person. Any man would be so lucky to have you." He could hardly believe the words coming out of his mouth. It sounded like they were coming from another person.

He reached up and brushed some stray hairs away from her eyes. He kept his hand there. Their faces were so close. "You know that, right?" he asked.

She smiled thinly, then nodded. It seemed like the space between them had evaporated. Her bright green eyes peered into his soul. He felt unmasked in front of them, exposed, free. It would be so easy to lean in a little more…just a little more.

Suddenly he was violently shoved back. "What are you doing?" Emily yelled.

"I…I'm…I…"

"Jesus, Alex. What the hell?" She stood up and backed away. "You kissed me!"

"I…I thought…"

"We're cousins!" she yelled, wiping her mouth in disgust. The look on her face was like daggers in Alex's heart.

"No, we aren't," he said desperately, trying to salvage the situation. "Not really."

She gave him a look of mixed horror and revulsion. "I can't believe…is this where you thought this was going? I'm married!"

"He's cheating on you!" Alex said, more anger in his voice than he had intended.

Emily looked like she had been slapped. "What do you mean?" she asked, clearly trying, but failing to control her voice.

Alex was breathing hard. It was amazing how a stressful situation could make the body react like it had just run a sprint. He took a breath. "Diamond isn't my girlfriend. She's an escort."

Emily tried to speak, but Alex cut her off, speaking quickly, the words coming out in a rush. "Rob knew her! That's why he was acting strange that night. He's been with her before. She told me he's been with lots of women. He uses them to entertain his clients for work."

Her mouth opened, then closed. She sat back down on the bench heavily. She looked…empty. "Go away."

"Emily, I'm so sorry." He reached towards her, trying to take her hand. She slapped him away.

"Leave me alone!" she screamed.

He stood up and ran, as fast as he could.

* * * * *

He ran until his legs felt like burning rubber. Fire coursed through his veins, and every rasping breath felt like needles ripping through his throat. With each passing step, his internal monologue became increasingly angry. *What was I thinking? How could I be so stupid? I'm such an idiot, such a fucking idiot.*

When he finally stopped, he leaned his full weight against a street lamp—doubled over and hacking continuously, struggling for breath. He felt like he should be coughing up blood, but somehow none came out.

After a few minutes of coughing and wheezing, Alex forced himself to start walking. He needed to get away from Emily, the café, and what had happened there. He tried to think about work, about TV, about anything else. But his mind kept coming back to the look of disgust on Emily's face after he had kissed her. That had been one of the most hurtful looks he had ever received in his life.

Is this what he had been waiting for? He had struggled all week in a sort of limbo, a strange feeling of being caught between action and decision; and if he'd waited a little longer, just a little longer, everything would have changed.

Well, he was done waiting. He was tired of suffering through a life of debilitating despair and loneliness. Tired of being the odd man out wherever he went, like being around him was some sort of chore. Most of all, he was tired of being rejected. Emily hadn't been the first person to push him away, but she would be the last.

Alex detoured into a convenience store near his place. He stalked up and down the aisles, picking at random items. He picked up a Coffee Crisp, it had been his favourite chocolate bar when he was a kid; he hadn't eaten one in years. He also grabbed a box of Nerds, another old favourite. He walked around to the back where the supplies were: motor oil, wiper fluid, coolant, and other automotive necessities lined the shelf, along with bottles of WD-40 and extension cords. He picked up an eight-foot long cord that looked about a half-inch thick; strong, and not likely to break. It would do.

He took his Coffee Crisp, Nerds, and extension cord to the front counter, where a bored-looking man who stunk of booze and cigarette smoke scanned Alex's items and tossed them into a white bag.

"That'll be seventeen ninety-five." His gravelly voice was like sandpaper to Alex's ears.

Alex gave him a twenty-dollar bill and picked up his bag; then dropped the change into the plastic Salvation Army donation box and left the store.

It took him less than five minutes to get home from there. By the time he sat down he had already finished his Coffee Crisp and was knocking back the box of Nerds.

When he was finished, he sat on his couch and stared at the corner of the room. Up on the ceiling, sticking out of the plaster, was a hook. When he had first looked at the unit, the landlord had informed him that the previous tenant had set up a punching bag in that corner, but if he wanted it removed it wouldn't be a problem. Alex hadn't bothered getting it removed. Now it stared at him from the corner, like a slightly cocked finger, beckoning him closer.

He pushed himself off the couch, walked over to his computer, loaded up the suicide note he had been working on for over three years, and printed it out. He read through it again, slowly, remembering how he felt as he typed it. Everything rushed back to him: losing his parents, living with his callous relatives—all of his life's anguish rolled into one rambling note.

He traced his finger over one of the sentences. *"Maybe the only coward is the person who can't do either."* It was true. He had been a coward his entire life, always afraid to commit to any one choice.

Well, he was done being a coward.

Alex propped the note up against his computer monitor, so it was easily visible. After that, he walked into his bathroom and pulled out his container of Aspirin. He unscrewed the top and poured out the contents: only seven pills. He took them into the kitchen, poured himself a glass of water and tossed the pills into his mouth. Three large gulps of water and the pills were successfully swallowed. Seven pills wasn't enough to do any damage, he knew that much; but it felt like the right thing to do, as much as anything could actually be considered *right* at this point.

Then he went back into the living room and pulled out his shiny new orange extension cord, ripping it out of its packaging and unravelling it. He dragged a chair across the room and positioned it underneath the ceiling hook; then climbed up and looped the cord around the hook. He knotted it off, making sure to loop the cord back on itself so that it wouldn't be too long; then made the noose at the other end. He wasn't an experienced noose-maker, by any means, but he was pretty sure what he had would work.

He yanked on the cord a couple of times to test his knot, made a few adjustments, and yanked again. It seemed like it would hold.

He looped the noose around his neck and looked around. The room looked different from up there. Everything seemed smaller, less important, and almost foreign, like it all belonged to some other person.

His heart was thumping, his breathing was heavy and, for the first time, he realized he was crying. He wiped his hand across his eyes and took a deep breath. He could do this. It would be over soon.

I'm not a coward.

Leaning to the left, he tilted the chair; then—with a sudden jerk to the right—the chair toppled. And Alex dropped.

TWENTY-FIVE
JOEL – PRESENT DAY

"HELLO, SON. IT'S been a long time."

Joel stared at his dad from the other side of the aisle, stunned. No, he decided, not *dad*; he was done calling him that. The man's name was Anson.

"Excuse me," said an elderly lady as she pushed past Joel. She stood in the middle of the aisle and surveyed packages of dinner buns for what felt like an hour, oblivious to the tension around her. Joel and Anson stood motionless, glaring at each other as the moment stretched.

Joel's mind swirled with questions. Why was Anson here? How did he find him? Was mom still safe?

"What are you doing here?" Joel asked when the lady finally left.

"What? I can't pay a visit to my long-lost son?"

Joel fought back the urge to spit. "I'm not your *son*," he said with derision, "not anymore."

Anson snickered. "You think you can un-become my kid? Your hate isn't strong enough for that. You are who you are."

"I've changed."

"Sure you have. Did you know your mom died?"

The words hit Joel like a fist to the gut. He struggled to breathe. "Wha...how?"

191

Anson ignored Joel's question. "Hmm, I can see from the look on your face that you didn't. That's a shame. You missed the ceremony, by the way. It was lovely. Your friend Uncle Frank was there too. Her death hit him really hard. Strange, considering she left him years ago. I guess he still loved her, even though she came running back to me."

Anson's words were like blows raining down upon Joel's head. He could hardly believe she was dead. And she'd left Frank? Why? Why did she go back to his da...to Anson? It didn't make sense.

"You're lying."

"Me? I've been many things in my day, but I've never been a liar, boy."

"I don't believe you."

"You can believe whatever you want. I'm telling you how it is."

"You did it, didn't you? You killed her."

Anson burst out laughing. "Really? You think I did this?" When no response was forthcoming from Joel, he continued: "No, it wasn't me. She had cancer. Nasty business, that was. She kept asking for you, though. Wanted to see you one last time."

Joel felt like his insides had been scooped out, leaving a giant expanse of nothing inside. "Why are you telling me this?" he asked. His voice was shaking.

Anson glared at him. "Don't you want to know? You cared so much back then, right before you disappeared."

"I still ca—"

"Oh, fuck off," Anson said, waving a dismissive hand, "Don't act like you need to apologize. I don't want your apology, boy."

"I'm not apologizing," Joel said angrily.

"Good," Anson gave him a feral smile.

"How did you even find me?"

"Wasn't hard. You know, there's a lot of information on the Internet. If you really wanted to hide, you should have changed your name. I know about you, your wife, and that little girl of yours. How old is she now?"

Joel felt his anger transform from a seething mass into a whipping torrent. "You stay the fuck away from my family," he said through clenched teeth. "I have a better idea, why don't you go die and leave us all the fuck alone."

Anson looked down at his maimed hand and squeezed it into a fist. "We have unfinished business, boy. I'm not going anywhere."

* * * * *

That night Joel sat in his study, lost in thought. Dim moonlight streamed through the window, glinting off the stainless steel Springfield 1911 in his hands. He ran his forefinger across the barrel, feeling the inscription: Springfield Armory. He caressed the logo on the copper-coloured hardwood grip, two crossing cannons inside a circle with a cannonball in between, and a flame on top. The bottom of the logo read *Since 1794.*

Killing people for over two hundred years, he thought, and shook his head ruefully. *But that isn't a fair judgement, is it?*

He was, after all, the one with the gun. And a gun is nothing if not a tool of the user, a victim of intent. *Guns don't kill people; people kill people.* That was the saying, and it seemed fair, especially now, with the weapon sitting in his hands and intent burning in his eyes like a barely constrained fire.

He lifted the weapon to his face, pressing the cold steel against his cheek. He closed his eyes and took a deep breath, moaning softly. *This is...* he struggled to find the right word: *a solution.* Yes, that sounded right. No argument, no negotiation; only cause and effect; this weapon and its function, a result.

Lowering it before him again, he stared hard at the gun. His fingers clenched tightly around the rubber grip. He turned it around, pointing at his face, losing himself in the inky blackness of the barrel. The safety was off, and a .45 calibre round— capable of ending his life with little more than a twitch of the thumb—sat in the chamber.

He imagined the shot. The explosive detonation as the gunpowder inside the bullet casing ignited and sped the projectile into his face at a killing velocity. The recoil from the shot would push the gun out of his uncomfortable reverse grip; so that even as the bullet tore through his skull, the weapon would be falling to the floor to land on its side, issuing a small tendril of smoke from its barrel.

The explosion of blood and brain matter from the back of his skull would paint the wall in an expressionist spatter pattern. Maybe someone could frame it, call it *Brain,* and hang it in an art gallery; then a bunch of puffed up upper-class assholes could argue over its hidden messages, all the while oblivious to the truth behind the macabre visual they so cheerfully dissected.

"It's a commentary on society," some might say. "The randomness of the image proves it. He's showing how we're all disconnected from each other."

"Oh no," others might argue. "There is a definite pattern here. See those dots? That's a line, and it means something; it definitely means something."

And if he could come back as a ghost, and see these people staring at what remained of his head, he would whisper in their ears: "It means fuck you." And maybe, just maybe, they would hear him; and their faces would darken with disquiet, but then they would move on. People always move on.

But not me, he thought. *I haven't moved on. I'm still in the same place I was all those years ago:sitting in a room with a gun, ready to decide a man's fate.*

He'd made that choice once, and he'd chosen wrong. He knew that now, had no doubt; the world would be a better place if he had shot and killed Anson Fischer that day. And if he had gone to prison for murder? Well, that probably would have made the world a better place too.

The return of his father had brought back many long-suppressed emotions; most notably, anger. He'd lived with it for so long that it had become a part of who he was, influencing his decisions, tainting every choice he made. Until Jenny, it was hard to think of any decisions he'd made that weren't in some way related to the burning rage inside of him. Still, was he really any different now? Past events leave an indelible imprint upon a person's soul; and while certain perceptions can be adjusted, that imprint will always remain.

He turned his attention away from the gun and looked out the window. From over halfway up the condo tower, the view commanded a wide array of sights. He could see inside neighbouring buildings, could see people watching TV, playing video games, eating supper, or like him—sitting and staring.

He watched, and he hated them all.

They sat there, oblivious, lost in their own little lives. Stupid grins plastered on their faces like an endless procession of toy-store dolls.

None of these people had suffered like he had. None of them understood how lucky they were to live in their little bubbles of lies.

He wanted to burst those precious bubbles. He wanted to stand over them and see the look in their eyes when they finally realized the truth of this world.

A knock at the door startled him out of his reverie.

"Yes?"

Another knock; Jenny's voice came from the other side of the door. "Joel? Can we talk?"

He closed his eyes and took a deep breath, then put the gun in a drawer and opened the door. "Hi, honey." She stepped inside and he shut the door behind her. "What's up?" he asked.

She picked up a photo of the three of them in front of the totem poles at Stanley Park: A happy family doing the kind of thing happy families do. "I wanted to see how you were doing. You seemed…stressed…when you got home from work today."

"Yeah, I…saw someone at work today."

"Who? Someone fr—"

"It was my father."

"Oh," Jenny said quietly. He had told her about his relationship with his father, enough for her to understand the kind of impact he'd had on Joel's life; but she didn't know everything. "What did he want?" she asked.

"He told me my mom died."

"Oh, Joel," Jenny said. She put the photo down and walked up to him. Her green eyes were wet and full of compassion. "I'm so sorry."

They embraced and, for a moment, Joel felt his anger begin to drain away, replaced with…sadness. He grasped at those retreating threads of anger and held on to them, wrapping himself in it like a spider's web. It was better than the alternative. He'd rather fuel his hate than sit in misery, crying over the shattered relationship he had with his parents.

"It's okay," he said, separating from Jenny. "It had to happen eventually, right?"

"Don't say that, Joel. She was your mother."

"I know, but what am I supposed to do? I haven't seen her in, what, ten years? Am I supposed to cry about someone I probably would never have seen again?"

"Don't be that way; you can't know that."

"I *do* know that. Did I tell you she went back to him? In spite of everything he did to her, to *us*, she still went crawling back. What was she thinking? It's *fucking stupid.*"

"Shhh! You'll wake Hayley!"

"Sorry," he said, lowering his voice. "But it's ridiculous. How could she do that?"

"Maybe she had a reason, maybe—"

"No!" Joel said, raising his voice again. He took a deep, calming breath. "He said it was cancer, but I'm sure he had something to do with it. I just...feel it."

"Joel, come on, be reasonable. Don't work yourself up. I know he's an awful person, but he can't be..."

"A murderer?" Joel said, finishing her thought. "I don't know, Jen. I really don't. You don't understand."

"Then help me. Help me understand. All I know is what you've told me, which isn't much."

"I...I don't want to talk about this," he said. He glanced at the clock on his desk. "I need to go."

"What? Go where? It's almost eleven o'clock!"

"For a walk. I need to clear my head." He started to open the door but Jenny put her hand on it. She looked scared.

"Joel?"

He realized why she had a look on her face like she was about to be thrown off a cliff. "I'm not going to buy anything. I haven't used in five years; I'm not about to start again now."

She put her free hand on his arm. "Please, stay here with me."

"I can't. I'm sorry."

He pulled the door and Jenny's arm dropped away. She followed him to the front door and watched silently as he put on his jacket. He put his hand into the inside pocket where his keys sat. "Oh, I left my keys in the office," he said.

Thankfully, she stayed by the front door while he went back to the office. He pulled open the drawer housing his gun and picked it up. He reached behind and stuck it into the waistband of his pants, suppressing a shiver when the cold steel touched his lower back. From the drawer, a glint of light from a four-inch fixed-blade hunting knife caught his eye;

he'd almost forgotten he owned it. He pulled it out and tested the edge. Still sharp. *Better be safe than sorry*, he thought, sliding the knife into its sheath before dropping it deep inside an inner-jacket pocket.

He met Jenny back at the door with his keys in his hands.

"Don't be long," she said.

"I won't." He kissed her on the forehead. "Go to sleep. I'll be fine."

She looked skeptical. "I wish you would stay and talk to—"

"Jen, please."

She bit her lip. "Okay. I love you."

"Love you too," Joel said. He considered saying more. He even considered staying home and explaining everything, like she wanted. But he couldn't do that; at least not now, maybe not ever. So he quashed the words before they could even form and walked out the door.

Anson would be waiting. It had to end, this *thing* between them, whatever the cost.

TWENTY-SIX
MELISSA

"HEY, MELISSA. THERE'S a delivery for you," Tam called out.

"For me? What is it?"

"Come see."

Melissa sighed. She was knee-deep in reorganizing the storage area and wasn't interested in distractions. "I'll be out in a bit."

She continued her work, peacefully sorting clothing, shoes, and makeup for another ten minutes before Tam interrupted her again.

"Hurry up, we're waiting for you," Tam said, standing in the doorway with her arms crossed.

"Fine, geez," Melissa said. She extricated herself from the stacks she was working on and walked out onto the store floor. "I don't know why you're in such a hu—" She stopped and stared at a large basket of flowers that sat on the counter beside one of the tills; a white card with her name written in ornate letters stuck out the side. "What's that?"

"Flowers," Amrit said with a bounce. "For you."

Melissa frowned. "Why?"

Amrit's face screwed up. "I don't know, why don't you read the card?"

Melissa picked the card out of the basket and opened it. The note inside read:

Melissa
Can we talk, please?
Mark

"So, who is it? Does it say? Do you have a secret admirer?" Amrit fired off the questions in quick succession.

"Yeah, I know him."

"Oooooooh, so it's a him. Ilsa, you owe me five bucks!"

"Really?" Ilsa asked, disappointment obvious in her voice.

"What are you talking about?"

"Ilsa thought it would be from a girl," Amrit said.

"Why?" Melissa asked, feeling lost.

"Ilsa thought maybe you played for the other team," Tam answered.

"I don't know what that means."

"Don't worry about it," Amrit said, stifling a laugh. "So what does the note say?"

"Nothing, really. He wants to talk."

"Who's 'he'?"

"Oh." She hesitated. "His name is Mark. We met at a birthday party on the weekend."

"Reeeaaaally," Amrit said.

"Don't get any ideas. It's not like that," Melissa said.

"Suuuuuure. Hey, Tam, do you know anyone who sends flowers when it's *not like that*?"

"Nope."

"That's what I thought," Amrit said. She bent over, stuck her nose in the flowers, then let out an exaggerated breath. "Ah, these smell wonderful. Yeah, it's definitely *not like that*."

"Okay, okay. I get it," Melissa said. "Maybe he has other ideas. But nothing happened between us." She picked up the basket and carried it to the back room, stopping just before the door closed. "Hey, wait a sec. Does Ilsa think I like girls?"

A burst of laughter sounded from the store floor. "Yes," Tam called out. "But can you blame her?"

"No," Melissa said back. "But who says she's wrong? Maybe I play for both teams. Did you ever think of that?"

She smiled and left those words hanging in the air as she shut the door.

* * * * *

Why did you send flowers to my work??? Melissa typed. She hit the send button and waited for a response. She didn't have to wait long.

Because I wanted to talk to you but you've been ignoring my texts.

One of Melissa's various regrets about that night was exchanging phone numbers with Mark. He'd been texting her multiple times a day since the party. She'd been just as persistent at ignoring him. *But why send them here?*

The guy at the flower place said he doesn't recommend sending flowers to condos, usually ends up in delivery delays. You're welcome btw.

Melissa frowned, then replied: *Thx. They're nice.*

Mark replied with a smiley face.

What did you want to talk about? Melissa asked.

I wanted to see how you are.

I'm fine. Is that all?

You don't have to be rude.

Melissa's eyes widened. It seemed he had a lot more backbone over text than when he was sitting beside her.

Another text from him came through. *I'm sorry, that was rude of me.*

Well, maybe not a *lot* more backbone.

I probably shouldn't say anything, but Luke told me you had problems in the past with men. If I had any idea I wouldn't have come on so strong. I feel awful about it.

Melissa tilted her head back and groaned. "Seriously, Luke? What the hell?"

I understand if you need some time to yourself. But I really wanted to tell you I was sorry and I'd love if we could be friends.

This was the problem with guys like Mark. It was hard being angry at them when they were so insufferably nice.

It's fine, she texted back. *Let's forget it ever happened, ok?*

Well, maybe not all of it. He followed that up with a winking emoticon.

The switch from somber to humour was jarring, but Melissa was happy to move on. *Maybe not. But don't get any ideas. We're just friends right now.*

Haha. That works. So how about we go for a drink some time? As friends, of course.

Before she even had time to respond another message came through.

I mean coffee or tea. Not booze. I swear I'm not trying to get you drunk again haha.

You better not be. Yeah, maybe this weekend. We'll see.

Great! I'll see you this weekend.

Melissa put her phone down. Did she really just make plans for the weekend? That hadn't been her intention when she texted him. But then again, she didn't really have a plan at the time.

She wondered if she should be angry at Luke for talking to Mark. In the past, she would have been more than ready to give him a piece of her mind. Now? Now she felt tired: tired of dealing with it alone; tired of hiding; tired of her own weakness. So maybe she would talk to Luke, but instead of ripping him a new asshole, as she might normally be inclined to do, maybe she should just thank him for caring.

She was starting to realize that life was a lot easier with friends.

* * * * *

A string of late customers left Melissa in a rush to close the store. She blew through the closing meeting with the girls with only a cursory look at the numbers. Melissa knew that when Lynn wasn't running the meeting, the other girls hardly paid any attention. The numbers looked pretty good anyway, so she saw no reason to waste time.

After locking the money in the safe and checking that everything was in order, she finally left. She checked the time on her phone to see if she could make the twenty-two bus. It would be close.

She had been walking fast, but when her bus drove by, she broke into a run. "Don't make me wait for the next one," she said, her voice reflecting a preemptive frustration at the possibility of not catching her ride home. It was only ten minutes until the next bus came through, but missing a bus had this inherent aggravation factor, like buying a lottery ticket where every number is off by one.

The bus stopped ahead of her to let a group of people on, then closed the door. "Wait, dammit, I'm coming." She waved, trying to get the driver's attention. She heard the bus shift into gear; the brake lights turned back on and the door opened.

"Thanks," she said when she reached the door.

"No problem," the bus driver said, smiling.

Melissa dropped a ticket into the fare box and started walking down the aisle looking for an empty seat. She had started to think that there might only be standing room, when she spotted a seat with a backpack on it next to a guy who rode the same bus with her every day. Privately, she had dubbed him The Creeper, because she could always feel his eyes on her. He seemed like one of those people who love to stare, but hated to be caught. He usually sat at the back where he could see and watch everyone else. When he wasn't watching people, his eyes were usually firmly directed at the floor.

Noticing her, he lifted his backpack from the seat and put it in his lap; smiling, he gestured for her to sit down. It was a nervous smile, and it caught her off guard. They'd travelled on the same bus for who knows how long, and that was the first time she'd ever witnessed a wisp of emotion from him.

Still, she didn't feel comfortable sitting beside him: he was The Creeper, so she shook her head and turned away, even though she could see the look of utter hurt on his face. Like a child who had been given the news—all at once— that Santa isn't real, the Easter Bunny is a myth, and his parents were splitting up. It was enough to cause her to question her characterization of him.

But not enough to make her sit down with him. Not this time, anyway. Maybe next time.

She stood near the front of the bus and held on to a pole for balance. Halfway home, she heard her phone ringing. She dug it out of her purse and answered: "Hello?"

"Melissa." It was Lindsay.

Something about her tone was off. "What's wrong?"

"It's Lacey. She's in the hospital."

"What? What happened?"

"She tried to kill herself, slit her wrists." She could hear Lindsay blowing her nose; she'd been crying.

"Oh my God. Is she okay?"

"I think so. They said she needed a blood transfusion, but she's stable now."

"I can't beli...why? Why would she do that? I thought she was doing better. She was going to meetings, she had a sponsor...I don't understand." The bus came to a stop and the guy she called The Creeper bumped her on his way out. She hardly noticed.

"I know. I don't understand either. Something must have happened. Visiting hours are until eight tonight. I think we should go see her."

"Yes, of course. Are you home right now?"

"Yeah," Lindsay said.

"Good. I'll be there in a couple of minutes. We can grab a bite, then head over to see her."

"Alright, see you in a few."

* * * * *

It was half-past seven when Melissa and Lindsay arrived at the hospital. Lacey, who'd been watching TV, turned it off when they entered.

"Wow, look who's here," she said.

"Hey, Lace," Melissa said. "How you doing?"

Lacey raised her bandaged hands in the air. "I'm doing fine. How about you?"

Melissa winced. "Sorry."

Lindsay sat down on the bed and hugged Lacey. "We were so worried about you." She pulled away but kept her hands on Lacey's shoulders. Tears welled in her eyes and her words began to flood out of her. "Don't you ever do that again, do you hear me? I know we don't talk much anymore, but you know you can call us, right? We're always here for you. Just call if you need to talk; we can help you work things out. We want you to be okay so this doesn't happen again."

Lacey opened and closed her mouth a few times, but couldn't get a word in edgewise through Lindsay's increasingly incoherent stream of babble. Eventually, her words merged with her sobs and she hugged Lacey again, who sat there with a guilty expression on her face.

"I'm sorry," Lindsay said, when she was able to speak again. "I wanted to make sure you knew…"

"I know," Lacey said. "I know."

Melissa put her hand on Lindsay's shoulder. "Hey, Lins, do you think you could do us a favour and grab a bottle of water? I saw a vending machine down the hall."

"Yeah," Lindsay said, wiping her eyes. "I'll be right back."

"She wears her heart on her sleeve, that one," Melissa said as soon as Lindsay shut the door behind her. She sat down in a chair on the far side of Lacey's bed.

"Yeah, she can be a bit emotional," Lacey said.

"But you know, I think we could learn from her. She doesn't hide her feelings, she lays them out there for everyone to see instead of hiding behind some sort of fake stoicism. I wish I was more like that. I think we'd all be better off if we stopped hiding all the time."

Lacey looked down at her hands and didn't say anything.

Melissa gave her a few moments, before asking the question they both knew was coming. "What happened?"

Lacey let out a breath that she'd been holding, licked her lips and shook her head slightly. "Where do I even start? You know what it was like when I was drinking, how bad I was. When I finally decided to quit, it was so hard. I didn't know how to function in a world where I wasn't drinking. Giving up alcohol was like sawing off an arm, only worse; it was like a part of my soul was being torn off, bit-by-bit."

"Then I met Richard. He was so amazing and kind. Do you remember him? He was my sponsor; you met him once."

"I remember," Melissa said.

"He introduced me to the beauty and meaning of God. He made me feel beautiful, special. I felt whole when I was with him. I don't know any other way to explain it, but that's how it was."

"I didn't even question it when he said we should make love. I trusted him. He said it would bring us closer to God, that in our moment of bliss we would be able to see and understand Him in a way we never could otherwise. And I believed him…I believed him."

Lindsay returned and shut the door silently behind her. She filled a plastic cup with water and handed it to Lacey, who nodded her thanks and took a sip.

"So we made love. And he was…so convincing, you know?

Eventually, I convinced myself that I could see God too. It was…magic. Like, an extraordinary feeling of being together, and connected. After a while, I got as addicted to that feeling as I'd ever been to alcohol."

"Then," she laughed softly to herself, as if she was telling a joke, "he left. Told me he had to go to Toronto—to be with his family—if you can believe it. Then *poof*," she made a gesture. "He was gone and out of my life."

"That's…horrible," Melissa said.

"What a bastard," Lindsay said.

"I felt so alone. It was even worse than when I stopped drinking. I wanted to die. I kept searching for that feeling, the feeling that would make me whole again. And I thought I'd found it…with someone else…but I was wrong. I don't know how I could have been so stupid." She started to cry.

Melissa and Lindsay shared a helpless look. What do you say to a story like that?

"I'm so sorry, Lacey."

Lacey looked at Melissa; her wet eyes bore into her. "*You* understand though, right? You know how this feels."

Melissa shifted in her seat. "Um, I don't know—"

"I know it's not the same as what happened to you, and I'm not trying to compare; but you were raped. And…in a way, I feel like I was too. But what's worse is that I let it happen, over and over again. Just thinking about it makes me want to die."

After years of referring to what had happened as *the attack* or *the incident*, it was disconcerting to hear someone say the word *rape* so openly. It had a stigma attached to it and hearing it made her uncomfortable; like someone was pointing out everything that was wrong with her life. *But why should it feel that way? I should be able to handle this by now, shouldn't I? Shouldn't I be able to say or hear the word rape without cringing?*

"You're right. I was," she hesitated, "raped. It was horrible and it did change me. So, I guess I do understand, a little, how you're feeling."

"How do you deal with it? How can you keep on living?" Lacey asked.

The way Lacey looked at Melissa, with such desperation, made her heart break. "I don't know. I don't know if I really am dealing with it.

There are days I wonder if that's even possible."

"But you're still here and getting on with your life."

"I am. But sometimes I wonder. Sometimes I feel like I'm still in that alley." She realized that none of what she was saying was helpful. If anything, her words might even be making the situation worse. "Not as often, anymore, but I guess I realize now that it's a part of me, a part of who I am, and that there's nothing I can do about that."

Lacey looked away from Melissa. She seemed disappointed. "I don't know if I can live that way."

"Don't say that," Lindsay said.

"I'm sorry," Melissa said. "I wish I had all the answers, but I don't. I look back now, and I realize I had no idea what I was doing. It's like I spent years in this fog where I let this one thing define my life, and now I'm waking up to the reality of it. I spent so much time waiting for something to happen, some sign to appear, telling me that I was going to be okay. But I realized I can't waste my life waiting for some sort of revelation. If I want something, I have to work at it, make it happen.

"What I wish, though, is that I hadn't spent so much time feeling afraid. I was so scared and ashamed. I funneled my energy into trying to find the person who raped me. I thought if I could find him, and make him pay, that it would bring closure. But I was wrong. All I was doing was using it as a way to keep from dealing with what happened. I wasn't facing my problem: I was avoiding facing myself. And now, well, now I wish I had been willing to accept the help my friends and family were offering; instead, I pushed them away. But now I realize I can't deal with this alone." She looked at Lacey and held her gaze. "You can't deal with this alone."

Lindsay reached over and held Lacey's hand. "That's what we're here for, Lace."

Lacey nodded. "Thank you." She wiped her eyes with her free hand and forced a smile. Her eyes were still sad, desperate, and exhausted; but for the first time since they'd arrived, Melissa saw what looked like hope.

* * * * *

"I'm going for a walk," Melissa said, after spending three hours restlessly pacing in her room.

"What do you mean?" Lindsay asked from the couch, interrupting the show she was watching. "What about everything you said earlier?"

"It's not like that. I'm not…searching. I need time to think. I'm going stir-crazy in here."

"It's pretty late, Melissa. Shouldn't you wait until tomorrow?"

"It's fine; I still have my bear spray. I'll be safe."

Lindsay turned off the TV and pushed herself off of the couch. "Okay, wait for me to get ready."

Melissa started to laugh. "You don't have to come with me. Honestly, I won't be gone long."

Lindsay stood there and sighed. "Are you sure? I mean, I know this is what you do, but especially after tonight, what with Lacey and everything. I thought—"

"I know, but I figured since I couldn't sleep, I might as well go for a walk to clear my head."

Lindsay stared at her for a moment, then sighed again. "Fine, but if you're gone for more than an hour, I'm calling your brother."

Melissa laughed again. "Okay, deal."

TWENTY-SEVEN
RICHARD

THE MORRISSEY PUB, which Richard and his friend had discovered by accident one day during training, had since become their favourite hangout: their haven, a place to get away from work and relax for a little while.

Richard wasn't relaxed this particular afternoon, but he sure wanted to be.

A glass of Crown Royal was on the table in front of him. He sat there, slowly turning it around, back and forth, watching the liquid swirl in the glass. He hadn't had any, not yet. But he wanted to, badly. He wasn't exactly sure why he hadn't drunk it yet. What was holding him back?

"Are you going to stare at that all day?" someone asked.

Richard looked up, surprised to see Lee, his former friend and current nemesis.

"I'm not in the mood right now, Lee."

Lee ignored him and sat down on the other side of the table. "You know, I heard you got sent to AA after having it out with a reporter."

"Yeah, so?"

"Just saying. So you gonna drink that?"

Richard gave him a hard look. "I haven't decided yet."

Lee looked like he was biting his cheek. "It's a damn shame what happened with that girl," he finally said. "A damn shame. You know—"

"I don't want to talk about this, Lee."

"It was nothing personal, Richard. All they wanted was the facts. If it hadn't have been me, it would have been someone else."

"You were my friend."

"Then, I guess it's bad luck that I got fingered to be their expert, isn't it?" Lee said.

"Yeah, I guess so."

Lee took a drink from his beer. "A couple of years ago I had this call; a guy overdosed and his girlfriend called it in. So we get there and the guy is on the floor, foam coming out of his mouth. And the woman is screaming. She looked about a half-step away from an OD as well.

"So we resuscitate this guy, and wouldn't ya know it, he's some sort of big shot dealer. The first thing the son of a bitch does when he sees us overtop of him is pull a knife out of his pocket and stab me in the stomach. Then he takes a swipe at my partner John, who barely dodges the knife. So I'm lying on the floor bleeding out and this guy, who knows where he got all this energy, starts beating the shit out of the poor woman, calling her a stupid whore for calling the cops.

"Obviously, we're not the cops; but he's so messed up he doesn't know the difference. So John takes a run at him and they tussle on the floor for a minute. Somehow the guy comes out on top, but he lost his knife so he can't finish it. By then, the girl's screaming brought some other people in, and once he sees the odds, he takes a run for the window and jumps out. No lie; the guy smashes right through, falls two stories, and lands on the pavement. Then he gets up again and takes off."

Richard stared at Lee, mouth hanging open. He'd never heard about this. "Holy shit, man. Just…wow. Are you serious?"

Lee lifted his shirt up to show the grisly scar on his left side. "Yeah, I'm serious."

"But what happened? Why didn't I hear about this?"

"The guy got away. It was an embarrassment, so they covered it up. The woman was a meth-head prostitute, so that wasn't going anywhere. Either she didn't know anything, or she was too scared to speak up. But that's not even the best part."

"Seriously? What else could happen?" Richard asked.

Lee laughed to himself and took another swig of beer. "I was out for about a month. Then my first week back, guess who I find coked up in an alley."

"No way," Richard said quietly.

"Same guy, half dead, suffering from another overdose. John and I looked at him and seriously considered walking away. I wanted to. I really did. The world would be a better place, right?"

Richard didn't disagree, but couldn't say so out loud. Their job was to save, not decide who to save.

Lee shook his head and smiled. "We didn't, though. Walk away, that is. We tied the bastard up and brought him back to life for the second time. And if he showed up at the police station with a few extra bruises, well, who's to say where they came from?"

Richard nodded. "Can't blame anyone for that."

"Nope," Lee said.

"Why didn't you tell us? We would have been there for you."

"Wasn't allowed. Still not allowed."

"So why tell me now?"

"Because you looked like you needed to hear it."

Richard didn't have a response to that.

"So, you're not the only one who's had a shitty go of it. I've spent my entire career working the Downtown Eastside while you, the golden child of the training class, got a cakewalk gig working south of False Creek. So you fucked up. We all have. Shit happens, man. It sucks, but that's the way it is."

"Did you come here to give me shit?"

Lee sighed. "No, I actually had something else to tell you; but you looked so damned morose, I thought I'd cheer you up with my story of woe."

"Thanks," Richard said without a hint of sarcasm. It actually had made him feel a little better, in a backwards sort of way. "So what did you need?"

"Well, we picked up a woman today who tried to kill herself: got drunk and slit her wrists. She's fine. She's over at St. Paul's. Funny thing, though, she kept asking for some named Richard. 'Where's Richard? Richard needs to save me.' Isn't that strange?"

"Yeah," Richard said. His heart had dropped as soon as Lee began the story. He knew it was Lacey. It had to be.

"I know there are thousands of Richards out there; but I had this feeling, like I knew who she meant. And I can tell from the look on your face that I guessed right."

"Did you find her ID? If her name is Lacey, then yeah."

"Bingo," Lee said.

Richard shook his head and sighed. He could hardly believe she had attempted suicide. Was it a cry for help? An attempt to get his attention? He couldn't live with himself if she died because of him. It would be too much.

"Thanks, Lee," he said.

"No problem." Lee looked concerned. "Is there something you need to talk about?"

"No." He smiled at Lee, surprised at the realization that he was sitting with a friend once again. Sometimes, a friend can come from the most unlikely place.

He stood up, extended his hand to Lee, and they clasped hands. "Thanks again," Richard said. "I hope..." He struggled with the words.

"Forget about it. The past is the past."

Richard left, leaving his full glass of Crown Royal on the table.

* * * * *

Richard had to work that night, but he was able to convince James to make a stop at St. Paul's Hospital so he could check in on Lacey. It was late, and visiting hours had long since ended; but he was able to talk his way in, a perk of being in the business.

He opened the door to Lacey's room and walked over to the bed. She was hooked up to an IV and blood pressure monitor, and her eyes were closed. The slow beeping sound of the monitor echoed in the sparsely furnished room.

"Lacey," he said quietly. She stirred at the sound of his voice.

He walked closer and called her name again. Her eyes fluttered open. After a moment she turned her head away from him and spoke, "What are you doing here?"

"I came to check on you. I was worried."

"Don't be," she said. "I'm fine."

"Are you, though? Why would you—"

"It was a mistake. I guess I got a little crazy."

"You were asking for me, you said I had to save you."

She turned back to him, eyes wide. "You? What makes you think I was asking for you?"

"They said you were asking for Richard. Who else would—" he stopped when she began to laugh. "What?"

Still laughing, she shook her head at him. "God! You're so arrogant. You think this is all about you."

"Isn't it? You said my name. You asked for me."

"No, Richard. I was asking for someone else."

"What? Then who?" he asked.

She closed her eyes and turned her head away again. Her lips pressed together tightly. She was holding back tears.

Richard suddenly realized who she was referring to. "No. You said he's in Toronto. There's no way you were asking for him."

"Does it even matter?" she said, voice cracking. The tears she'd been fighting so hard to hold back broke free, tracing wet lightning bolts down her face. "It's over. Him, you. It's all over."

"No, no. It's not over. We can still be friends. I'm here for you, let me help."

She looked at him with squared shoulders and red-rimmed eyes, and took a deep breath. When she spoke, her voice was steady. "I don't want your help. I can't be around you anymore, Richard. When I look at you all I can think of..." She paused, shaking her head slightly. "I can't get past this. Not with you around."

"What do you mean? I want to help."

"Then leave. And never come back." She looked at him with grim determination. She was serious.

Her words were like a hot branding iron on his skin. But they made sense. She would never heal with him around. He had been a part of her downward spiral, a piece of the addiction.

Alcoholics are taught to remove temptation, to pour their stock of booze down the drain and throw away the bottles. That was him, now. To move forward, she had to leave him behind. If he was serious about helping her, he would need to accede to her wishes.

He grabbed her hand and squeezed it. "Okay," he said. "I

understand."

She wiped her eyes with her free hand and said nothing.

He walked to the door and turned around before leaving. His heart felt like it was skipping beats. It was hard to breathe. He forced out his final words to her: "Good luck."

She nodded and gave him one last smile. As he closed the door he heard her exhale and begin to cry.

He sighed and walked away to where James was waiting. They still had half a night of work ahead of them.

TWENTY-EIGHT
ALEX

ALEX STOOD IN a bright meadow; an array of multicoloured flowers and short, green grass, blanketed the undulating hills that rolled into the distance. The entire sky was a deep, unchanging shade of blue; like something from a child's drawing, with not a wisp of cloud in sight, and a large, yellow sun in the centre. The sweet fragrance of spring filled his nose: the smell of wet loam and grass, mixed with daisies, poppies, clover and marigolds. There was no sound, as if a preternatural stillness had settled over the landscape: no birds chirping, no insects buzzing; no wind rustling. It was just him, standing in a cone of perfect silence.

Alex.

He spun around, searching for the source of the soft whisper, but he didn't see anything

Alex.

It came from everywhere, and yet nowhere. As if instead of an external source, the call came from within. He turned again, scanning the meadow, continuing to search.

In the distance, atop one of the hills, stood two people. It looked like a man and a woman. The woman was waving.

He started walking in that direction. He couldn't recognize the faces; they were blurred, as if drawn by an artist who hadn't decided on their identities. As he neared, their features resolved and, piece by piece, the two faces that he knew better than any others in the world came into focus; perfect, unchanged from the last picture they had posed for, a picture he had spent countless hours looking at since the accident.

"Mom! Dad!" he called.

His mom smiled and continued to wave. He began to run towards her.

Alex.

"I'm coming!" He ran faster, the landscape whipped by in a blur; but for some reason, he wasn't getting any closer. He pushed harder, grunting with the effort. The world stretched, pulling them away. He felt like he was running on the world's longest treadmill, and the speed kept pushing higher.

They were farther away now, their faces began to change. His mother opened her mouth to scream, black scribbles covered her face; she reached out to him.

He stumbled and fell face first into the grass. He sat up, ears ringing, while the world around him spun, like he was on some sort of a carnival ride. He shook his head to try and clear it, but it didn't help.

Al-ex.

The call was different now, taunting, and growing louder. Dozens of voices mixed together, calling to him; indistinguishable shadows formed all around him, carrying large drums that they banged repeatedly.

Al-ex. Bang, bang, bang. Al-ex.

The shadows were everywhere now, stacked one on top of the other, so that the sun disappeared behind the dark void of their large faces, dimming the entire meadow. The banging of the drums reverberated in his skull. He bent into a fetal position and covered his ears. But it didn't help, as before, the sound was coming from within.

Al-ex. Bang, bang, BANG.

* * * * *

"Alex!" a muffled voice called, followed by the sound of knocking. "Alex!"

Alex opened his eyes. He was on the floor of his apartment, covered in bits of drywall. Directly above him, a hole in the ceiling exposed a beam; thin strips of wood jutted out from the ragged hole where the ceiling hook used to be.

God, his head hurt. He felt like someone had tethered his neck to a horse; then dragged him up the side of a mountain. He put a hand to his neck, the cord was still there. He struggled for a moment to loosen it and pulled it off his head; the skin on his neck burned where it had been wrapped. As soon as it was off, he rolled over and began to cough violently, his burning lungs sucking in life-giving air.

"Alex!" the voice outside his door called again, followed by more banging. The sound bounced inside his skull, slicing through his brain matter like a sharp knife. He held his head and groaned.

Slowly, he struggled to his feet and stumbled to the door. He looked through the peephole; it was Emily. She was leaning toward the door, listening for sounds.

"I can hear you," she said. "Please, open the door."

Alex sighed. She was the last person he wanted to talk to right then. He opened the door a crack. "What do you want?"

"Alex…what's wrong with your voice?" she asked. "Can you just let me in? We need to talk."

"Why? I think we've said all we needed to say."

"No, we haven't." She pushed on the door, but he held it firm. "Please, I came all the way here."

"I didn't ask you to," he said. "How did you get in anyway?"

"I followed one of your neighbours in; I told them you were expecting me. And your unit number is listed on your mailbox in the lobby. It wasn't that hard."

"They shouldn't have done that."

"You weren't answering your phone, I was worried. Are you going to make me stand out here all night?"

He considered. The idea had some appeal.

"I'm not leaving," she said.

He sighed and pulled the door open the rest of the way.

She walked in and immediately noticed the mess on the living room floor. "Jesus, what happened?" she said, turning to Alex. Then she saw his neck. "Oh my God, Alex." She reached towards him. "What did you—"

He pushed her hands away. "Why don't you sit down; I'll get you a glass of water."

She nodded, eyes watering, and did what he asked. She sat down on the couch, hands in her lap, watching him. He filled two glasses and brought them into the living room, handing one to Emily before sitting down with his own. He took a sip; the cool water flowing down his throat felt amazingly soothing, like putting aloe vera on a burn. He realized his glass was already empty and got up to refill it. He could feel her eyes follow him, filled with hurt, confusion, even anger. Her intense look weighed on him like a granite block: crushing, suffocating. It demanded a truth he didn't want to share, didn't know if he *could*.

After sitting down again, he began to watch her. She looked at the corner with the overturned chair, extension cord, and damaged ceiling. Looking back at him, her face was tense, and her eyes burned with questions. When she raised her glass to her lips, her hands trembled.

Finally, she spoke: "I...I came here to apologize. I—"

"Why? I did something stupid. I deserved it."

She shook her head, red face scrunching up like she was holding back a sneeze. "No, Alex. You didn't. I'm so...I'm so sorry if I hurt you. I really didn't—" He could tell this wasn't the first time she'd cried that night.

"I hurt you," he cut in. "I'm the one who kissed you. I'm the one who threw Rob's cheating in your face." He paused for a moment, letting his own words sink in. He had been so focused on how bad *he* felt, that he hadn't considered how Emily might be feeling. A wave of guilt washed over him. "I'm the one who should be sorry."

She lifted her hand, gesturing towards the ceiling and, in a voice that was barely a whisper, asked, "Why?"

"Why kill myself?" he asked, not wanting to dance around the topic. "Because I hate my life, I hate myself, and I can't stand the thought of living anymore. I'm just tired of being alone."

"But you're not alone. You have me, you have Uncle Phil and Aunt Nikki, and your bro—"

"Oh come on. I already screwed up whatever you and I had. And Uncle Phil and Aunt Nikki? Please. They can't stand me. They've always treated me like some sort of burden that they got saddled with and couldn't wait to get rid of. And the people you call my brothers?

They were terrible; they never treated me like a brother. They treated me like...like, you know, when you have someone at school who is your worst enemy, and you hate them with a passion and do anything you can to make their lives miserable? That's how they treated me. The worst part is that Uncle Phil and Aunt Nikki just let it happen; they didn't care!"

"Oh, Alex," she said, with a look of compassion. "I know it was hard for you to lose your parents. I know you felt abandoned. It's certainly not what your mom and dad ever wanted for you."

"Did you know them?" Alex asked.

"Yes. Not well. We met a few times at family gatherings: at my brother's wedding, and at *their* wedding. I was pretty young at the time, but I remember them."

"I can't remember them anymore," Alex said. "I used to, but I can't now. I know their faces, but I don't remember anything else."

"They were great people," Emily said, smiling. "And they were so proud of you. You used to run around and bother everyone; you were such a little shit. But you made everyone laugh." She chuckled softly.

"That doesn't sound like me," Alex said.

"Maybe not now, but back then that's how you were. And then you changed—we all did—after the accident. It was like you had gone into a cave and refused to come out. No one knew what to do. Nikki had a hard time of it too; she was so close to your mom. Did you know she suffered from depression? She saw a therapist for years after the accident, and I think she still takes some kind of medication, even now."

"I didn't know that..."

"She tried to hide it from you. Listen, I'm not saying what they did was right. I know that for a long time, she resented you. You were a constant reminder of the sister she lost. For a long time, she couldn't look at you without crying. That's what the therapy was for, to keep her from heaping all of her anger onto you. I know she regrets it now. Even back then, when she had control of herself, she felt terrible. She once tried to convince Phil to give you up to foster care because she was worried she was hurting you. He convinced her that keeping you was the best thing to do. He didn't want you growing up in a foster home because he thought it would be too hard. The boys...I don't think they understood why you were always in such a shell. They knew their mom had a problem with you, and it rubbed off on them. I know this doesn't excuse what happened, but…I thought you should know. No one meant to hurt you, Alex. They've been worried about you for so long. They just didn't know how to reach you; you never accepted them as parents. That's…that's why I wanted to spend time with you after Thanksgiving: they asked me to, thought you might open up to me."

Alex was horror-stricken. Had she only befriended him because his aunt and uncle, who had just been revealed to have really hated him all along, had asked her to? That meant…

"So this was all a lie?" he asked, "You were checking up on me? That's all this was?" It felt like the perfect punctuation on his shitty life.

Now it was Emily's turn to look surprised. "No, no no no. We care about you, Alex. That's what this is about. Don't you see? I didn't do this just because they asked me to; I did it because I *wanted* to. This wasn't a chore. I had fun. *We* had fun, didn't we?"

"Yeah," he said, "I guess." He wasn't even sure what he felt anymore. All this time he had been so angry at Aunt Nikki and Uncle Phil. They were the embodiment of everything that had been wrong with his life after the accident. And now…

"I was so angry at them, at *him*."

"I know," Emily whispered. "I know."

Emily knew exactly who Alex was referring to: Sean Banks, the drunk driver who'd had a few too many beers while watching a hockey game at a friend's house; then decided he was sober enough to drive home: one poor decision that changed so many lives. After a short trial, Banks was convicted of vehicular manslaughter. Alex watched him hug his wife and four-year-old daughter in the court before they took him away. His daughter cried, and kept crying. But at least she got to see her dad again.

Alex *hated* him. He hadn't wanted Banks to go to jail; he wanted him to die. He wanted him hung from a crane in the middle of a busy intersection, his body a piñata that drivers could try to break open.

Would that have been justice? No. And it wouldn't bring his parents back; nothing could change that. And so he had stayed angry. But instead of acting out that anger, he turned it inwards, on himself; like an acid that slowly ate away at him from the inside, creating a void in his life that he'd never been able to fill. He used to think that Sean Banks didn't kill just two people that night.

Yet, somehow, he was still here, having failed at trying to end it all. Did that mean something? Was he going to remain a suicide risk? Or was he going to do something with the second chance he'd been given?

This isn't only a second chance at life, he thought, looking at Emily. *This is a second chance with her, as well.* Not in the way he thought it could be before: that option was gone now. Maybe it had never existed. What he felt for her, that puppy-dog infatuation, was nothing more than a misguided attempt to fill the gaping void in his life; and now he felt ashamed of his behaviour.

But here she was, sitting on his couch, ready to move on and forge a real friendship with him.

"Thank you," he said.

"For what?"

"For forgiving me."

Smiling, she reached out and took hold of his hand.

Now, with the rift between them resolved, Alex and Emily spoke for hours: about his parents, about Rob, about their lives and where they were going now. It was the most honest conversation they'd ever had and, for the first time, Alex felt freed from the past. After what felt like a long, steep climb, he had finally made it to the summit where, instead of something stunning, he was greeted by a massive blank canvas that awaited his creation. He had the tools now; all he had to do was make the first brushstroke. The view would be what *he* made it.

Emily decided not to go home. She didn't want to confront Rob, not yet. So Alex brought her a pillow and she dozed off on the couch around midnight. He watched her sleep for a while, observing the rhythmic rise and fall of her chest. Even with her tousled hair, she looked peaceful, like all the stresses of her life had simply disappeared. He wondered if everyone looked like that when they slept.

He couldn't sleep. Didn't want to. So he cleaned up the mess in the corner. The ceiling would need fixing. Maybe Uncle Phil knew how.

He sat down at the computer desk and read over his suicide note again. It looked childish now, filled with misplaced anger and resentment. He flipped the pages over, picked up a pen and wrote a note on the back.

Satisfied, he put the pen down and stood up. It was late, but he felt like going for a walk. He needed fresh air. He pulled out a blanket and covered Emily. She shifted slightly as he tucked her in, but was otherwise undisturbed.

He put his shoes on and turned the lights off. As he left, he stood in the doorway and looked back at her one last time, her body illuminated by the moonlight streaming in the window. The lighting made it seem surreal, like the whole night had been a dream.

He closed the door.

TWENTY-NINE
JOEL

JOEL WALKED TO the False Creek seawall and turned east. He followed the path through Coopers Park, under the Cambie Street Bridge, and through the Plaza of Nations where BC Place loomed to his left like a giant monolith. When he reached the north arm of False Creek, he turned towards Carrall Street. The Georgia and Dunsmuir viaducts stretched out in front of him while the Skytrain's elevated guideway ducked under and around the viaducts like a vine snaking around a tree.

In the space between the viaducts was a small field guarded by a barbed wire fence and an abandoned Atco trailer. Graffiti-covered concrete blocks were stacked inside the field, forming a large U-shaped wall.

Joel snuck through a break in the fence and cautiously looked around. A large truck rumbled by on the viaduct overhead. An oncoming Skytrain screeched as it rounded a nearby corner. The sound of the passing train drowned out the crunch of his footfalls on the gravel-strewn ground; it also prevented him from hearing any other noises nearby. He felt vulnerable; he braced himself and scanned the area. As the train receded into the distance, he relaxed and continued to scout the area. He seemed to be alone. He pulled out his phone to check the time.

A shadowed body stepped out from behind a concrete pillar barely ten feet away, startling him.

"A little jumpy?" the mocking voice of his father Anson asked. He stepped out of the shadows, revealing his face.

"You're here." Joel stated after recovering.

"Yeah, nice spot by the way," Anson said. "I didn't have to walk very far. You know how many hookers there are a few streets over? I was just with this one, my God she could suck like a vacuum. Cheap too. I can see why you like it here."

"I didn't pick this place for that."

Anson grinned. "No? Guess I'm lucky then."

"Lucky? Maybe, but not because you found some coked up whore willing to go down on you."

"Actually, I think she was using meth—"

"You're lucky because I didn't kill you ten years ago. You should be rotting in a forgotten grave somewhere!"

"And yet, here I am," Anson said, smiling and spreading his arms. "You couldn't do it then; what makes you think you can do it now?"

"I've changed," Joel said.

"Oh yes, I can see that. You've got yourself a wifey, and a kiddie too. Isn't that nice? You keeping them in line?"

"I'm not like you, I don't need to—"

Anson laughed. "Of course not. You're too much of a pussy for that. I'm surprised you were even able to seal the deal with her. Did she charge you for it? How much?"

"Don't talk about her like that," Joel said through gritted teeth.

Anson laughed again. "You know, you seemed so surprised to see me here, but to be honest, I'm more surprised to see *you* here. I thought for sure you'd run away and hide like you did before."

"I wasn't hiding."

"Sure you weren't," Anson said. "But that doesn't matter now. It's long past time you were punished for what you did." He balled his hands into fists and took a menacing step towards Joel.

Joel pulled out his gun. "Ah, ah, ah. Don't you fucking move."

"What are you going to do with that, boy? You couldn't do it before, you won't do it—"

"I'll kill you. I swear to God I will," Joel said, shaking. This is what he came here for. This had to end.

Anson spoke slowly, levelling a powerful glare towards Joel. One of his hands slipped into the side pocket of his jacket. "Then, why, don't, you DO IT!" And with that, his hand came whipping out and he threw a handful of gravel at Joel's head.

Joel reflexively turned and closed his eyes. He fired the gun where Anson had been standing. The sound was high-pitched, closer to the short, sharp sound of a plate smashing on concrete than the low, bass-filled blasts guns made in the movies.

He opened his eyes again just as Anson bowled into him. They both tumbled to the ground and began punching and kicking at each other, with Anson ending up on top. Anson grabbed Joel's gun-hand and smashed it into the ground: once, twice, then a third time. Joel's grip finally weakened and the gun went flying.

He swung his free hand and connected with Anson's jaw. He didn't have enough leverage in his position to put everything into it, but it was enough to knock Anson back. Joel took the opening and kicked him off. He looked for the gun, but it was hard to find in the dim light, and Anson was already attacking him again.

They grunted as they wrestled on the ground. Joel realized Anson was bleeding from his shoulder. The first shot must have hit him, though it hardly slowed him down. He stuck his finger in the wound and pushed. Anson growled and took it. He grabbed Joel's head and shoved the side of his face into the gravel. The sharp rocks cut through Joel's skin and one just missed his eye. He let go of Anson's bullet wound to defend his face from further abuse.

Anson let go of Joel's head and hammered a fist into his side, sending a searing shock of pain through Joel's body. Joel lashed out with his leg and managed to connect his knee with Anson's groin, making him gasp. His eyes looked like they were about to pop out of his head. They both rolled in opposite directions and turned to glare at each other, Anson cupping his wounded privates, while Joel wiped the blood off his face.

Then Anson broke into a feral grin. He reached under his leg and pulled out the gun. He spit out some blood. "Look what I found," he said.

Joel lunged forward, but Anson pistol-whipped him across the side of the head. A flash of blinding whiteness followed by loud ringing; then blackness began to close in and threatened to overwhelm him.

"Now it's your turn, boy," came Anson's voice from far away.

Joel had a vague sense of his hand being grabbed and someone stepping on his wrist; then came the gunshot.

He screamed as a burst of pain like nothing he'd ever felt before shot up his arm. He writhed and tried to pull away but Anson's foot held him fast.

"How does that feel, *boy*?"

"F…Fuck you," Joel said between gasping breaths; then he remembered what he'd hidden inside his coat. It was still there.

Anson laughed.

Joel rolled onto his stomach, hiding his free hand while he pulled the hunting knife out of its sheath.

"I told you I would find you, *boy*. I told you—"

In one motion, Joel rolled over and swung the knife at Anson's leg. It caught him below the knee, slicing through his pants and into his calf. Joel felt it nick bone before bursting through the front of Anson's leg in a shower of blood.

Anson screamed and fired, narrowly missing Joel's head.

Joel scrambled to get up. He dove behind the pile of concrete blocks as Anson fired again.

He crawled along the ground until he reached a point where the blocks were stacked high enough for him to stand up. He glanced over the top to see if Anson was following him. He wasn't; he was struggling to stand up. He had ripped a part of his shirt off and wrapped it around his calf like a tourniquet. Blood was everywhere. His face was pale and covered in a glistening sheen of sweat reflecting the meager light from the lamps on the viaduct overhead.

Joel's head ached. His adrenaline was beginning to wear off, making him feel woozy, but his hand was also bleeding profusely. He took a cue from Anson and ripped at the bottom of his shirt until he had a strip that was long enough to wrap around his hand. It was saturated with blood almost instantly.

I have to get out of here, he thought. He looked back over at Anson who was still labouring to stand.

"I'll get you, you son of a bitch," Anson said. "You won't get away."

This is my chance. I have to go now. GO!

Joel burst out of cover, running as fast as he could towards the Atco trailer. He heard a gunshot, but didn't turn to look. He took shelter behind the trailer and stopped to catch his breath. To his left, back towards False Creek: that was the fastest route home, but there was a lot of wide-open space in that direction; he'd be an easy target. To his right was Andy Livingstone Park, a much safer route with lots of cover. Once he lost Anson, he could take a circuitous route back home.

Home. He thought of Jenny and Hayley. He hoped they would be safe. Anson undoubtedly knew where they were, but he would be focused on Joel now. *I hope*, Joel thought.

He looked back; Anson was limping towards the trailer muttering a string of curses. He saw Joel's head pop out and he raised the gun. Joel ducked before Anson could shoot.

"I'm coming for you," Anson said.

Joel ran for the park, using the trailer and Anson's angle of approach as cover. He hoped he could reach the park before Anson saw him again. *Run.*

He heard Anson yell from behind him: "You hear that, *boy*? I'm coming for you!"

Just run.

THIRTY

ALEX SHIVERED AND hunched in his jacket. He hadn't realized how cold it was. His breath misted in front of his face, like steam rising from a boiling kettle. He clenched and unclenched his hands in an attempt to keep the blood flowing. He shifted his neck uncomfortably. The collar of his jacket was rubbing against the burn around his throat, a painful reminder of what he had tried to do earlier that evening.

He didn't feel any shame over what he had done. At the time, it seemed…logical, like it was the only outcome that made any sense. He'd spent a lot of time thinking about it, so it certainly wasn't a spur of the moment decision. Recent circumstances had changed the timeline, of course, but in the end he'd only done what he thought was best.

That was the thing about depression. It fogged the mind, making good things seem bad, bad things seem awful and, yes, it could even make suicide seem logical.

Now, some of that fog had dissipated, and Alex could see more clearly; but on some level the depression was still there, probably always would be. It wasn't the sort of thing that would go away because of a botched suicide attempt and a nice, long talk with Emily. He'd barely been keeping his head above water for so long. Maybe now he had a piece of wood to hold on to, but that didn't make the water any less treacherous.

There was, he realized, no such thing as dealing with problems on your own. All that really meant was that you were suffering by yourself.

But he didn't need to be alone anymore. He had Emily, and he had his family, such as it was. He needed to talk to Uncle Phil and Aunt Nikki; he owed them an apology: for doubting them, for hating them, and for never, ever thanking them. He felt a wave of sadness as he contemplated everything that had gone wrong in their relationship. What a horrible child he had been. The thought made him nauseous, and his chest tightened and spasmed as though it wanted to discharge its contents. He closed his eyes and fought the feeling.

It had all gone wrong; but he still had a chance, a chance to apologize and make things better. He could mend these bridges. It would take time, but he had hope now that it was possible.

He rounded a corner and nearly bumped into another person. "Oh…" he started to say.

* * * * *

Melissa took a deep breath, formed an *O* with her lips, and exhaled, opening and closing her mouth, over and over like a fish. Her breath blew out in the same stream she'd gotten on all of her other tries, making her frown with disappointment. *How do smokers manage to make those rings?* she wondered.

She sighed and stopped trying. It was obviously an acquired talent, and she had no interest in taking up smoking just to learn how to blow rings.

It was a beautiful, crisp night. Cold, but not too cold. Melissa felt like she was one of only a few people in Vancouver who actually enjoyed these temperatures. Something about the chill made everything seem sharper, more focused, more real. The air also felt fresher, like the city's stink was being held down by a layer of frost, and wouldn't escape until the air warmed.

She would have to invite Lacey on one of these walks one day, Melissa thought. She had an image of the two of them walking together in silence, both feeling refreshed and renewed by the simple power of companionship and the crisp, cool air.

That was probably a pipe dream, though. Not that Lacey wouldn't join her, she probably would. But Lacey was wired differently than

Melissa. When it came to her ability to enjoy a companionable silence, she was more like Lindsay: as in, no ability at all.

What about Mark? She didn't really know him that well yet. But he seemed like the kind of guy who would follow her lead. If she indicated a desire to walk, but not speak, surely he would oblige.

But why was she thinking about bringing Mark, anyway? This was her time. Her time to think, reflect, and figure things out. Inviting Lacey made sense; she needed those things too. But Mark? There was no reason to bring him, was there?

No, not really. She was still uncomfortable with the idea of having a boyfriend, and she wasn't sure she could get past what happened in her bedroom during the party. It wasn't his fault, of course, and maybe she was being unfair, but the simple fact was that being with him had brought out something very painful for her. Even the thought of his touch made her shiver uneasily. Could a relationship ever recover from something like that? She wasn't sure.

She'd kept her head down, eyes on the ground, while she chewed on these thoughts. But as she neared an intersection something on the opposite corner caught her eye, breaking her reverie and bringing her to a standstill. Her chin dropped.

* * * * *

Joel walked down the street laboriously. His good hand, sheltered by the inside of his jacket, had a white-knuckle grip on his blood-slicked knife. The blood was drying, getting stickier with every passing second. He could feel his skin peeling away from the handle every time he adjusted his grip, as if it had been covered in a layer of glue.

His left hand throbbed, a feeling that intensified as his adrenaline wore off. The series of cuts on his face were beginning to burn as well, along with what felt like the world's worst charley horse in his thigh. He wasn't even sure how that happened, but it was making it difficult to walk.

His only solace was the knowledge that Anson had to be in as bad shape, if not worse. If anything, having taken a bullet to the shoulder and a knife to the leg, he should be lying on the ground somewhere bleeding out.

Joel didn't believe that, however. Anson wasn't the type of person to go die in a corner quietly. He would be loud. He would make a fuss. And he would take someone down with him.

As long as Anson didn't get anywhere near Jenny or Hayley, Joel could live with that. They were the ones who mattered. Without them, Joel didn't think he'd be able to go on.

A noise behind him caused Joel to spin around. Nothing. Just a car crossing an intersection in the distance. The sound of his heavy, ragged breathing filled his ears. He turned and continued walking, his charley horse-induced limp becoming more pronounced with every step.

His eyes went fuzzy, forcing him to stop and lean against a tall, wooden pole. He blinked rapidly and shook his head, to no avail. The world started spinning. Multicoloured lights left trails across his vision like a swarm of fireflies in a long-exposure photo. A traffic light changed from red to green, abruptly changing the hues of everything around him.

He closed his eyes and tried to steady his breathing. *No, this can't happen now.*

He pushed himself off the pole and continued walking. Anson could be anywhere now. He had to be careful, he had to be ready.

Joel reached an intersection, and a tall figure abruptly rounded the corner in front of him. Joel lifted his hand in defense.

"Oh, excu—" the person began to say, but the words died on his lips. He looked down, then looked at Joel with shock and confusion.

Joel took a step back. His hunting knife slid out of the man's body, covered in bright, red blood.

The man looked down and lifted his hand to his chest. He pulled it away and stared at the blood. His face twitched, like he was fighting to find the right expression. He opened his mouth. "Why?" he asked, then he stumbled back, and fell.

Oh no!...No!...no no no no. Shit. SHIT!

He stood over the man, frozen in place. A droplet of blood ran down the blade of his knife— around the hilt, down his knuckles and, finally, onto the sidewalk.

Somewhere in the back of his mind he felt a familiar surge of power, control, and dominance. But this time it was tempered by very real feelings of shock and fear.

Who the hell was this? How could he have thought, for even a second, it was Anson? The kid was too short, too thin, too young.

Oh God. "What have I done?" he whispered.

Then someone yelled from across the street.

Joel looked up at the sound, and realized that all of his nightmares were coming true.

* * * * *

"Hey!" Melissa yelled.

The man with the knife turned to look at her. Their eyes met and they both froze. Melissa's heart lurched in her chest: the face from Playland, no doubt this time—it was him. He looked like he had been tied to a car and dragged down a gravel road. One eye was red, puffy, and half closed. His cheek was ripped open in various places, streaks of blood ran down his neck. One of his hands was wrapped in a red cloth; his other hand, trembling, held a bloody knife.

Melissa's pulse quickened. She tried to move, but her feet felt rooted to the ground. She opened her mouth and all that came out was the rough sound of her breathing. It was like a cat had clamped its claws around her larynx.

For his part, the man seemed transfixed as well. A flurry of emotions battled for control of his expression, shock and horror leading the way.

They stared at each other for what felt like an eternity. A half decade of pent up emotions transferred between them with nothing more than the power of each other's eyes.

He broke first. He glanced back down at the body at his feet, then turned and ran.

Melissa was suddenly freed of the force that had been holding her in place. She ran after him, the force of her anger giving strength to her legs. He was slow: stumbling, and obviously in pain. She could catch him, easily. And then she would—

The body on the sidewalk rolled onto its side and began coughing as she ran past it.

She stopped in her tracks, heart beating furiously. She looked over at the injured man, surprised that he was still alive; then turned to see the retreating form of her attacker.

Two sides of her warred with each other: one wanted to keep chasing the bastard, to run him down and exact all of her anger onto him.

The other side of her saw the struggling victim on the sidewalk—who, without her help, would probably die. Watching him there, alone and in pain, reminded her of her own horrible helplessness after being left alone in the alley. She couldn't leave him, not like that.

But saving him meant letting her attacker go, and she didn't know if she could do that, either.

Melissa looked down the road at her fleeing attacker, the boogeyman that had been terrorizing her dreams for half a decade. He wasn't too far away yet. She could still catch him.

A few long and agonizing seconds passed; finally, she let loose a ragged breath. She turned and, with that motion, felt as if a part of her ripped away. She ran to the injured man.

* * * * *

A shadow descended over him. At first, Alex thought it was the stranger, back to finish the job. But the form resolved into a woman with short, blonde hair, and large, concerned eyes, and small, red lips.

It's Kate, from the bus. "What are you doing here?" he asked in disbelief, or tried to ask. All that came out was a bloody gurgle.

She pulled out a cellphone and made a call. "Hello? Hello? I need an ambulance."

Oh, she was calling for help. Good idea.

"My name is Melissa." She looked up. "We're at the corner of Nelson and Homer."

Melissa? Wow, he wasn't even close. Did he have to call her that? He had grown pretty fond of her as Kate.

He groaned as another wave of pain washed over him. He was getting cold, really cold. His hands and feet felt like they were being held inside a freezer of crushed ice. And the cold was spreading up his arms and legs. He began to shiver uncontrollably, hardly noticing when Melissa pulled off her jacket and covered him with it. Then she put her phone between her ear and shoulder and started pushing on his chest where he'd been stabbed. He gasped in pain, and she reduced the pressure.

Suddenly, he thought of Emily, still at his place, sleeping peacefully on the couch. She needed to know.

He tried to speak. "Mm…my, ph…phone." He laboured to form the words. It was so hard to breathe. It was like trying to catch a breath while his head was under water.

Melissa leaned forward, dropping her phone and cursing. "What was that?" she asked.

"Ph…pho…ne, E…e…em—"

She tried to piece his words together. "Phone Em?" she asked, slowly enunciating the sounds he'd uttered, putting them together like a set of lego blocks.

"Emily," he finally managed to say. He coughed and large, red globs of blood splattered on the sidewalk. "C…c…call, h…h…her."

"Emily? Emily! You want me to call Emily!"

He nodded. "T…tell her…"

Ambulance sirens blared in the distance. Melissa looked up, then back at him. "They'll be here soon. You're going to be okay."

No, I won't be.

He reached for his pocket. He had to look down to see if his hand was in the right place, because he couldn't feel anything. The cold had moved far enough up his arm that it felt like he was moving ice blocks attached to his shoulders. But he was still able to pull his phone out, barely. He put the phone down on his chest, beside her blood-soaked hands. "T…take it." He coughed blood again. He felt like his lungs were filled with it, like he was suffocating.

"T…t…tell her…I'm…s…sorry," he said. "Th…thank y…you."

"No no no, you don't need me to tell her that. You'll be able to tell her yourself, okay? Look, the ambulance is here." She gestured to the side where an ambulance pulled up. The sirens blared in his ears.

He tried to respond, but couldn't. He felt a powerful urge to speak, to yell, to scream out everything he'd ever wanted, but hadn't had the courage, to say. He felt a pressure building inside his chest and knew beyond a doubt that he would never get that chance.

He felt the world pulling away. Or was he the one pulling away? He tried to hold on. But there was so much pain. And coldness like nothing he had ever imagined. He just wanted it to stop.

He thought back to the conversations he'd had with Emily, and how hopeful she was. "Everybody should have a happy ending sometime," she'd said. "Even you, Alex."

Is this it, then? Is this my happy ending?

* * * * *

As soon as he saw the patient, Richard knew the odds were bad. Other than the pool of blood on the ground, he was coughing blood and struggling to breathe, his hands and lips also showed obvious signs of cyanosis. They had been told it was a stab wound, and Richard could tell right away the knife had penetrated the lung.

"We need to get him hooked up, quick," James said. He put the patient in a neck brace and started cutting off his jacket. Once it was off, they cut open his shirt to assess the wound.

"Yeah," Richard responded. James put an oxygen mask on the injured man, while Richard attached the AED sensors to his chest; then they lifted him onto the cart and rolled him to the ambulance.

"Wait," the young woman who had called them said. "I want to come."

"Are you family?" Richard asked.

She hesitated. "I'm his girlfriend."

"Okay, get in," Richard said as he and James lifted the cart into the back of the ambulance. She nodded and hopped into the back of the ambulance with Richard, then sat down and held the injured man's hand.

The beeping AED monitor indicated a problem with heart rhythm. No surprise there, thought Richard. He prepared an IV.

"What's his name?" he asked.

The woman didn't respond.

"Hey, what's his name?" Richard repeated.

She blinked. "I...I don't know."

"You said you're his girlfriend." He braced himself on the wall for balance as James swung the ambulance around a corner.

She nodded after they straightened out. "I know."

"Dammit. His jacket is in the corner; check for a wallet."

She picked up the jacket and searched the pockets while Richard proceeded, with some difficulty, to set up the IV: the patient— who would be in unbearable pain by now, and feeling like he was drowning with all the blood in his lungs—had started struggling.

"Alex...Alex Phillips," the woman said, reading from the licence she held in her shaky, bloody hands.

"Okay Alex," Richard said. He always spoke to his patients. He had no guarantee they could hear or understand him, but a steady voice was always helpful in a tense situation. "I'm giving you a bolus of normal saline. Hopefully, this will get your blood pressure under control, okay?"

He checked the AED monitor, hoping the heart rate would even out. It didn't. Instead, it continued to rise in an attempt to perfuse the major organs with blood. It had been one-fifty beats per minute when Alex was first hooked up; now it was approaching two hundred.

And then it stopped.

* * * * *

Melissa kept a firm grip on Alex's hand while the paramedic performed CPR. With every push on Alex's chest, bits of blood flew out of his mouth and caught on the inside of the oxygen mask.

"Come on, Alex, stay with me. Come on!" the paramedic said. After thirty compressions, he stopped and squeezed the bag attached to the oxygen mask on Alex's face; then checked the reading on the AED monitor: *Continue CPR.*

Melissa's hand hurt; Alex had banged on the side of the cart during a particularly bad fit of twitching. But she hadn't let go; she couldn't have even if she'd tried: Alex's grip was too tight.

What a surprise it was when she ran to the injured man and recognized him as The Creeper from her bus commute. She felt a twinge of regret now for having thought of him in such a negative way, and for turning down the seat he offered her on the bus.

Her decision to tell the paramedic she was his girlfriend as a means to get on the ambulance was also a surprise. She didn't know for sure if it was guilt that drove her decision or not, but it had felt right.

She remembered how alone she felt in the alley. Even after the police and paramedics arrived, she still felt as if she was alone, riding an ocean storm in a tiny boat. That suffocating feeling of solitude was something she would never forget.

She could see that same feeling in Alex's eyes when he was lying on the ground trying to speak to her. And she knew she would do anything to help him through it.

His hand loosened at the same time the machine went wild. But she was sure she could still feel something there.

Come on, Alex, she thought, echoing the words of the paramedic. *You can make it through this. Don't give up.*

His hand was freezing. She cupped it in both of her hands then, suddenly, his arm went completely and utterly limp. What little strength he had had was gone. *No!*

She shook his arm. *Alex. No!* She could feel the tears flowing down her face.

The machine continued beeping. The paramedic continued compressions.

But she knew it was over.

* * * * *

Richard stood outside the ambulance and watched as Alex's body was rolled away by a doctor and team of nurses. As a paramedic, he didn't have the authority to declare anyone dead, so he'd continued to do his job, even when it was hopeless.

He looked over at the woman standing beside him, nagged by the feeling that he knew her.

"You're not his girlfriend," he said, still a little annoyed that she'd lied to him.

"No."

"You shouldn't be here."

She turned to him; fresh, wet tracks ran down from her eyes. "Yes, I should," she said evenly.

He was taken aback by the conviction in her voice. He frowned. "But why?"

"Because," she said quietly, "no one should have to go through that alone."

He looked at her again, really looked at her. And finally it hit him: he *did* recognise her. It wasn't some trick where people with similar features blended together. What threw him off was her hair; the last time he'd seen her, her hair was long, and red.

James and Richard had been the first responders on the scene years ago after she had been beaten and raped. Richard remembered how they'd found her, shattered and terrified; remembered wondering how anyone comes back from something like that. It had broken his heart.

Now here she was, breaking his heart all over again. Not because of what had happened to her, but because of the phenomenal strength of character she displayed by doing what she had just done. It was the sort of courage that he only dreamed of having.

"Let's go inside and get you cleaned up," he said.

She looked down and noticed for the first time that she was covered in blood. She nodded. "Okay."

* * * * *

Joel ran from the woman as fast as his broken body would allow. The shock of seeing her, along with the realization he had likely killed an innocent man, gave him a renewed burst of energy.

He went down to the seawall and, after looking around to make sure no one was watching, threw his knife into False Creek. Back at his building, he was careful to leave as little blood as possible on the door handles and elevator buttons as he made his way inside. He reached his condo and pulled out his keys. The key caught in the lock for a moment, causing him to catch his breath. He looked around the brightly lit corridor, hoping no one was there. He jiggled his key and, finally, the lock clicked open.

He stepped inside, shut the door behind him, and breathed a sigh of relief.

The first thing he needed was to get cleaned up. He was an absolute mess, covered in blood and dirt, with torn clothes and a *hole in his hand*. He should have disposed of his clothes before coming home. But where? Besides, it was chilly out.

He settled on a plan: clean up, put on new clothes, take the old ones outside and burn th—

"Joel?" came Jenny's voice from the living room.

He froze. What was she doing out there? Why wasn't she in bed?

He saw the silhouette of her form rise from the couch. "I heard the door. I know you're here."

Joel's mind raced. If she saw him like this, he didn't know how he would explain it. "Yeah, sorry, I thought you'd be sleeping so I was trying to be quiet. You should be in bed."

"I wanted to see you when you got home, to make sure you were okay." She reached for the light.

Joel looked around for somewhere to hide. Jumping in the closet wasn't going to do him any good. In that moment, more than at any time since he'd moved into Jenny's condo, he hated that the bathroom wasn't at the entrance.

Jenny turned the light on and gasped. "Oh my God, Joel! What happened?" She rushed towards him and started looking him over.

"It's...nothing. I got into a bit of a scrap."

"A scrap? This doesn't look like a scrap, Joel. What happened...oh God !...look at your hand. We need to get you to a hospital."

"No," Joel said firmly. "There's no need. I'll be fine." He pushed her away and started walking towards the bedroom.

She wasn't giving up so easily, though. She grabbed his arm and held it with a strength that belied her small stature. "No need? Are you kidding? Joel, you're a mess. What were you doing?"

"I...I saw my father, okay? We got into a fight. It's over, leave it alone."

"Look at your hand, Joel. He shot you!"

Joel grinned maliciously. "Yeah, but I got him too."

Jenny let go of his arm and took a step back. "What? What did you do?"

"I did what I needed to keep you and Hayley safe," Joel said, louder than he intended.

She looked him over again and put a hand on her mouth. "There's so much blood," she whispered, and then realized something. "How much of it is yours?" Her voice wavered as she asked the question.

He looked himself over and shrugged. "Some. I don't know." He put his hands on her shoulders. "It doesn't matter now."

She shrugged out of his grip. His hands left red stains on her white top. "Is...is he dead?"

"I don't know. He might be by now."

"We need to call the police," she said, voice rising in pitch as she became more rattled. "We need to explain what happened. Tell them he attacked you and you were defending yourself. It'll be okay." She picked up a cordless phone and started dialing.

"No! Don't do that!" Joel reached for the phone and she pulled away. He grabbed her arm and dragged her back, yanked the phone out of her hand, and smashed it on the counter. "I *said* not to do that."

"Joel, you're scaring me." She tried to pry his fingers off her arm, but she couldn't budge them.

He yanked her close and grabbed her neck with his other hand. "You listen to me, missy. Everything will be fine—"

She kneed him in the midsection, then pulled away. He tried to keep his grip on her arm, but his hand was weak from the injury and he wasn't able to maintain his grip. She stumbled at the sudden release and fell backwards, her head slamming into the side of the coffee table with a loud *crack*.

"Bitch!" Joel yelled. He towered over her, clenching his fists, and breathing heavily. She groaned on the ground. He pulled his arm back to strike.

"Daddy, NO!"

Joel stopped and looked over. Hayley stood in the hallway wearing her pyjamas, tears coursing down her face. She ran over to her mom and dove on top of her, protecting her from Joel. "You said you would never hurt us. You promised!"

Joel took a step back, and then another. Hayley cried and held her mom. "You promised, you promised."

Joel's rage faded, leaving him breathless. He felt a pain in his chest, like his heart was being squeezed. He realized he'd been here before in this exact position, except this time, he wasn't the one on the ground shielding his mother. And the one looming over them wasn't Anson.

"Hayley..." Joel said. "It was an accident. I..."

He turned and saw his reflection in the TV. He looked...*evil*. Like a monster. *No. I'm not my father. I'm worse.* His vision became blurry as tears pooled in his eyes.

"I'm so sorry, Hayley," he said. "I never meant to hurt her."

"Then why did you?" Hayley yelled.

"Because," Joel said, feeling a wave of despair wash over him. And everything he'd ever done wrong in his life flashed through his mind: abandoning his mom; raping a woman; killing a man; betraying his wife and daughter. "Because I'm a bad man."

"I wish you weren't."

With those words, Joel knew what he had to do. He went and slid open the glass door to the balcony, a gust of cold air brushed across his face.

He looked into the living room. Jenny was on the floor, groaning and holding her head. Hayley stared at Joel, a mixture of anger and disappointment in her eyes.

"I'm sorry, Hayley," he said, hoping she could understand.

He opened the balcony door then pulled the curtain shut before stepping outside. With his two hands gripping the railing, he took a deep breath and exhaled. *They don't deserve this. I have to end the cycle.*

He climbed over the railing, reversing his grip and catching his heels on the edge of the balcony. His breath came in ragged gasps as his heart beat faster and faster. *This is the right thing to do. All this time I wanted to protect them, when I should have realized I was the one they needed protection from.* Anson had told him years ago that he should kill himself. Perhaps he was right, after all.

He closed his eyes and let go, leaning forward and beginning to fall.

At least I made one good thing before I died, Joel thought, thinking of Hayley. She will recover from this, she has to.

In spite of you, Dad. That means I win. I wi—

* * * * *

Richard leaned against a wall in the hospital corridor. He and James had decided to take a short break and get a bite to eat. Now James was in the bathroom while Richard waited. Richard was still shaken up over losing the stabbing victim named Alex. Losing people was part of the job, but it never got any easier.

Melissa sat across the hall from him. When they exchanged names earlier, Richard didn't mention that he already knew hers.

"Do you want us to drop you off somewhere? We're leaving soon," he asked her.

"No, thanks. I'll be fine."

Richard fought back the urge to ask her more invasive questions. Whenever he worked on someone, he always felt a connection with them and felt legitimately concerned about their well-being. Her case had affected him more than most. Most patients had something he could fix, like a cut or a broken bone. With her, most of the damage was internal, out of reach. It made him feel helpless.

But she was here now. And she seemed okay. She'd obviously found her way through the darkness and come out a stronger person. She was…an inspiration.

He took a few steps to the side and pulled out his phone. It was late, probably too late, but he had to do this before he lost the nerve. He dialed the number for Natalie's phone.

A sleepy voice answered. "Hello?"

"Natalie, it's Richard."

"What are you doing calling at this time? Do you reali—"

"I know. I'm sorry…I…had to talk to you."

He heard sounds from the other end of the line—a shuffling movement, the click of a lamp being turned on. After a few seconds, Natalie asked, "What do you want, Richard?"

"I…How are the kids doing?"

"They're doing fine," she answered in a flat voice.

"That's good," Richard said. After a few seconds of silence, he took a breath and continued. "I wanted to say I'm sorry—for everything. I've been a shitty husband, and I don't know if I can ever apologize enough to you and the kids. I got so caught up in everything that was happening that I wasn't seeing straight, you know?"

He waited to see if she was going to say anything, but when it became apparent that she wasn't going to, he plunged onward. "I want you to come back. I need you, Nat. I can't function without you."

"It's not that easy," she whispered.

"I know," he said. "But we can work on it, right? I'm prepared now. I'll do anything to make this work. I promise."

He could almost hear her shaking her head. "You were with another woman. Am I supposed to forgive you?"

"Nothing happened between us. It almost did, but I stopped it. I swear."

"How can I believe you? How do I know you're telling me the truth?"

He paused and sighed. "You don't. You have to trust me."

"I don't know if I do," she said. She made a sniffling noise, the one she always made when she started crying and was trying to hold it back. He wiped away a tear of his own.

"So," he said after a few moments. "Where do we go from here? I still love you. I want to make this work. Don't you?"

Silence on the other end.

"Natalie?"

* * * * *

Melissa sat in the hallway watching Richard talk on the phone. She couldn't hear what he was saying, but he was obviously stressed out about it.

She felt exhausted, both physically and mentally, by everything that had just happened. But at the same time, she felt different, as if a great weight had been lifted from her shoulders. Something happened out there, in the street and in the ambulance. Something that changed her. Seeing her attacker and letting him go, followed by the powerful connection she'd felt with Alex, holding his hand while he died. Moments like these could change anyone.

James came walking down the hallway, nodded at Melissa, and walked up to Richard, who was putting his phone away.

"Holy shit, did you hear?" James asked Richard.

"Hear what? I was on the phone," Richard said in a somber voice.

"Some guy offed himself over in Yaletown. Took a swan dive off a building, apparently fell seventeen stories. I heard it on the radio."

"Damn. Do we need to go?"

"No, they don't need us. Just thought it was crazy."

"Yeah."

"Well, we better get going."

Richard looked at Melissa. "You sure you don't need a ride? It's not a problem."

"No, it's okay. But thanks," Melissa said. *There's still something I need to do.*

Once Richard and James had left, Melissa pulled Alex's phone out of her pocket. It was covered in dried blood.

She cleaned the screen as best as she could and turned the phone on, hoping he didn't have a password. He didn't. She opened the contact list and scrolled through until she found the name Emily. She pressed the green call button and lifted the phone to her ear.

The phone rang four times before a groggy voice answered. *She must have been sleeping.* "Hello? Alex?"

"Hi, is this Emily?" Melissa asked.

"Yes. Who is this?"

"My name is Melissa."

"Why are you calling from Alex's phone?"

"Alex asked me to call you."

"Why? What's going on? Is he alright?" She sounded wide awake now, frantic, even.

"I'm so sorry, Emily," Melissa said. She tried to keep her voice as calm as possible, but it still broke on the words. "Something terrible has happened…"

EPILOGUE

Melissa breathed in the cool morning air and started walking across the perfectly manicured grass towards a small group of people. A short, blonde haired woman left the group to meet her. They hugged.

"Hi, Melissa," Emily said. "Thank you so much for coming."

"No, thank you, for giving me the chance to come," Melissa responded.

Emily smiled; she looked nervous. "I have to speak soon. You want to do it for me? I wrote everything down. I'm terrible in front of crowds."

"Trust me, I'm even worse. You'll be fine."

Emily shook her head. "I still can't believe it."

Melissa put a hand on her arm. "I know. I'm so sorry."

Emily took a deep breath, seeming to steel herself for what was coming. "Well, I'd better start."

Melissa watched her rejoin the group, remember the night she'd met Emily at the hospital. Their bond had been instant. After hearing the doctor's official confirmation of Alex's death, they had hugged and cried together. More members of Alex's family arrived and, even though Melissa felt like an outsider intruding upon their grief, they didn't treat her like one. They shared their pain with her like she was a part of their family. And they thanked her for being with Alex at the end. They were comforted by the fact that he hadn't been alone. So much so, that they invited her to take part in the funeral preparations. She was humbled.

The next day, Melissa went for lunch with her mom and, for the first time in years, they talked, really talked.

"You changed your hair," a man's voice said.

She turned to see Richard, dressed in a black suit and a white shirt. It didn't look like something he wore very often; it was at least one size too small, and she could see fold lines on his pants.

"Yeah, just this morning," she said. "I got tired of blonde; thought I'd go back to my natural colour."

"It looks good."

"Thanks." They stood in silence for a few moments while the group in front of them arranged themselves.

"What brings you here?" Melissa asked. "I didn't know you knew the family."

"I...didn't recognize him at first. But I knew his parents, I guess. Sort of."

Melissa looked over at him, curious.

Richard pointed at two slabs of granite about twenty feet from where they stood. Melissa could just make out the names: Mitchell Phillips and Eve Phillips.

"Those are his parents. They died in a car accident a long time ago. I was there when it happened. His mom...died in my arms. That was actually when I decided to become a paramedic. I still come here from time to time, to pay my respects and to apologize."

"Apologize?"

"For not knowing how to save them," he said, looking down. "Now their son is dead, and I couldn't save him either. This entire family died on my watch...and I couldn't stop it."

Melissa felt her heart constrict. "It's not your fault. There was nothing else you could have done."

"I don't know. There's always a shred of doubt when you lose someone. You keep thinking: maybe if I had done this differently, I could have saved them." He sighed. "I guess I'll never know." He fidgeted with his wedding band, twisting it back and forth.

Emily stood beside a large, cherry-coloured casket with a handful of papers in her hand. Directly in front of her, Alex's aunt and uncle, and their three sons sat on fold-out chairs.

"Welcome," Emily began. "Thank you, all, for coming." She waited until the last murmurs of noise died down before she continued, reading from the sheets of paper she held. "I didn't know Alex as well as I would have liked to. None of us did. He was the lone wolf of the family, always going off on his own. He seemed to like it that way, and we accepted that.

"When I finally got the chance to get to know him, I realized what a great guy Alex was: funny, intelligent, and compassionate, even though he didn't like to show it." She smiled slightly at a private memory. "The reason I bring this up is...because Alex tried to commit suicide a week ago." An audible gasp rose from the small crowd, followed by murmuring.

"Obviously, he failed. But I'm telling you this because it concerns us all." She shuffled through the sheets of paper in her hand and, finding the ones she'd been looking for, held them up. "This is his suicide note. He had left it on his desk the night he tried to hang himself. When I read it, it made me cry, because I hadn't realized until that very moment just how lost and alone Alex felt. And it was heartbreaking to know that he'd been feeling this way, and that we had no idea!"

She took a few steadying breaths and wiped a tear from her cheek. "It kills me to think he was living like this. It really does. And...if we can learn anything from this it's that we should appreciate each other more. We should listen, and talk to, and just love each other so much more than we do right now. In the end, Alex didn't choose to die. But if things had been different— if we had been more supportive, more loving towards him—maybe he wouldn't have been out that night. And we wouldn't be here now."

She looked around at the tearful faces.

"Before Alex went out that night, he wrote me a message. I want to share that with you."

She flipped one of the pages over and began to read. Her voice trembled at first, gaining strength as she continued.

"Emily,

I don't know if you realize, but you've given me a gift tonight. I've spent so much of my life in despair, thinking how I wanted to die. I forgot what it felt like to hope for something. I don't know that I could have done anything differently in the past. And I can't change it, anyhow. But I know that I can start over now. I hope it's not too late.

Thank you so much for showing me that life can be better, and that maybe there is a reason to look forward to the future.

Alex."

She lowered the page and looked at everyone. "He was ready to move on, and now he will never get that chance. God, it makes me so angry that he was taken away right when he was getting better. Life isn't fair. It doesn't wait for us to get over our mistakes, get past our problems with each other, or come to the realizations that could change our lives. It just happens, and it leaves us with regrets and missed opportunities.

"I think if Alex could tell us anything today, he would tell us to stop waiting. Stop worrying. Stop being scared. Just go out, go out and live your life. That, in my mind, is his legacy. That is how I choose to remember Alex."

She stepped away from the casket and gave Alex's aunt a long hug. After a few minutes with the group, she walked over to Melissa and Richard.

"That was beautiful," Melissa said.

"Very," Richard added.

"Thank you," Emily said. "I wanted to say something that showed how he changed my life."

"You did great. I'm sure he would have appreciated your words," Melissa said.

A man standing behind the casket leaned down and flipped a lever, lowering the casket into the freshly dug earth.

Emily, Melissa, and Richard stood together, watching woefully.

An eagle soared overhead.

The sun appeared through broken clouds.

The casket sank, lower, lower, and then it stopped.

The End

ABOUT THE AUTHOR

Bryan Clegg's love affair with writing began at the age of 7 with a famous (among his family) story about 'a dog taking a wack in the forest'. As he assumed their laughter meant the story was good, he decided to never stop writing.

He lives in New Westminster with his partner, Kathryn, and a ridiculous cat named Kibbles.